NO SECOND CHANCE

DIVISION SERIES #5

ANGUS MCLEAN

Published 2020 by Smoking Gun Publications

ISBN 978 0 473 56088 1

ALSO BY ANGUS MCLEAN

Chase Investigations Series

Old Friends

Honey Trap

Sleeping Dogs

Tangled Webs

Dirty Deeds

Red Mist

Fallen Angel

Holy Orders

Deal Breaker

The Division Series

Smoke and Mirrors

Call to Arms

The Shadow Dancers

The Berlin Conspiracy

No Second Chance

Nicki Cooper Mystery Series

The Country Club Caper

Early Warning Series

Martial Law

Getting Home

Stand Fast

NO SECOND CHANCE

BY ANGUS MCLEAN

1

———

Auckland, New Zealand
Monday, 1100 hours

Archer sat across the desk from the Director and waited.

In a tailored charcoal pinstripe suit, crisp grey shirt and navy-blue silk tie, he looked sharp. He had a good shave, his hair was neat and tidy and his cologne was subtle.

He appeared relaxed, one ankle crossed over the other knee. His face was blank, showing no sign of emotion.

Inwardly, he was seething.

A late call back from London on a flight that arrived at dawn, a quick cab ride to a chain hotel in downtown Auckland for an early check-in, and just enough time to freshen up before another quick cab ride to the Director's office.

The Assistant Director, to be more accurate, but nobody ever called him that. He was known simply as the Director. The head of the Auckland field office of the Security Intelligence Service and, more importantly, the head of Division 5 of the SIS.

Officially, of course, the Service didn't have a Division 5. There wasn't even a Division 1, hence there was no need for any other divisions beyond that.

But Division 5 was real, and the work they did was very dangerous. The black operations world called for such units in a time of turmoil, and even in a time of peace, as such units often kept a lid on the subversive activities of militants and terrorists that could otherwise disrupt economies, overthrow governments and lead to innocent blood being spilled.

The intervention of Archer and his colleagues had directly prevented such catastrophes, and the existence of the unit remained a closely guarded secret even within the Service itself.

While some of his colleagues were retained as contractors, Archer filled a role at the New Zealand High Commission in London, ostensibly as a standard Intelligence Officer. His secondary role, which as far as he was concerned was in fact his primary role, fitted in around that.

Of late, to his disgust, the opportunities given to him by the Division had been few and far between. A close target recce here, a surveillance detail there, and very few direct-action missions. For a man of Archer's experience and nature it had become a constant sore point.

It was, however, not the only source of his moodiness, and he had no doubt that he was going to hear all about it from the short, soft-bellied man across the wide mahogany desk from him.

'You are in something of a rut, Craig,' the Director finally said. His pale blue eyes flicked from his desktop to Archer's face. Seeking a response, perhaps. Or simply assessing.

The Director was a shrewd old bugger, and Archer was determined to give him nothing that could be used against him. One of the first things he had learnt upon moving from the Special Forces into the shadowy world of intelligence was to believe nothing and trust no one. And to Archer, that included his colleagues.

'You have not got any closer to tracking down Viktor Kozlowski,' the Director continued. 'Your work in London is boring you. And your relationship with Ms Graf has ended somewhat unfortunately.'

Somewhat unfortunately was an understatement, and Archer felt himself visibly rise in his seat at the mention of it all. He forced himself to get a grip and clamped his jaw shut, knowing that he'd just given the Director all the reaction he could want. He cursed himself for being so foolish.

'Does that about sum it up?' the Director inquired, watching Archer like a headmaster watches a naughty pupil.

Archer shifted uncomfortably in his chair. 'You could say that, sir, yes. Unfortunate is one way of putting it.'

The Director cocked an eyebrow, still watching him, saying nothing.

'If by unfortunate you mean that your counterpart in the BND disciplined her, threatened her with dismissal and forbade her from seeing me like she was some bloody schoolgirl, then yes sir, it was bloody unfortunate.'

Archer stopped, feeling his fists clenched, his heart hammering in his chest.

Jesus fuckin' Christ this was embarrassing. Discussing his love life with the Director, a man old enough to be his father? A man who he'd never had a personal conversation with in his life? He felt like a schoolkid himself now, a silly teenage boy whose girlfriend had been banned from going out with him by a strict father.

Which was pretty much what it had amounted to. They had both known going into it that it had been an unlikely alliance, being officers of different intelligence services, albeit allies of sorts.

'Well,' the Director said ponderously, 'while I appreciate your strong feelings on the matter, Captain Archer, that wasn't really what I was wanting to discuss.'

Archer felt his face flush red hot, the humiliation threatening to physically scald him. The room was closing in around him and it was all he could do not to get up and storm out.

Not what he wanted to discuss? Of course he didn't want to bloody discuss it. The bastard across the desk from him was just as much to blame for it as Eva's own boss, Dieter of the BND. There was no doubt at all in Archer's mind that the two men had colluded, both knowing that it was the smartest and safest way of dealing with a conflict of interest for both their agencies.

No matter the effect on the two people involved, two people who had been through hell for their masters, who had spilled blood to protect their countries and save innocent lives. No bloody regard for them whatsoever. Just protect the national interests and pick yourselves up, move on. There's always another mission waiting for you.

Archer's jaw was so tight he knew there was no chance of speaking right now. He pushed his hands into his lap and slowly sucked a breath in through his nose. *Grip it and fast. If you don't, you'll be eaten alive.*

He looked across the desk at the Director. It was like eyeballing a reptile. Cold, emotionless and deadly.

'Sorry sir,' he heard himself saying, 'my mistake.'

'Quite alright, Captain Archer.' The Director gave the slightest hint of a smile. 'I was a young man myself once, you know. And a squaddie, to boot.'

Archer knew that.

The Director had, a long time ago, been a member of Archer's own parent regiment, the Queen Alexandra's Mounted Rifles. Gone now, merged and rebranded, but a formative part of young Second Lieutenant Craig Archer's life. Well before he became Captain Archer of the 1st New Zealand Special Air Service Group, the legendary 1NZSAS, a Tier One SF unit that had trained and fought with the best in the world.

Hence the Director's use of Archer's rank, a professional acknowledgement from one officer to another.

Archer gave a short nod. His cheeks and neck still burned and he willed the older man to hurry up and get to the point. That, or put him out of his misery.

'Viktor Kozlowski.'

The name hadn't left the forefront of Archer's mind in over a year. The man was evil, a criminal genius. The worst kind of terrorist, as far as Archer was concerned; a terrorist for hire. With no particular agenda of his own other than hurting the West, he planned and orchestrated terrorist atrocities for the highest bidder. Not above getting his own hands dirty, he was a natural-born killer who had served with distinction in the US military before his psychopathic traits had got the better of him.

A fall from grace led to an obsession with hurting his former masters, and Archer had crossed his path by foiling an airline hijack that would have led to a strike on Los Angeles International Airport, an atrocity intended to rival that of 9/11.

More death had followed and along the way Archer had joined forces with Eva, the lovely Eva. Together they had hunted Kozlowski, nipping another strike in the bud at the Berlin Gate, the very heart of the German nation.

But, ultimately, they had failed to capture or kill the terrorist mastermind.

He had narrowly escaped them in a plane crash in Bavaria and had taunted them ever since. Emailed cards on their birthdays, photos of them sunning themselves together in the Maldives, anything to needle them that he had won and they had lost.

And still the terrorist activities continued.

Archer hated the man with every bone in his body and he would give anything to choke the life out him with his own hands. Nothing would give him greater pleasure than to kill the bastard. Or almost nothing.

Eva.

The woman he had dared to imagine spending the rest of his life with. What a fool he'd been to allow himself such a dream. Men like him didn't settle down. There was no white picket fence and family home in his future. Men like him were men of action, not domesticity. Domestic bliss was for other men.

Archer snapped back to the present, realising he had tuned out to the Director.

'Sorry sir?'

'I said, Viktor Kozlowski. It appears that we may have a lead on him.'

Archer sat upright, dropping his cocked foot to the floor. His attention was focussed on the older man.

'We have intelligence that he may have had some hand in our recent trouble with our friends.'

The Director didn't need to expand on that. Even if it hadn't been in the media, Archer would have had to be blind not to have noticed.

The Five Eyes network, such an important partnership in signals intelligence, was crumbling. New Zealand, Australia, the US, the UK and Canada, squabbling amongst themselves amidst accusations of backroom deals and the withholding of vital sig int. Irritation and suspicion had led to distrust and was barrelling at top speed towards a full breakdown. If that were to happen, not only would one of the most important partnerships against terrorism and international crime be lost, but New Zealand would find itself out on its own, forced to feed off the scraps it was thrown by its former friends.

The world was a lonely place for such an orphan, and it was not a position the government – regardless of their naivety or effectiveness – wanted to be in.

Archer had about as much faith in his political masters as he did in real estate agents or used car salesmen, but he had to concede they were right on this count.

'Exactly how does he figure into that, sir?'

'The int we have is that he has provided advice to Ethan Capstick, who has in turn leaked information via his *blog*' – the Director emphasised the word as if just saying it gave him a foul taste – 'that could only have come from within the intelligence community.'

Archer nodded. He knew Capstick by reputation. A skinny, repugnant little man with no formal training who touted himself as an investigative journalist, he wrote books based on little more than speculation and whispers.

How such a creature had been allowed to flourish for so long remained a mystery to him.

'Makes sense,' he said.

'Not only that, but this advice and information is directly influencing the actions of the Aotearoa Freedom and Liberation move-ment.' The Director's nose wrinkled at the mention of the AFL, the high profile activist group.

Archer frowned. 'What's the link there? Capstick's always seemed to be more of a lone wolf than that lot.'

The Director gave a harrumph of disgust. 'Perhaps he was at one time, Captain Archer, but a lone wolf he is no longer. The int we have is that he is in a relationship of some sort with Krystal Raines.'

'Excuse me?' Archer couldn't hide his surprise. 'That can't be right. The woman might be barking mad, but she's an absolute stunner.'

The front person for the AFL was a former model with a few minor acting credits – usually the scantily-clad bimbo – who purported to have turned her back on the material existence she had led to fight for freedom and liberation. Specifically, the freedom of animals from torture by scientists and slaughter by meat eaters, the liberation of women from sexual slavery and servitude to men, the promotion of environmental causes and the downfall of capitalism.

Being a man who spent a lot of time in the outdoors, Archer had some sympathy with environmental causes. However, he had no sympathy with the execution of AFL's actions. Burning down chicken factories, throwing buckets of blood at shop owners, and vilifying every man as a kindred soul whenever a rape case made the news.

Strangely enough, she had never been above using her beauty to bring attention to her causes. The thought she was with the vile crea-ture Capstick was absurd.

'I can assure you it is absolutely right,' the Director replied. 'Oddly enough, the source is sig int itself.'

'Really?'

'GCSB, or perhaps one of our partners, have identified a burner phone that Capstick uses to communicate with his lady love. It's the age-old tactic of meeting in chat rooms and using a joint email address to write drafts to each other.' The Director snorted. 'I would have expected more from someone as paranoid as him, so quite frankly the man is begging to get caught.'

Archer nodded. It was basic but reliable tradecraft, and he wasn't surprised that Capstick and Krystal Raines knew such tactics.

Accessing an email address and saving a draft without sending it allowed the other party to then log in and read the message. It didn't leave an email trail that could be tracked, and chat room conversations were equally difficult to obtain, since they were automatically wiped.

The fact that the Director had mentioned the GCSB told Archer who had really secured the sig int. Legally, and in most circumstances, the Government Communications Security Bureau could not spy on its own citizens. Practically, those lines could become blurred. Often it was a matter of "don't ask, don't tell".

'So,' Archer said. 'What is it you want me to do?'

'I want you to follow the lead to its natural conclusion, of course.' The Director's tone was irritable. 'Take what you've been given and run with it. See where it takes you. It's better than anything you've come up in the last year on your own, Archer, so give it the attention it deserves. I'll have Mr Ingoe send you all the relevant information.'

With that the older man folded his hands on his desk and looked at Archer. The dismissal was clear.

'Right sir, very good.' Archer rose to his feet. The jet lag was starting to hit him, but his mind was buzzing. No point trying to sleep now. 'I'll go and see him.'

Jed Ingoe, or Jedi as he was known, was the Operations Manager for the Division. The Director's right hand man, he was a former SAS Regimental Sergeant-Major who had lost a leg in Afghanistan.

He started to turn, but the Director halted him in his tracks.

'Oh, and Captain Archer?'

'Sir?'

The Director's face was like stone.

'There will be no second chances. Is that clear?'

Archer raised an eyebrow, resisting his natural reaction to bite back.

'Yes sir,' he said, giving a short nod. 'Understood.'

He turned and headed for the door.

2

Having grown up in the provinces, Auckland had never really been home to Archer. He'd spent his schooling years in and around Palmerston North and Blenheim, due to his father's Air Force postings.

His own military career had taken him to Waiouru – colloquially known as the arsehole of New Zealand – back to Linton base near his hometown, and on to Papakura in south Auckland when he joined the Group. Overseas postings during this time had ensured he'd never put down roots anywhere for too long, the closest being a small house, more of a bach really, in Beachlands. The small satellite town on the city's southeast coast had become wildly popular in recent times, attracting city dwellers who still fancied a beach lifestyle, and prices had skyrocketed.

Archer had sat on his house, renting it out when he moved to London, and had not laid eyes on it for two years.

He sat now, parked a few doors down in the hired Honda, a take-away coffee cooling in the cup holder. The stereo was on low, playing some soft jazz that he'd stumbled across while scanning for anything decent. It seemed to suit his mood, the wave of melancholy that had crept up steadily since being back in Auckland.

He should have been at the hotel catching up on some sleep today, but he felt too distracted. Coming back here felt like a mistake. He wanted it to be home, but it no longer felt like that.

It was like seeing an old girlfriend again, the one who broke your heart or ended it badly, wanting it to be more but the damage was irreparable. It would never be the same and the realisation weighed on his shoulders.

He shook his head. He was tired and body sore.

The day before he'd got back to London from Wales, two days spent tabbing in the Brecon Beacons. The training ground for UKSF, it was a bleak, rugged landscape that took no prisoners. Men had died training there, and it had been a long time since Archer had had such a workout. Accompanied by a mate from a British unit, he'd thrashed himself across the mountains, doing the "Fan Dance" across the Pen-y-Fan in a respectable enough time. Not respectable enough to avoid the abuse from Jack who, when it came to physical training, was a sadist among sadists.

'Platform 4, sunshine,' he'd shouted at Archer as his Kiwi counterpart struggled up a scree slope. 'You're out of shape and out of time!'

Platform 4 at the Hereford train station was where failed applicants were sent from Selection, to wait for the next train out of town, carrying their kit and misery with them.

Still, Archer was satisfied enough. The fact that Jack could dance across the Fan like a mountain goat on Viagra was ridiculous; the man was nothing short of a machine, and Archer felt no guilt about not keeping up with him.

And so he sat, staring down the suburban street at his old weatherboard bach, noting that the fence needed a bit of a tidy up and the lawns had to be mowed. The property manager would be getting an email to get it sorted before he left town.

There used to be a girl living next door, an artist named Jazz. He'd had a long-standing on-off thing going with her after he left the Army, but that ended horribly when her drunk ex turned up and got rough. Archer had got rougher, and Jazz had seen a side to him that she didn't like.

He hadn't seen her since, and wondered if she still lived there. Even though it had never been serious between them, it had been comfortable and convenient. Just another failed attempt at the good life, he mused.

Life had been simple back then; the work on the security circuit usually entailed six or eight weeks in country and a couple off. Unless he had other plans overseas he would fly home, go fishing, catch up with mates, and hook up with Jazz. The V8 Monaro he'd driven back then was in storage, no use to him while he was in London.

So many things had changed since then.

'Fuck it,' he muttered, starting the engine. 'What's the point?'

He shifted the car into gear and pulled away from the kerb.

3

The AFL's headquarters was in Grey Lynn, a stone's throw from downtown Auckland.

It was on the second floor of a former menswear store, sharing the building with a legal chambers, a yoga studio, and a web design company. The next door down was a vegan café. Upstairs from that was a shosha shop that sold pipes and bongs ostensibly for smoking legal herbs, although from the look of the customers that drifted in and out it was an obvious cover.

No doubt the AFL members used the services of all their neighbours, Archer mused as he watched from a vantage point in a café across the road. This café was not vegan and made great coffee, a bowl of which he was slowly working his way through. Nor did it have the same sort of desperate-to-be-noticed clientele of the one he was watching.

Not that it excluded the middle-aged hipsters from Grey Lynn or the neighbouring Ponsonby, but Archer could live with them if he had to.

The sun was warm on his face as he enjoyed the solitude of a small table on the footpath, his back to the glass frontage of the café. It was late February and the country was in the midst of an Indian summer. Forecasters claimed it would run through until April, water restrictions were already in place and no doubt soon there would be droughts. The rugby season had already started, of course. That stopped for nothing.

The road was narrow, a single lane each way but cramped by cars parked badly on both sides of the road. The gap between Archer's table and the subject of his surveillance was about fifty metres, easily within range of the listening device he was deploying.

What had started out as a simple recce, a desire to lay eyes on the people he was tasked to look into, had taken a sudden turn as soon as he had driven past just ten minutes ago.

Ethan Capstick had exited the vegan café with another man in tow just as Archer was finding a park. They had taken a seat outside and were deep in conversation. Coffees had arrived at the same time as Archer grabbed a seat across the road. The other man was heavily overweight with a scruffy beard, unkempt hair and thick glasses. His pants were either long shorts or short longs, it was hard to tell.

Archer's "go bag" included a couple of basic items of surveillance kit, one being a small but powerful boom mic. It sat in his man bag – even carrying it made him feel uncomfortable, but it was very Grey Lynn – on the table top beside his bowl of double-shot flat white and a half-eaten date and walnut scone.

The Bluetooth earpiece Archer wore looked like any other, and allowed him to listen in to the conversation at Capstick's table, which was also being recorded. Fortunately there was little passing traffic, however the background noise of the vegan café interfered with the quality.

Still, it was enough to get some insight into one of his targets.

And an insight it was. Within two minutes of tuning in, Archer was having doubts about the quality of the intelligence he'd been given. It wasn't that he expected to pick up on a plot to overthrow the government, or hear Capstick passing on the details of how to make a pipe bomb. Or even some salacious gossip about a public figure's sexual fetishes that Capstick was planning to expose.

No, none of that was expected at all, and nor did it transpire. The thing that Archer picked up on, and which brought the doubt to his mind, was that Ethan Capstick was clearly a homosexual.

Archer had had little contact with gays in real life – at least, as far as he knew – so he was the first to admit that his knowledge of what to expect was limited at best. There were plenty of butch lesbians in the armed forces and on the security circuit, but as far as he knew, the only openly gay bloke he'd ever worked with was an office junior at the embassy.

It simply wasn't something that was encouraged in the world he'd come from.

The way Capstick spoke and moved, his voice being soft and more than slightly effeminate, his hands expressive and limp wristed, all screamed at Archer that there was no way this bloke was giving Krystal Raines the good news. As if that wasn't enough, the only thing he called his companion was "sweets".

He pondered this as he watched and listened, half tempted to give Jed Ingoe a call and ask him what the hell was up with their intelligence.

He held fire for now, finishing off the scone in a couple of bites and washing it down with the dregs of his coffee. The caffeine was doing its thing and he wanted another hit, but the bloody waiter was nowhere to be seen. He'd have to go inside to place another order and he didn't want to lose his spot, lest some Ponsonby wanker in a Panama hat and loafers should come along to rest his weary bones after a hard session of yoga.

He focussed on the two men across the road instead, his hands folded across his waist and his head cocked back as if enjoying the sun. Which was also true, given that it had been eleven degrees when he'd left London.

The other upside to it, as far as he was concerned, was the girls were wearing less. A case in point walked past, two blondes with tanned legs and ponytails hanging out the back of their caps, toned arms pumping as they strode past, chatting away. Neither of them had probably hit twenty one yet, probably lived with mummy and daddy – him being a corporate soul and her being a lady that lunched – or maybe with their moody boyfriends who used too many products and covered up their low self-esteem with tribal tattoos and beards that barely qualified for the title.

Again, Archer didn't care. He lingered on their taut backsides as they went past, knowing they were completely oblivious to his presence. And if they were, he was just another man over thirty – *eeewww!* – perving on them as they exercised.

He turned his attention back to the task at hand. The conversation between the two men had turned from a discussion on the latest tweets in American politics to the pending announcement of tax changes.

So far, so mundane. And then she appeared.

The door to the AFL office opened and Krystal Raines stepped out onto the footpath. Even at this distance, Archer could tell she was quite something.

She was the better part of six foot, slim and toned, with honey-blonde hair falling loose to her shoulders. She wore a simple red summer dress with thin straps, sandals and had a satchel hanging on a long strap from her tanned shoulder. She wore wide sunglasses pushed up on her head.

She paused and glanced around, seemed to linger on Archer for a moment – or was he just imagining that because she was beautiful? – before moving right towards the table where Capstick and the other man sat. Capstick started to wave for the waitress' attention, but Raines waved her away.

'Come on,' she said, her tone impatient, 'we need to get a move on.'

'I was just...' Capstick started to say, but Raines cut him off.

'We haven't got time. Let's go.' She glanced at the other man. 'Sorry Sweets, we'll have to catch up another time.'

His reply was muffled by a passing car and as soon as it was gone another car pulled up, double-parking right in front of Archer to drop off a couple of middle aged ladies. Their chatter and farewells to the man behind the wheel blocked the rest of the conversation and

Archer felt his frustration rise. He stayed where he was, willing them to hurry up and get out of the way.

By the time they ambled past him into the café, the targets across the road had moved off. He watched from the corner of his eye as they headed towards the next corner, walking together but not holding hands. The other man stayed where he was, finishing his coffee, still treating the rest of the world to a glimpse of his Grand Canyon.

As soon as the two targets disappeared from view around the corner, Archer moved. He put his phone away and grabbed his ridiculous man-bag, throwing it over his shoulder as casually as he could while he crossed the road.

Not that he was tasked with tailing them – it was supposed to be just a recce, after all - but he felt himself drawn to them like a hunter to their prey.

Capstick's companion was still sitting there, finishing off his coffee, and Archer saw more of him than he'd ever wanted to. The man was a fat slob, and while his black T-shirt hiked up to reveal a thatch of lower back hair, his pants slid down to reveal a good two inches of arse crack to the world. Archer reached the footpath and angled across it, digging his phone out again and activating the camera on video mode.

He moved to the front window of the café and peered in as if deciding whether to enter, the phone to his ear as he gave the odd "uh-huh" to his imaginary caller.

He angled it around, hoping to get a decent facial of the fat man, before moving off again in the direction his targets had taken.

Rounding the corner, he found himself in a residential street lined with cars, more side streets running off it. There was no sign of either Capstick or Raines anywhere.

Archer put his phone away and continued walking as if he belonged there and knew where he was going. Turning back would make it obvious to the fat man or anyone watching that he had been following the other two, so he pushed on, taking the first side street and working his way back towards his car.

As he walked he felt the heat of the sun on his exposed skin and the top of his head, reminding to cover up properly. He wasn't in London now.

He wondered if Eva would like it here. She loved the beach almost as much as she loved skiing, and the outdoors was always an attraction. The shopping would be a let down though, he figured. There were only so many pieces of fake greenstone jewellery and rugby jerseys one could buy.

They had talked about a trip out here, even got to some loose planning, but work had got in the way. In a couple of months' time, they'd say. It was always a couple of months away. He had wanted to take her on a road trip, show her where he grew up, take her to the mountains and the beaches and the rugged coast, even bloody Hobbiton if she'd wanted to.

Eva. Gone.

Archer felt his jaw clenching. She could have fought harder. He'd pushed, putting himself at risk with his agency, but it felt like she hadn't. She'd given up. Given up fighting and given up on them.

He felt his chest constricting and forced himself to take a long slow breath. No point getting wound up about it now. He had a job to do, something to take his mind off her.

He walked on.

4

———————

Auckland, New Zealand
Tuesday, 0800 hours

The hotel Ingoe had booked him into was right in the city, part of a large anonymous chain where he could melt into the background.

The basement gym wasn't deserving of the name so Archer skipped it and went for a run instead, heading down the city streets to the water front. He'd grabbed a short nap when he returned from his recce in Grey Lynn, had a bite to eat and felt the need to get energised.

Soon he was striding it out along Tamaki Drive, the harbour to his left, blue and crisp and dotted with boats of various sizes. Soon he could see kayaks out there, people paddling about for fun, just part of the scenery in Auckland these days. He made it to Mission Bay and turned back, feeling good with a sweat on and the blood pumping. Up ahead was a woman in black running tights and a grey singlet, her dark hair short and her limbs long and toned, ear buds in.

She was maybe a hundred metres ahead and he made her his target, putting in a little extra effort to catch up, challenging himself to pass her by the time they reached a camper van he could see further up. She was moving at a decent clip but he drew her in, and as they got closer he could she was toned in all the right places. Her arse was firm enough to bounce a coin off and he contemplated slowing down for a chat, maybe see where it took him.

No, he decided, not today. His recent track record was not good and he had more pressing matters than scratching an itch. He did hesitate, though, before giving himself a mental uppercut and carrying on.

She glanced at him as he edged by. Her smile was polite and slightly quizzical as she gave him a quick once-over. She was certainly worth slowing down for.

Clear skin, deep brown eyes, white teeth. A button nose that suited her pixie cut. Very cute, and he second guessed his decision to carry on.

A few paces on and he realised it didn't matter what he'd decided anyway – she was matching his pace, running shoulder to shoulder.

'Hello Craig,' she said. 'We need to talk.'

THE MERCEDES VAN was decked out as good as a limo, with wide comfortable seats, plenty of head room and thickly carpeted floors.

Archer was seated in the front seat beside the sliding door, turned to face the other occupants across the aisle.

The driver was a slim young man with perfectly-coiffed blonde hair. He sat motionless, eyes front, temporarily unemployed since the van wasn't moving.

Directly across from Archer sat a middle-aged man with the weathered skin of a smoker, a large bald patch surrounded by a ribbon of grey, and a paunch. His dark suit was off the rack and he was in need of a shave. The man beside him was younger, maybe late thirties, with cool blue eyes and clipped dark hair. He was dressed in jeans and an open necked shirt that accentuated his sculpted upper body. He regarded Archer across the aisle with practiced indifference.

The girl was in the front seat closest to the driver. She had pulled a hoody over her running top and was sitting quietly, waiting.

The boss, the muscle, and the beauty, Archer figured.

'So what's this about then?' he said, ignoring the other two for now and focussing on the boss. 'You obviously know who I am. The lady here tells me you represent the Canadian government, so I'm guessing you're CSIS.'

The older man gave a nod. The Canadian Security Intelligence Service was a good, experienced outfit, but Archer had never worked with them before.

'You're a long way from Ottawa. Do you fancy getting aboot?'

The older man acknowledged Archer's jibe at their accent with the slightest smile. The younger man's eye twitched. Archer grinned inwardly.

'You're right, Mr Archer,' the older man said. 'On both counts. My name is Pierre, this is Michael and Isabella.'

They both gave short nods.

'We have a common interest right now,' Pierre continued. 'We would like to share information and see if we can't work towards a common goal.'

'That's probably something better done through the proper channels,' Archer said coolly, 'than abducting someone off the street in their own country.'

Pierre feigned shock. 'Abduction is a bit strong, I would say Mr Archer. A friendly chat between colleagues is more accurate, don't you think?'

Archer tilted his chin towards the younger man, Michael.

'Well, considering your mate here's got a Sig on his hip, and whatever else the young lady and your driver have at hand, friendly's not the term I would use.'

'And you don't have a Glock on your own belt?' Michael retorted.

Pierre shushed him with a lift of his hand, and Archer gave a smirk.

'I don't, as it happens. Look, we could have this cock fight all after-noon mate,' he said, 'but it's my country. Even without that' – he looked Michael up and down – 'I'm pretty sure I'd win anyway.'

Michael flushed and was ready to bite back, but Pierre lifted his hand again.

'There is no need for this cock fighting, as you put it Mr Archer. We are what we are and we do what we do, isn't that right?'

'Fair enough,' Archer agreed, 'but this is still something you need to speak to the higher-ups about, not me. I'm just a worker, and you know I can't talk to you about operational matters. The government tends to frown on treason these days.' He shrugged nonchalantly. 'What can you do?'

Pierre smiled. 'I understand completely, and this is in no way some kind of attempt to corrupt you, Mr Archer. Please don't think that for one minute. We are simply trying to get to the heart of the matter as soon as possible, for all our sakes. And trust me, others from our organisation, further up the food chain, are doing the same with their peers within your own organisation.'

The Canadian smiled again and extended his hand. 'Please, no hard feelings. We are a bit like you Kiwis – we like to get to the point without having to muck around. No hard feelings?'

Archer shook the hand. 'None from me. See you around.'

The girl, Isabella, rose and slid the side door open. She stepped outside and waited while Archer debussed. Straightening up, he looked at her, close enough to smell the faint traces of a subtle perfume. She was watching him, her dark eyes giving nothing away.

'Nice to meet you,' she said, a hint of a smile playing on her lips. They were nice lips, full and plump and pink.

Beyond her he could see Michael watching them from his seat, his face stony.

Archer gave a small grin. 'Maybe we'll bump into each other again some day,' he told her.

She cocked an eyebrow. 'Perhaps.'

Isabella stepped back into the van, pausing in the doorway to close the door. Her butt was right there, definitely firm enough to bounce a coin off. Archer took a breath and stepped back as the door closed. The van began to move off.

He watched it go, and wondered what the hell that had all been about.

5

Auckland, New Zealand
Tuesday, 2130 hours

'Clumsy,' Ingoe said, 'fucking clumsy. That's not like them. They must be seriously rattled to try a direct approach like that.' He ran a hand through his clipped greying hair. 'The boss was far from impressed.'

Archer took a sip of his bourbon. 'They went to him too though, didn't they?'

Ingoe nodded. He toyed with his glass. 'They did.'

'And?' The former RSM was being unusually coy today and it, coupled with the onset of jetlag, was leaving Archer feeling irritated.

The hotel bar was nearly empty and they had a corner table where the lighting was dim and they both had a good view of their surroundings. Old habits die hard.

'And they have agreed to cooperate if needed on a mutually-beneficial operation.' Ingo lifted his glass, looked at Archer across the rim, and paused. 'You leave tomorrow.' He tilted the glass to take a sip.

Archer felt a boost inside. This was what it was all about – missions, not meetings. He needed to get out on the ground and get busy. He took another hit of bourbon. It wasn't great stuff but it served a purpose for now, warming his throat on the way down.

'Briefing?'

'At base. 0900.' Ingoe threw down the rest of his drink in one hit, indicating the conversation was over. He stood. 'See you there.'

With that he disappeared. Archer sat back, contemplating the last of his drink. It didn't inspire him, but there was bugger-all else to do in a hotel when you were staying on your own. He cast an eye around the bar, noting the distinct lack of females. Certainly nobody he would consider taking a shot at; an older couple together, a pair of girls in their early twenties, and a pair who were maybe forty. He eyed the 40-year olds first, noting the masculine cut of their clothes, the short hair and the lack of any feminine touches.

Probably not playing the same game as him, he figured.

The younger pair had potential, if he could ignore the loud chatter and hair flicking. Both were slim and pretty, hair carefully manipulated to within an inch of death, almost identical outfits. Each had a cocktail in one hand a phone in the other, and were constantly checking both their own and each other's phone. Maybe they were texting each other, or Instagramming or whatever the hell they did. Maybe sexting.

One caught him staring and whispered something to her friend, who looked over and gave an exaggerated impression of being embarrassed.

Archer rolled his eyes inwardly. No, he couldn't stand either of them, even if the game was on. He wanted a woman, not a bloody schoolgirl.

He threw back the last of his drink and called it a night.

6

Auckland, New Zealand
Wednesday, 0900 hours

The briefing from the Director was short and sharp, just how Archer liked them to be.

'Capstick is booked on a flight to the Cook Islands tomorrow,' the Director said. 'Departing Auckland at 08.55 hours and landing in Rarotonga at 13.45. He's booked a room at the Horizon Resort for two nights, then flies back. He has booked for one adult only.'

The Director peered over the top of his spectacles at Archer.

'You will fly out today at 1630 hours. He's on Air New Zealand. You're on Virgin Australia.' He pulled a face. 'Get there ahead of him and surveil him when he arrives. We've organised a local contact to meet you there, and your equipment will go ahead of you via the diplomatic bag. Mr Ingoe will organise that for you when you're finished here.'

Ingoe was seated off to the side, listening and waiting. He nodded his agreement but said nothing.

'This is a surveillance op only,' the Director continued, 'but I want you armed. We don't know why Capstick's going there or who he's going to meet, and for all we know it could be Viktor Kozlowski himself.'

Archer felt his heart pick up a beat. He certainly hoped so. If it was, it wouldn't end as a simple surveillance op, that was for sure. He would put the bastard down without batting an eye, and the consequences be damned.

The Director seemed to have read his mind.

'Being a surveillance operation only,' he said firmly, 'there will be no need for Rarotonga to be torn apart and the organisation to have to try and bail you out, will there, Mr Archer?'

Archer kept his face blank. 'Of course not, sir. I'll be prepared for every contingency of course, and will deal with things as I find them.'

The Director was silent for a moment, eyeing him warily across the desk. 'As long as we understand each other. Stay in comms with Jed, and I'll see you when you get back.'

He turned towards his computer screen. Archer paused, unsure if there was more to come. The Director glanced back at him with his fingers poised over the keyboard. 'That is all,' he said.

'Very good, sir.' Archer stood and followed Ingoe to the door.

They took the lift down to the basement range, where the smell of cordite and gun oil hung in the air. It was Ingoe's man cave, the place he came to reconnect with his past and get away from the politicking and schmoozing that took up more of his time than he liked.

'I suppose you left your 26 back in Haymarket?' Ingoe said, moving across to the heavy steel door to the armoury. He punched in an access code and swung the steel wheel.

'I didn't think I'd need it to meet the boss,' Archer said.

Ingoe opened the door and gave him a disapproving look. 'Don't I always tell you guys to be prepared?'

'I know you've always got spare toys to play with, Jedi,' Archer grinned. 'Let's hit the candy store.'

For ex-soldiers, the armoury was just that. It contained longs and shorts of several different makes, models and configurations, everything carried by the conventional police and military and many that weren't.

Ingoe plucked a Glock 26 from a rack and tossed it to Archer, who caught it neatly in one hand. It was a compact, reliable 9mm sidearm with a 10-round double stack magazine, and was Archer's favourite choice for everyday carry. He rummaged in a box and found three magazines.

'Heads up.'

He looked up just in time to catch the small pistol sailing towards his face. He opened his hand to look at it, recognising the weapon as a Kel-Tec P-32.

It was a fraction of the weight of the Glock and was chambered in the lighter .32 calibre.

'What d'you want me to do with this paperweight?' Archer said quizzically.

'Shoot it,' Ingoe said bluntly. 'You'll like it, it's a damn good gun. Ideal for a back-up for the likes of you.'

'The likes of me?' Archer raised his eyebrows. 'As opposed to the likes of anyone else?'

'The likes of you,' Ingoe said, 'who always gets himself into the shit then struggles to get out of it.'

'I'm still standing, Jedi,' Archer said. 'Besides, I didn't know you cared.'

'I don't, but it's a shitload of paperwork for me every time you get your arse in a sling. Perhaps if you've got a back-up weapon that won't happen so often.'

Archer shrugged and tossed the pistol back to him. 'If you love it so much, you can load it.'

Minutes later he was on the underground range, putting rounds down from both weapons.

Ingoe stood back, watching, and controlling the lights and targets. Once Archer was comfortable with each weapon Ingoe put him through a series of drills, varying the number of targets and frequently changing the lights so that one second he was shooting while back lit, the next second he was in low light or facing headlights.

The Glock was like a familiar old friend and he was happy with it.

The Kel-Tec took more time since he'd never fired one before, but after he'd emptied a hundred rounds from it he could see why Ingoe was so impressed. It was small and light, which seemed at first to be a hindrance, but he soon realised that it was probably the weapon's biggest drawcard.

Easy to conceal and easy to use, his only concern remained the stopping power. A .32 was nothing these days.

'True enough,' Ingoe agreed. 'But when your back's against the wall, would you rather have seven rounds of bugger-all or a hundred rounds of nothing?'

Archer couldn't argue with that, so he loaded three magazines for the Kel-Tec and put them with the three for the Glock. He and Ingoe stood at the workbench outside the armoury and cleaned the weapons, stripping each one before carefully wiping down the surfaces and getting rid of the burnt powder.

They chatted while they worked, catching up on gossip about who was where and who was doing whom. Ingoe was still very well connected with the Group and ran a couple of names past Archer of potential recruits to Division 5. Archer knew both of them and gave him his approval – like anyone who came through the unit, they were highly skilled and extremely motivated.

Archer reassembled the Kel-Tec and worked the slide before dry firing the trigger. He put the pistol down and looked across at his former Sergeant-Major.

'You miss doing this, Jedi?' he asked.

Ingoe eyed him. 'I'm right here,' he said. 'I'm down here most days.'

'I mean getting out there yourself,' Archer said. 'Deploying on ops yourself.'

Ingoe paused, put the Glock down and looked him in the eye.

'Every fuckin' day,' he said quietly. 'I deployed on practically every op in the unit for almost twenty years until some jihadi cunt blew my leg off. If that hadn't happened I'd still be out there.'

'You haven't lost the skills,' Archer said.

'I know. But I'm slower because of the prosthetic, and nobody wants a cripple on their squad do they?' He gave his head a shake as if brushing away a bad dream. 'No. My days of doing that are gone. These days I do what I can by sending you young fellas out into the field to do the fighting, while I keep the bosses out of your way and do the wining and dining.' His face softened ever so slightly, if that was possible for the old warrior. 'There comes a time for everyone, Arch. Your time will come one day, too.'

Archer tried to wave it away with a grin, but Ingoe was having none of it.

'It will come,' he said. 'The important thing is that you recognise it and act accordingly. Guys that don't either die or end up as sad bastards trying to keep up with the next generation. Know yourself, Arch.' He pointed a gnarled finger at his chest. 'Know yourself and accept it.'

7

———————

Rarotonga airport was humid and busy when Archer disembarked, yet it still managed to remain calm and laid back in the quintessential style of all Pacific islands.

Archer shuffled through Immigration – for what it was worth – in the midst of his fellow travellers, taking his time and melting into the background.

He wheeled a small carry-on bag and clutched his passport in his other hand, looking to any onlookers like just another tired but happy passenger. He was sweating by the time he crossed the tarmac from the plane to the building.

The four hour flight across the international dateline had been easy – a drink, a meal and a movie – and he had managed to avoid chatting to anyone aside from a fat Australian couple who had the seats across the aisle from him. They had insisted on introducing themselves – *Pat and Matt from Melbourne, good to meet ya cobber* – and he had done his best to shut the conversation down as fast as possible, putting his headphones on and absorbing himself in a Will Ferrell comedy that he couldn't remember the name of.

The line snaked forward and he eventually made it to the Immigration desk, handing his passport to the fat woman waiting there. She barely glanced at it before waving him through and Craig Anderson, freelance travel journalist from Auckland, was on his way.

He grabbed his suitcase from the luggage rotunda and exited into the Arrivals Hall, scanning for his contact.

Tumaru Aitu was someone he'd never met, but he recognised him immediately from the photo Ingoe had shown him. He was broad and strong looking, wearing cut off denim shorts, a Rip Curl T-shirt and jandals. He looked to be in his late forties. He stood right in front of the doors holding a handwritten sign in front of him – *Anderson* – mirrored aviators and a big grin on his face.

He spotted Archer at the same time and came to him, extending a big hand to crush Archer's.

'Kia ora bro,' he grinned, 'welcome to Raro. Steve's the name, hospitality's the game.'

Archer hesitated a second. 'Steve?' he said, suddenly unsure if there had been some mix up.

Steve waved his hand and grinned again, pushing his aviators up onto his head. 'Only my mum calls me Tumaru, bro,' he said. 'Oh, and my missus when I'm in trouble.' He paused and thought for a moment. 'Oh, and my ex-wife. Come to think of it, she called me that a lot.'

He gave the big grin again, his dark eyes sparkling. 'Prob'ly explains why I traded her in for a newer model, eh? Younger, sexier,' he cupped his hands out from his chest to illustrate his point, 'bigger boobs.' He laughed. 'It's all good bro. See if we can get you a island princess while you're here, eh?'

Archer grinned, immediately warming to the islander.

'Sounds good to me.' Archer passed him the litre of rum he'd picked up duty free on the way through. 'I hear you're a fan.'

Steve checked the label and his eyes creased into slits. 'Brother, you know the way to a man's heart.'

Steve grabbed Archer's suitcase from him and led him outside to a battered green Suzuki jeep. He tossed the bag in the back and fired it up, Archer climbing in beside him.

Other tourists were wrestling with their bags and bustling about the vans from the various resorts and hotels, cramming in to be taken to their holiday destinations.

The night air was warm and humid and buzzing with insect life. Soon those insects were barrelling past the open-topped jeep like incoming rounds as Steve hit the road. There was only one main road on Rarotonga, a 32 kilometre circuit all the way around the island. It was sealed and in reasonable condition, but some of its users were not so hot, ducking and weaving without too much consideration for the other chunks of steel whizzing by.

Their destination was on the south eastern side of the island, the most popular area for holidaymakers and tourists.

Steve chatted away as he drove with one hand, a smoke in the other hand which he also used to point out landmarks as they went by. Archer had read up on the place earlier in the day so he had some idea of the geography and history, but his driver's insight was not one found in the travel guides.

He pointed out the homes of a couple of political figures, the place an All Black had got drunk and run naked through a bar, the hotel frequented by the local organised crime figures – 'They're here bro, don't you worry about that,' – and the house where, aged 14, he'd lost his virginity. He had laughed at that one. 'My mate's mum,' he said. 'Her dog had just died. She was sad; I was glad.'

Archer laughed with him, finding the man's humour infectious.

'She even cooked me a feed afterwards,' Steve said. 'Not the dog though, bro. We're not Tongans.'

They soon pulled in the driveway of the Horizon Resort and Steve took him into the reception area to check in. Naturally Steve knew the man on the desk so the process took twice as long as normal as they chatted about how good the fishing had been lately.

The guy eventually handed over a key and Steve showed Archer to his room, narrowly missing the group of tourists who were piling out of a taxi van out the front.

'I'll see you in the morning bro,' Steve said, putting the suitcase down just inside the door. 'I'll prob'ly bring my assistant with me too.'

'Sounds good. What time?'

Steve grinned. 'Island time, bro. Or maybe five past.' He grinned and shut the door.

The room was called an executive suite, which meant it had a separate bedroom and a tiny kitchenette. Aside from that it was fairly standard – cold tiled floors, a fan lazily circling on the ceiling, an ancient air con unit that rattled like a tractor, and floral-patterned bedding.

Archer quickly unpacked what he needed, ensured the door and windows were secure, and threw the covers back off the bed. Despite the best efforts of the air conditioning unit it was still humid inside the room.

He took a quick shower with the cold on full before hitting the bed and staring at the ceiling. Another fan did what it could above him and he closed his eyes, waiting for sleep to take him.

Thoughts jumped about in his head and he focussed on processing them so they would leave him in peace. The new mission. Eva. His contact, Steve – jovial and obviously a real character, but could he be trusted? What would tomorrow bring?

A cicada sang its raspy song somewhere outside and other tourists banged about as they made their way to their rooms. None of these things he could do anything about right now, so he put them aside, bade them goodnight and slowed his breathing.

But even as he slipped under the warm blanket of sleep, one face remained in his mind's eye, laughing with child-like glee as she danced away from him.

8

———————

Rarotonga, Cook Islands
Wednesday, 0600 hours

Dawn was breaking over the island when Archer slipped into the clear water of the lagoon.

The resort was behind him, just a few metres of sandy white beach separating it from the warm waters of the Pacific. Nobody else was up this early and the ocean was calm, tiny waves rippling across the wide lagoon. Beyond the coral border bigger waves curled and crashed on the reef, and as he swam out he could see a handful of early-morning surfers out there, taking their chances of smashing onto the razor sharp coral for the thrill of a ride.

Archer built a steady rhythm, long strokes of freestyle that carried him the 150 metres or so out to the edge of the lagoon. He paused there for a few moments, treading water as he breathed in the clean, fresh air and let the waves wash over him. Tiny fish darted around beneath him, the dawn light catching flashes of their silver and rainbow colours in the water below.

Beyond the beach he could see the volcanic peaks that formed the centre of the island, covered in dense rainforest.

He set off on a breast-stroke journey the width of the lagoon, cutting back towards shore and rolling over so he could backstroke into shore. He pushed out again, floating on his back and looking up at the sky, the water muffling his hearing as he absorbed his surroundings. There was something special about being in nature like this, away from the world of technology and business, a raw calmness that nothing else rivalled.

He floated back out to the coral before turning and swimming into shore, taking as few breaths as his body could stand before his hands hit the sand and he pushed up in the shallows, his lungs heaving and his muscles buzzing from the exercise.

He lay there until he got his breath back, watching as the resort staff started getting ready for the day. Nobody moved fast but they had a well-practiced routine that soon had the outdoor dining area set up, sun umbrellas up, loungers ready and the pools free of leaves.

Archer grabbed the towel he'd left on the sand and dried himself before padding across the paved pool area, past the restaurant to his room. The air con was on full blast and the room felt cool to walk into. He stripped off his togs and tossed them into the bathroom before dropping to the floor.

Naked and with cold air blowing onto his skin, he spent half an hour on a set of exercises, bending, stretching, lifting and lowering himself using only his own body weight. He worked all the major muscle groups and soon they were singing. The last exercise was hand stands against the wall, carefully lowering himself until his head touched the tiled floor then pushing up again. One set of eight was enough and after the last one he flipped his legs back down and came onto his feet, breathing hard.

His muscles were screaming for relief and he spent the next ten minutes stretching them properly, getting the maximum benefit from the session that he could. He hadn't bothered finding out if the resort had a gym, and had come to realise that most hotel gyms were rubbish anyway, so he had developed this set of exercises that he could do anywhere. Usually not naked, of course.

Twenty minutes later Archer was the first guest to be seated for breakfast, taking a table at the edge of the dining area with an unobstructed view out over the water. It was a buffet set up and he happily helped himself. Breakfast had always been the most important meal of the day to him and he made two trips to the serving area. Fresh pineapple juice, strong coffee, wholegrain toast and peanut butter, fresh tropical fruits with muesli and natural yoghurt, with scrambled eggs for the main course.

He had pushed his plates aside and was working on a green tea when Steve ambled towards him. He was wearing battered board shorts and an old Balmain Tigers rugby league shirt. He had a black day pack over his shoulder and a grin on his face.

He stopped at the serving area to grab a coffee and brought it to the table, sitting across from Archer and putting the bag under the table.

'Up to your standards, bro?' he said with a grin, indicating the empty plates with a toss of his chin.

'Did the trick.' Archer took a sip of his tea. He wasn't a great fan, but he couldn't argue against the health benefits of it. 'Did you bring me a present?'

'Yep. I haven't opened it.'

Archer nodded and felt the smiling islander push the bag over to his feet under the table.

They sat for a few moments in the quiet of the morning. It was shaping up to be another hot day. The surfers were still out but the tide was receding, so the swells were easing off. Steve finished his coffee and waved to one of the waiters, pointing at his cup.

'One of my cousins,' he said to Archer. 'Well, my mum's cousin's grandson, anyway.' He gave the big grin again. 'We're all cuzzies here, bro.'

The waiter brought him a fresh cup and Steve went to take a sip, then paused.

'You are paying for this, eh?'

'All on the government ticket, mate,' Archer assured him. 'So, what's your story then? How did you end up here doing this kind of work?'

'Was gunna ask you the same thing,' Steve said. 'You're not the usual pencil-neck they send over here. You in the unit?'

'Long time ago,' Archer said vaguely. He didn't know how much to trust this guy just yet; no point giving away too many details. 'You?'

'Na, I know some boys who were though.' He mentioned a couple of names that Archer recognised. 'I was in the cops back there,' he continued. 'Did ten years, undercover and all that shit. Got myself in the shit though, so I jumped before I was pushed. Come back over here and put my money into a bar with my cuz.'

'What kind of shit?' Archer said.

'You're pretty blunt, bro.'

Archer shrugged. He wanted to know who he was dealing with.

'Just liked my piss too much. Got caught drink-driving, way over the limit. The bosses don't like that, so that was me done. But I got to come back here.' He gestured at their surroundings. 'This is paradise, bro. I grew up here. I live to fish and swim and sleep and serve drinks.' He grinned. 'My kids grow up between here and New Zealand. They know how to fish, they know to live in the bush. It's a pretty sweet deal.'

'Can't argue with that,' Archer said. He drained his green tea. The dregs were cold and bitter.

Steve leaned forward and lowered his voice. 'Even paradise has a dark underbelly though, bro. This is a tax haven, did you know that?'

Archer did know that, in fact, but he shook his head.

'And you know what tax havens attract? Organised crime. You know those criminals they're deporting from Aussie back to NZ? Some of them are here now. And those are some bad motherfuckers, bro. Bad motherfuckers.'

He was right. The Australians had been deporting NZ-born criminals back to their homeland, many of them having barely stepped foot in the place. Some had never been convicted but were known as criminal associates. Others were hardened members of outlaw motorcycle gangs, educated by the worst that Australia had to offer and with no respect for the law or their fellow man. The number of gangland hits and execution-style killings in New Zealand had noticeably increased since the deportees started hitting the shores.

Archer nodded, keen to hear more. It probably had nothing to do with his mission, but you never knew. They were just the sort of thugs that Viktor Kozlowski liked to use – brutal and motivated by greed.

'You have much to do with those sorts of dudes?' Archer said.

Steve pulled a face. 'Not if I can help it. They come into the bar sometimes, but we don't have any issues with them any more. Not since they first started arriving here.'

Archer cocked an eyebrow and smiled. 'Any more? So you did but you sorted them out?'

To his surprise, Steve didn't grin. 'Not like you mean. There's no point scrapping with these guys, bro, they'll kill you. In fact the only murder we've had in Raro in the last few years was from one of those pricks, beat a guy to a pulp for trying to stand up to them. Stomped on his head right in front of his missus, bro.'

His face darkened and Archer saw his edge then. Gone was the smiling island boy, replaced by a hard man who had seen and done things most people never dreamt of. 'You know what they did then? Two of these fuckers, they laughed in her face then they pissed on him. He's lying there with his head smashed in, dying. She's standing there watching, can't do a fuckin' thing to help him. And these cunts fuckin' piss on him.'

Archer felt his jaw tighten. He'd never liked bullies in any shape or form. 'Disrespect,' he said, and Steve nodded.

'Exactly, bro. Disrespect.' He took a deep breath. 'So that's the other side of the paradise you see. I just thought you should know what's real and what's not.'

Archer nodded slowly, his mind ticking over. He always liked to know what was around him. The environment played a big part in his situational awareness.

Most people wandered through life in a perpetual state of obliviousness. Men like Archer, who lived in the danger zone, never dropped below a readiness state of "yellow". Yellow meant they were aware of who was around them and what was going on nearby, without necessarily being on edge. As soon as things changed, their state of readiness moved with it. Yellow was relaxed.

"Red" was a state of high alert and action-taking. The general populace bumbled about in a "white" state with their eyes glued to their phones or thinking about what shoes to buy or what had happened at work today. They walked past threats having no clue they were even there.

They inadvertently placed themselves at risk. They constantly had near-misses. And sometimes they died.

Archer reconsidered the man across from him. He was confident now that Steve was a man he could rely on, and he understood why he had been picked by the Service as a contact point.

'I need a vehicle,' Archer told him.

'Sorted. That jeep I picked you up in is out the front.' He put the keys on the table in front of him. 'Rental, got it for however long you need it.' He grinned, the hard edge disappearing back behind the gleaming white teeth and smiling eyes. 'My cousin works at the rental company.'

'Of course he does. Thanks. And I take it you're my back-up?'

'You know it. I'm free until you go back.' He gave Archer his cell phone number.

'Sorted. So my target lands at 13.45 today. I'll get you to take him from the airport and I'll stand off. No point him laying eyes on me too soon.' Archer chose his words carefully. 'Do you have much experience in surveillance?'

Steve gave no hint of being offended. 'Yeah bro, I spent some time on a team when I was in the cops. I'm all good. Besides,' he grinned, 'I fit in better here than your pale face.'

Archer chuckled. 'Fair call.'

'Plus, I've enlisted my own back-up.'

'Let me guess, another cousin?'

'Na, my sister. Dee Dee. She works here anyway, so she's made sure she's working this afternoon and tomorrow.'

'What does she do?' Archer wasn't convinced on using an untrained helper. It was a risk that could easily blow the operation.

'She's a shift supervisor, helps out wherever they need a hand. Don't worry, she just sits in the background and you won't even know she's here.'

'Okay.' Archer gave a short nod, still not convinced. 'But if she's not up to it she comes off as soon as I say, right?'

'You da boss,' Steve grinned. 'But don't worry bro, it'll be sweet. I'll tell her to come see you before this dude gets here. Who is he, anyway?'

Archer gave an indifferent shrug. 'Just a guy who might meet someone. I'm interested in anyone he talks to, but I don't know who that will be.'

'All good.' Steve stood and gave him a toss of the chin. 'Catch ya later, bro.'

Archer watched him go, strolling away as if he owned the place. Maybe he did. Or at least one of his cousins might have.

9
____

With Capstick due to arrive at the resort about 15.00 hours, Archer took advantage of the down time to get his bearings.

He walked through the resort, eyeballing Capstick's room and all possible escape routes if things went wrong. He picked up the jeep and drove past the neighbouring resorts, getting a basic idea of their layout, having already done the same from the beach side.

With that done he hit the road and drove into downtown Avarua, the capital of the Cook Islands on the northern side of the island. He dropped the jeep at the kerb, preferring to walk to get his bearings.

It was hot and getting hotter, and the back of his shirt was soon soaked. The Glock was comfortably holstered on his hip under the loose shirt and he wore trainers in case he needed to run. With the requisite cap, shades, shorts and daypack of a tourist, nobody gave him a second look.

Downtown Avarua was typical of the islands – dusty roads, loose dogs, beat up trucks and SUVs and slow-moving locals. There was also a surprisingly number of new or newish commercial buildings with the older shops and business premises interspersed between them.

Archer stopped at a shop to grab bottles of water and downed one in a minute, binning the bottle and cracking another one. It was a while since he'd been in such humidity and he realised he hadn't been hydrating properly.

He found a tired supermarket and stocked up on dried fruit and nuts, chocolate bars and the few power bars he could find. The pickings were slim unless he wanted corned beef, anything with coconut or some strangely-packaged items he didn't immediately recognise. He added a pair of ugly Hawaiian-style shirts and a wide-brimmed straw hat to his purchases, all three items guaranteed to make look like just another idiot tourist.

The drive back to the resort was only a few minutes and he took the time to enjoy it now, having completed what he wanted to do. The ocean was sparkling and inviting off to his right, access blocked by the native palm trees and undergrowth that surrounded the resorts lining the coast. The wind was cooler in the open-topped jeep than the town centre and it carried with it the scent of native flowers.

Motor scooters buzzed about like insects, some carrying terrified-but-excited tourists, others casually piloted by locals. One kid raced past the others with his feet up on the handlebars, throwing Archer a cheeky grin and a wave as he went by. As if that wasn't unnerving enough, his little sister was perched behind him facing backward, her hair blowing in the wind.

Archer shook his head in amazement and carried on to the resort, backing the jeep into a slot out the front and gathering his purchases. The heat was draining and he could see why the locals never seemed to move very fast.

The laidback island lifestyle was certainly attractive, and as he unlocked his door he made a mental note to look into coming back for an actual holiday at some stage. Under a different name of course and at a different resort, and definitely not if things ended up going noisy.

His first mission for Division 5 had involved a trip to Samoa, which ended in the deaths of several bad guys and with himself and the British agent he was partnered with being tortured. Enough time had passed that he could probably go back, but he'd never felt the pull to do so. Despite some plastic surgery he still carried a scar on his chest where a red-hot steel poker had been pressed into it.

He locked the door and put his bags down, thinking for a moment about the British girl, Tracy. She was still with MI6, or so he'd last heard, but no longer active in the field. She'd been a tough cookie and had handled herself well, but the threat of being gang raped and having her teeth pulled out with pliers had been too much for her.

She had finished the mission in a fragile state and Archer had carried on without her. She had been a good girl and a good agent, but ultimately the sort of life he led was not for her.

Problem was, he didn't know how to do it any other way. Ingoe's words back at the armoury had been bouncing around in his head the last day or so. *Know yourself and accept it*. It was good advice, and Archer believed that he did. He did things his way, he knew what he was and he was comfortable with it.

He had left the air con cranked up, blatantly ignoring the instruction sheet pinned to the wall, and the room was cool to walk into. He downed another half bottle of water and put the others into the tiny fridge, along with the chocolate bars and the bottle of peach iced tea he had grabbed.

He peeled the sticky shirt off his back and stripped naked, stepping into the shower to freshen up with the intention of heading to the pool afterwards. It seemed silly showering first but he knew he would feel better for it.

He stepped out of the shower and reached for a towel, glancing through the open door into the living area.

A woman stood there, her hands on her hips and an amused smile on her face. She was a Rarotongan in her mid-twenties, with thick black hair and smooth milk chocolate skin. She was curvy in all the right places, perhaps carrying a little puppy fat, and her dark eyes danced with laughter at his embarrassment. She wore a white corporate uniform blouse over a black skirt.

She looked him up and down before settling on his face.

'Hi,' she said, 'I'm Dee Dee. I thought we should...make contact.'

'I DON'T NORMALLY greet visitors naked,' Archer said, placing a glass of iced tea on the coffee table beside the two-seater where Dee Dee sat.

It was several minutes after their awkward introduction and he was now fully dressed and almost over his embarrassment. He took the single armchair and sipped from his own glass. It was almost lunch time and he was hungry.

Not that he was in too much of a rush to show her the door. She was certainly an attractive girl, with long legs that went all the way to heaven and hefty breasts that placed an unreasonable strain on the buttons of her blouse. He wondered if Dee Dee was a nickname that originated with her breasts.

'Don't worry,' she said, trying to hide a smirk, 'I've seen worse. I grew up with five brothers, and you've met one of the tamer ones. And every other fat tourist here wants to have a little coconut before he goes home, so believe me Mr Anderson, I've seen worse.'

Archer put his glass down. 'Well, I'll try not to do that,' he said. 'And it's Craig.'

She gave an indifferent shrug and a smile. 'It's okay, Craig.'

He wasn't sure what that meant, so he played safe and pushed on. 'So what's Steve told you about why I'm here?'

'Not much. As much as he thinks I need to know.' A flicker of annoyance crossed her face. 'He can be a little bit over-protective.' She rolled her eyes. 'Island men are like that; they think they're the big chief until shit goes wrong, then they come running to their mummies or their wives. Or their sisters.'

Archer chuckled. 'Fair enough.' He gave her a short version of why he was there and what he wanted from her.

'Just eyes and ears,' she said, nodding. 'Sweet as. I start work at twelve so I'm here all afternoon until the night shift guy comes on. I get off at nine.' She tossed back her iced tea and stood, smoothing down her uniform as she looked him in the eye.

He stood, almost face to face with her. Her cleavage was wide and inviting, just inches away.

'Maybe we could have a drink after work?' she suggested softly.

Archer felt a grin tugging at his lips. 'Let's see how we get on today,' he said. 'I'm not sure if Steve would like me having a drink with his little sister.'

She wagged a finger at him and gave a tsk-tsk. 'Remember, it's not the men round here who call the shots. The Island ladies are the ones you need to listen to.' She gave a flirtatious smirk. 'I'll see you later, *Mr Anderson.*'

With that she headed for the door, leaving Archer to watch the sway of her hips and wonder exactly how much trouble he could get himself into in just two days.

10

———

The afternoon passed slowly at the poolside.

Archer had claimed a lounger that was back from the edge, and he moved it sporadically to chase the shade of an umbrella. He kept hydrated with a water bottle and ordered non-alcoholic drinks from the bar, all the while listening to an iPod on low or working his way through a paperback thriller.

Across the pool Ethan Capstick sat at a sheltered table, working on a laptop and slurping rainbow-coloured drinks with umbrellas and straws. He wore a Panama hat, a Hawaiian shirt with flamingos on it, baggy shorts that went below the knee and sandals. He spoke to no one, the only human interaction he had being the wait staff that brought his drinks to him.

Dee Dee herself tended to him on occasion and tried to engage him in conversation, but he brushed her off and made it clear he didn't want company or conversation. She pulled a face after the last time and left him to it. Archer watched her go and took a long draught of water; she certainly had some fire in her belly, this girl.

The other loungers were mostly occupied by couples and he let his eyes wander behind his shades, lingering on the bikini-clad forms that were soaking up the sun or slicing through the warm water of the pool.

One of the men caught him looking and gave him a scowl. Archer mentally shrugged and looked elsewhere. There was no point drawing attention to himself. Besides, there was plenty to look at besides that guy's wife with her tramp stamp and saggy arse.

Archer let his mind wander, the heat combining with the chilled-out environment to make him sleepy. The book wasn't enough to hold his interest and he felt his eyelids drooping. He tried to fight it but before he knew it his head was nodding and he was going under.

Fuck! He sat upright with a jerk, having no idea how long he'd been out for. It could have been seconds or several minutes. He glanced around quickly, checking to see what had changed from what he last remembered seeing. A few people had moved, but the most obvious thing he noticed was the woman beside him. Leaning over as she placed a coconut with a colourful umbrella and straw protruding from the top on the small table beside him.

It was Dee Dee in her crisp white blouse and he was eye level with her inviting cleavage. He lifted his gaze to see the amused look in her eyes. She glanced down at her cleavage then back at him, grinning mischievously without a hint of self-consciousness.

'Wakey-wakey,' she said, 'I thought you needed some stimulation to stay alert.' She lifted the coconut drink and handed it to him. 'And I brought you a drink, too.'

Archer gave a chuckle and sat up straighter, taking the drink from her. She was flirtatious and enticing and it was working. Not to mention she'd just saved his arse.

Fuck it, he decided, he was going to have to do something about this. But that was for later. He couldn't afford to be distracted again.

'What's he doing on the laptop?' he said. He took a sip of the drink; it was sweet and creamy, the coconut milk laced with something fruity he couldn't quite place. Hopefully the sugar would wake him up.

'Some kind of document,' Dee Dee said, leaning her hands on her knees so she could stay in position. Archer could see past her to where Capstick was typing away at his table. 'I couldn't see what it was but he's been at it for hours.'

Probably one of his so-called investigative assignments, Archer presumed. God only knew what the subject of that was. Perhaps the man had found signs of alien life that had been suppressed by the New Zealand government, or the SAS were really involved in the Kennedy assassination. The man was a lunatic.

'He's quite rude, too,' Dee Dee continued. 'I tried to make small talk with him but he's not interested.'

Archer crooked a grin around his straw. 'Maybe you're too much woman for him,' he said.

'I know you're taking the piss out of me, but it's the only possible explanation. Unless he's queer.'

Archer chose to keep his thoughts on that to himself, still not convinced either way.

She straightened up. 'I'll see you later.'

He watched her go, the sway of her behind drawing him in like a magnet.

Yes, he definitely needed to do something about that, he decided. An image of Eva bounced into his head and he felt a momentary stab of guilt before pushing it away. She had made her choice, so he had no need to feel guilty about his. No point in having regrets over things he couldn't change.

It was time to live in the here and now.

It was nine by the time Archer got back to his room, having spent the last two hours in the restaurant and bar.

The food had been excellent – scallops fresh from the shell, lobster drizzled with butter, a light salad, and a coconut cheesecake that was so rich and sweet it had set his teeth on edge. He'd washed it down with a Tiporo pilsener from the local Matutu brewery, followed by a bourbon and ginger ale at the bar.

Capstick had dined alone, spoke to no one and wandered off to his room with three stiff drinks in his belly and a wobble in his step.

There seemed little point in posting a guard on his room overnight, and with no electronic kit to assist, there was nothing to do but get his own head down. Steve had been in the bar but stayed away from him, talking with a couple of off-duty staff instead, and Dee Dee had finished work a little earlier. She had given him a coy smile as she walked past him at the bar and he had felt a kick of excitement in his chest.

Unlocking the door to his room, he wasn't surprised to find that he had a visitor. Tealights had been lit around the living room and in the bathroom. He moved down the hall to the bathroom doorway.

An ice bucket sat on a stand beside the bath, which was full of frothing bubbles, and a very naked and smiling Dee Dee.

She crooked a finger at him. Archer went gladly.

11

Rarotonga, Cook Islands
Thursday, 0930 hours

With Steve on deck to keep eyeball on Capstick, Archer took advantage of a few hours' down time to explore the island with Dee Dee.

Her offer of being a tour guide was too good an offer to pass up, and he had to admit that perhaps his eagerness to accept was coloured by her enthusiasm the previous night. She was a sensuous lover who took full advantage of their time together, leaving them both satisfied before falling asleep in each other's arms and waking with the dawn to do it all over again.

Archer knew it was nothing more than a fling and that he would probably never see her again after he flew out the next day, but that was okay. It was what it was and it served a purpose for both of them, and neither was bothered.

After checking in with Steve they hit the road, Archer at the wheel of the jeep while Dee Dee navigated. She took him the whole way around the island, pointing out her family home, the church they attended every Sunday, her school and various places of interest. The day was warming up nicely and there was a light off shore breeze that rustled the trees they passed and flicked up white caps on the ocean's surface.

After an hour or so of sight-seeing Dee Dee directed him off the main road onto an unsealed road that ran towards the centre of the island. He slowed to navigate his way, avoiding the odd chicken that ran loose from the undergrowth on either side, and they bumped their way to a dead end. He turned the jeep around and switched off the engine, silence falling on their green surroundings.

'Now we walk.' Dee Dee grabbed the flax bag she had brought with her and led the way up a narrow foot track that went further into the bush.

'Where exactly are you taking me, young Dee Dee?' Archer enquired, brushing aside the large green leaves that hung over the track. The track was well worn but still overgrown and narrow, indicating to him that it wasn't on the tourist maps.

The mountains loomed above and he could hear the tinkle of water.

'You'll see.' She shot him a cheeky grin over her shoulder. 'Just go with it, okay?'

He raised a quizzical eyebrow but said nothing further, following her up a short slope to a clear mound, breaking the ceiling of bush that had enveloped them. Straight ahead was a rocky pool of clear water, with a short waterfall cascading down the mountain side into it, maybe ten metres high.

'Wow,' Archer said, taking it in. 'It's beautiful.'

'But wait,' she said, heading off again, 'that's not it.'

She led him around the side of the pool and up a sharp incline that took them to the top of the waterfall. There lay a much wider pool, fed from a stream that flowed from above before washing over the edge to form the waterfall below them.

It was quiet and surreally beautiful, with the gentle waters framed by dense rain forest on two sides.

'This is it,' Dee Dee said, gesturing with open arms. 'This is the secret of the island. Tourists don't know about it unless locals tell them, and nobody does. If they did it wouldn't be special anymore, would it?'

'Too true.' Archer walked to the edge of the water and bent to swish his fingers. The water was cool and inviting.

When he turned to stand up he saw Dee Dee loosening the halter neck of the cotton dress she was wearing. She let it fall to her waist, exposing her large bra-less breasts, chocolate brown with dark, wide areolas. She unzipped the back to drop the whole dress to the ground. She saw him staring and smiled unashamedly. She stripped off her knickers and stood naked before him.

'Are you coming in or what?'

He quickly stripped off and followed her into the water, feeling only a little self-conscious about his nakedness. He swam out to where she was treading water and reached for her, but she duck-dived away and left him grasping air. She came up laughing and came to him with her arms open, pressing herself against him and wrapping her legs around his waist. She kissed him on the mouth, her tongue probing. He put his hands on her thighs and held onto her as he bounced on the rocky floor of the pool.

'Interested, Mr Craig?' she giggled, wriggling her hips. 'Yes, I see you are.' She wriggled again and he responded. 'Let's do something about that.'

She kissed him again, with more urgency now, and he entered her, bringing a moan of pleasure from her as he manoeuvred himself backwards for a better foothold.

Several minutes later they lounged on the rocks in the shallows of the pool, getting their breath back.

12

Dee Dee was tracing a finger through the hair on his chest when Archer heard a vehicle approaching below.

He listened for a few moments until the sound of the engine died, followed by the metallic thud of doors closing. Two doors, presumably two people.

'Sounds like we're about to have visitors,' he said, pushing up to his feet. He helped Dee Dee up, pulling her in for a last naked cuddle before they hurried for their clothes.

'Better not be bloody tourists,' she grumbled, struggling to pull the dress on over her wet legs.

Archer did his shorts up and helped her with her dress, then bent and tied up his trainers. He checked his watch. It was nearly eleven anyway, and he really should be getting back to help out Steve.

He checked his phone, but there was no signal. Hopefully he hadn't missed a call from Steve to say that the meet had gone down while he was busy off screwing Steve's sister at a tropical waterfall. That would take some explaining to the Director.

He surreptitiously slipped the holstered Glock from his pocket and secured the black nylon inside-the-pants holster on his hip under the loose flaps of his shirt.

He turned to see Dee Dee watching him and realised she had seen the gun.

'Jesus,' she said with a tremor in her voice, 'you really are an action man.'

He gave her a wink and a grin. 'I like to think I'm pretty good with my weapon,' he said and she laughed out loud.

'Well, there are no complaints from me, Craig.'

She led the way down the steep track beside the waterfall, the water hitting the rocks and spraying them with mist as they made their way in the sticky heat. It reminded Archer of jungle training – minus the enchanting waterfall and the sex with a beautiful local girl, of course.

They reached the bottom just as two more figures emerged from the track onto the clear mound overlooking them.

Dee Dee continued moving but Archer stopped and stared. Michael and Isabella from the Canadian SIS did the same, and even with the distance between them Archer could see the embarrassment in their faces.

'Well, well, well,' he said, moving towards them, 'fancy meeting you two here.'

Dee Dee stopped, turned and gave him a questioning look. 'You know these two?'

'We're sort of professional acquaintances,' he said. He edged past her on the narrow track. 'I didn't think I'd be seeing them so soon, though.'

He reached the bottom of the mound they stood on, a metre or so lower than them, and assessed them. Both were fit and athletic looking. Both wore shorts and trainers with T-shirts. Michael had a baseball cap on and a daypack over his shoulder. He looked mighty pissed off, to say the least.

Isabella's legs were smooth and toned and the faded old black Alannah Myles T-shirt she wore had ridden up slightly to show a hint of flat, tanned abdomen. Archer had seen worse. He glanced up to see her amused look. She shrugged and pulled a face as if to say "Whaddaya do?"

'So what're you playing at Archer?' Michael said, his tone testy.

'I'm not playing at anything. I'm on holiday, mate. You're a long way from home though. And fancy going away with a work colleague.' He grinned, knowing it was winding the other man up. If Michael was going to successful in this business, he really needed to get a better game face.

Michael glanced at Isabella then back at him. His face was dark.

'Okay, cut the crap,' he said. 'We need to talk.' He gestured towards Daisy. 'And who the hell are you?'

Dee Dee wasn't sure what was going on, but she knew rudeness when she saw it. 'I'm Dee Dee,' she snapped, planting her hands on her hips and giving him the full attitude. 'Who the hell are you?'

He scowled and made to snap back, but Isabella shot him a warning look. 'Michael,' she said softly, 'chill.'

The Canadian woman looked back to Archer. 'But we do need to talk.'

He shrugged. 'I'm guessing we're here for the same reason. And I'm guessing you followed us, so presumably you have more troops back at the resort?'

There was a telling pause before Isabella replied. 'All due respect to you Dee Dee, but this needs to be a private conversation.'

Dee Dee harrumphed under her breath, but the woman-to-woman communication was far more effective than Michael's effort. She turned to Archer, still looking pissed off, and he gave her a reassuring nod.

'No dramas,' he said. 'Just wait at the jeep, I'll come get you shortly.'

She stepped in and kissed him on the mouth, then started to move.

And that's when the shooting started.

Archer was looking towards the two Canadians when he saw Michael stumble forward as if he'd been pushed from behind. There was a slapping sound at the same time then Michael lurched again, his face registering surprise and pain. Hs grabbed at the air as his balance went, his body juddering with a third impact.

Isabella twisted at the same time as her colleague was falling forward, her legs going from under her and they went down simultaneously.

'Down!' Archer grabbed for Dee Dee but she was just beyond his reach and still moving.

'What the fuck...'she said, then there was the slap of a bullet hitting skin.

Archer saw a spray of blood from Dee Dee's head and lunged for her.

Michael came down off the mound like a falling tree, colliding with Dee Dee and knocking her backwards into Archer. Isabella tumbled down under more control, letting out a shriek as she did so.

Archer was knocked sideways by the impact of both Michael and Dee Dee, hit the undergrowth at the side of the track and tumbled. He rolled to his feet, hearing voices from just beyond the mound, and crouched, scanning and assessing.

Neither Michael or Dee Dee were moving, but Isabella was scrambling to her feet. There was blood on her left arm.

Archer pushed himself back into the undergrowth, waving at the Canadian girl to hurry up and come to him.

He had no idea who or what was on the other side of the mound, aside from at least one person with a suppressed weapon and an urge to kill. Isabella was scrambling towards him but it would be too late.

He saw a head starting to come into view above the dirt of the mound and lunged out of the greenery, the Glock in a two-handed grip. He stepped to the side past the girl, moving around the dirt mound in a crouch, and laid eyes on the attackers.

There were two bearded men, both white, in their forties and dressed in fatigue pants, shorts and baseball caps. Both had suppressed Diemaco assault rifles in the shoulder. One was coming up the mound, seeking targets, the other covering him from several metres back down the track.

The guy up front spotted Archer at the same time as Archer stroked the trigger of the Glock. The first 9mm round took him in the side of the neck, the second through the left ear. The guy dropped without a word and Archer turned his attention towards the second guy, realising as he turned that rounds were already incoming.

They zipped past him, close enough to feel the wind against his skin, and he dropped lower, stepping back left behind the cover of the dirt mound. He heard impacts against the dirt as he crabbed sideways, moving fast but placing his feet carefully so he remained stable. He heard Isabella calling out to him from behind and ignored her – the threat was in front and he needed to deal with that before he attended to her.

Several more shots buzzed overhead a good two metres to the side, and he eased around the edge of the mound with the Glock up. The guy had advanced closer and had his rifle up, but was scanning in the other direction. He never saw Archer as the Glock cracked off a double tap. Both rounds took him in the side of his torso and he staggered, trying to swivel to confront the threat, but he didn't stand a chance.

Archer put another double tap into him, one round shattering the stock of the Diemaco and the other punching through the guy's throat. He fell backwards and made like a starfish, his legs twitching violently. Archer moved up, kicked the rifle aside and stood over him while he scanned for more threats.

Seeing none, he crouched down and locked eyes with the guy. Blood was frothing from his lips into his beard and his eyes were wide. He was in a world of pain and knew his time was up. More blood was bubbling up from the hole in his throat.

'Who are you?' Archer said.

The guy continued to twitch and his lips moved soundlessly. His eyes went glassy and still and his lips stopped moving. Archer patted him down, finding nothing but a spare magazine for the Diemaco and a lock blade knife.

Archer moved back around the mound, finding Isabella kneeling beside Michael's still form. Blood soaked his shirt and her hands, and she looked up with wide eyes as Archer approached her. She had rolled her colleague onto his side into the recovery position, but

Archer could tell he was beyond that. He quickly checked the guy's pulse, finding nothing.

'I'm sorry,' he said softly, 'he's gone.'

He left her to check on Dee Dee, already knowing what he would find. A pool of blood had darkened the dirt around her head and she was lying on her back, her hair partially covering her face. Her eyes were closed and she almost looked peaceful. He knew it was futile but he checked her pulse anyway. Nothing.

Even if she was still alive, he doubted she would have survived very long considering the head wound she had received. Archer gently touched his fingers to her face.

'Oh Dee Dee,' he whispered. 'I'm sorry. This wasn't supposed to happen.'

13

Archer went to the first attacker he'd shot, quickly frisked his pockets, and found exactly the same as what the other guy had carried. These men had been sterilised. Coupled with their choice of the Diemaco as their weapon, it told Archer they were professionals of some sort.

He heard a shout from further down the track. He snatched up the fallen Diemaco, shoved the Glock into its holster, and checked the chamber on the rifle. There was one up the spout and the safety was off. He dropped out the 30-round mag and pressed down on the top bullet. It only had a couple of rounds missing. He slapped it back into place, ready to go. The whole process had taken only a few seconds.

'We need to move.' Archer grabbed Isabella by the arm, causing her to cry out in pain. He yanked her to her feet anyway and hustled her off the track into the undergrowth, pushing her ahead of him into the dense greenery. Running feet sounded behind them and he pulled Isabella down, dropping flat to the forest floor. He heard muted cursing and the squelch of a radio, followed by muffled speech.

Peering through the fronds, Archer could just make out the shape of another man. Fatigue pants and desert boots. These guys were definitely para-military of some sort, and he had a horrible feeling in his gut. Black Star employed dudes like this. Ex-soldiers looking for a buck, not too choosey about how they earned it. Archer had worked for private security companies on the circuit, and he knew that some were better than others. The top of the range outfits employed only ex-Special Forces guys like himself, most were somewhere in the middle, and then there were the bottom feeders. Security guards, wannabes and Walter Mitty-types.

Black Star had provided services to the CIA, including doing some of their wet work, and they were rotten to the core. Viktor Kozlowski was tied to them, and if they were here in Rarotonga, then Archer's gut told him he was on the right track.

'Come on out,' the guy called out. 'It's safe now.'

His Boston accent was another strand of evidence for Archer.

'Come out guys,' he continued. 'We've saved you, it's okay. We'll get you back to safety and on the next plane to Ottawa, okay?'

Archer frowned for a moment before it dawned on him. The guy had mistaken Michael's body for him, and thought the two Canadians had escaped. That told him that these guys knew who the Canadians were, and also that he either hadn't checked Michael's body properly or didn't know Archer by face.

Whichever way it went, it was sloppy work, and Archer reconsidered his assessment of these guys as professional. He gently eased the Diemaco around until the barrel was pointing towards the vague shape he could see. Isabella caught his eye and he could see the fear there. Hopefully she wouldn't blow a gasket and put them both in the shit.

'Come on guys, hurry up.' The guy was more insistent now. 'We ain't got all day. Get your asses out here so we can get you to safety.'

Archer lined up the shot through the undergrowth, sighting on the only part of the guy's body that he could see properly – his left leg. The distance was only about eight metres and elevated from the forest floor.

He stroked the trigger and the rifle nudged his shoulder. The guy fell immediately to his other knee, screaming as he clutched at his leg. Archer could see his torso now and put a second round into his side, knocking him over like a bowling pin.

Archer pushed up and went forward, pausing inside the bush line to check for other targets. Nothing. The guy was gasping and moaning, writhing on the ground. His rifle was out of reach and he was out of the game.

Archer went to him and jabbed the suppressor of the Diemaco into the guy's wounded leg. The guy moaned loudly and glared at him.

'You guys fucked up,' Archer told him. 'You shot two unarmed people.'

'You're Archer,' the guy rasped. He gripped his wounded leg and hissed with pain as Archer put some pressure on it.

'That's right. And you're with Black Star, right?'

The guy looked away, saying nothing. Archer ground the suppressor into his leg and he grunted with pain.

'I ain't sayin' anything,' the guy said, looking back at him. 'You're gonna kill me anyway.'

'I was thinking I'd hand you over to the Canadians,' Archer said. 'After all, you killed one of their officers.'

'I didn't...'

'You didn't pull the trigger? Doesn't matter. Or I could hand you over to the villagers, let them deal with you for killing one of their girls.' Archer felt an unexpected surge of anger as he said it, and he leaned hard on the guy's leg wound, making him squeal. 'She had nothing to do with this and you fuckin' animals just murdered her.'

'It's a job.' The guy's hand moved to the wound in his side, and he hissed through his teeth when he touched it. 'It wasn't meant to happen like that. These turkeys...' He glanced towards his dead colleagues.

'Amateurs? Is Black Star scraping the bottom of the barrel these days?'

The guy eyed him, wary of saying too much but perhaps seeing a glimmer of hope.

'Close to it,' he said. 'You're SF too, you know how it is.'

'Where's Viktor Kozlowski?'

'I don't know who that is, man.'

'Yeah you do.' Archer pressed down on his leg. 'You just need to think harder, *man*.'

The guy made a guttural growl. 'I don't. This is just a quick job, man. Last week I was in Kabul, this week I'm here.'

'Who for? Who's calling the shots?'

'I don't know.' He shifted his body weight and groaned. 'Fuck man, I need some help here.'

'Like how you helped these two?' Archer nodded towards the bodies of Dee Dee and Michael.

'Fuck man…' The guy's eyes were screwed tight in pain. 'Do it then. Just shoot me.'

Archer bent and picked up the radio the guy had dropped. 'Who's on the end of this?'

The guy squinted at him. 'You know I ain't gonna tell you that.'

'Then tell me your name,' Archer said. 'I'll tell them where you are, they can come get you.'

The guy looked doubtful.

'Mate, I live this life. I know what it's like. We're all just pawns in a bigger game.'

He was still wary but he was also desperate to grab onto any wisp of hope that floated by. His leg wound wouldn't kill him, but the bullet through his side was probably causing problems inside and they both knew it.

'Porter,' the man said.

'Porter what?'

'James Porter. Jimmy.'

Archer nodded. 'And what was your unit back in the day?'

'Second D.'

'2nd Infantry? South Korea?'

The guy nodded.

'They teach you much in the 2nd D, Porter?'

Porter eyed him, wary again. 'A little.'

'They ever teach you not to trust the guy holding the gun?'

Archer pumped a round through Porter's forehead and the body flopped back, a small red hole between his eyes beginning to trickle blood.

'Jesus,' Isabella said from behind him. 'What the fuck?'

Archer turned, lowering the Diemaco. He'd almost forgotten she was there. 'He had his chance,' he said.

They took photos of the three dead mercenaries and their kit, as well as of Michael and Dee Dee. Isabella's arm wound was just a nick, a flesh wound that bled a lot but wouldn't cause any real problems. Archer bound it with a strip of cloth ripped from Porter's shirt.

'We need to call this in and get some help here,' he said.

Isabella nodded, gingerly touching her arm wound.

'Isabella?'

She looked up at him. Despite the grime and sweat on her face she was cute. 'Izzy,' she said.

'Okay, Izzy. We need to call this in, but first we need to make sure we're safe. Stick close to me, we're going to check their vehicle and make sure no one's waiting for us.'

He turned down the volume on Porter's radio and shoved it in his thigh pocket, the spare magazine in a front pocket, and led the way. The track was clear and they soon made it back to the turning area where he had left the green Suzuki jeep. Parked behind it was a much newer blue Nissan SUV and alongside them both was a similar Nissan in maroon, with tinted windows.

'Yours the blue one?'

Izzy nodded. 'Yep. I've got the keys.'

Archer tried the doors of the maroon Nissan, finding them locked. He couldn't see anything of interest through the windows, and presumed it would be sterile like the men themselves. Chances were it would be alarmed so breaking a window would only attract attention – although the unsuppressed shots he'd fired from his Glock didn't seem to have raised any alarm bells so far.

He was about to crack a window when he heard another vehicle approaching up the road. It sounded like another SUV and it was coming at speed. It could be the cops or it could be more bad guys. No point putting themselves at risk until they knew.

'Quick, in here.'

He ushered Izzy into the undergrowth near the vehicles and they hunkered down, pulling branches and leaves over themselves.

She started to speak but he shushed her, the new vehicle tearing up the path and skidding to a halt a few seconds later. It was yet another Nissan SUV, this one white.

Three doors opened and men with rifles got out.

The driver stayed by the vehicle and the other two took off up the track, quickly disappearing from sight. They were all dressed similarly to the other three and had the standard beards and sun tans of security contractors the world over.

Archer had no doubt what would happen if they got their hands on him. Or Izzy, for that matter. He waited a few beats until he was sure the other two were out of sight and checked the driver. He was standing by his door, a Diemaco in his hands, looking alert.

As the guy scanned towards them, Archer raised the Diemaco and pumped three rounds into his chest, the shots so fast the guy barely twitched before the last one hit him. He grunted and fell back against his SUV, smearing blood down the white wing as he slumped down. Archer was up and over him quickly, kicking the rifle aside and checking for any sign the other two had heard the action.

Nothing.

Archer took a moment to put a round into the two nearside tyres of the white Nissan, then did the same to the maroon one. He swapped out the partially-spent mag for his spare and tucked the partial into his pocket in case he needed it.

He waved Izzy out and handed her the keys to the Suzuki. He climbed in the back and covered their rear while she took the wheel. As soon as she cranked the engine he saw movement up the track, and the other two guys came racing back, weapons up in the shoulder.

He started putting rounds down and they returned fire as they took cover.

'Go, go!' he shouted to Izzy.

She gave it a kick in the guts and they leaped forward, dirt spraying from the tyres. Archer continued pumping the trigger, his aim jumping with the motion of the jeep, but it wasn't so much about well-aimed shots right now. He just needed to stop the fuckers from killing them.

Suppressed bullets whizzed by them as they bumped and lurched down the rough track before hitting the side road and getting a better grip.

'Keep going,' Archer said, leaning over the back of Izzy's seat and putting his hand on her shoulder. 'Where are you staying?'

'Lagoon View,' she shouted back.

'Go there. They know where I am and probably you too, but they'll expect me to go back to mine.'

'What about the cops?'

'Not yet. Gotta make a phone call first.' He swayed as she hit a pothole and decided it might be better to sit down.

The main road was coming up fast. Archer started climbing over to the passenger seat, and saw movement from his peripheral vision at the last moment.

There was no time to shout a warning before the nose of a grey Land Cruiser smashed into the front passenger-side wing. The impact threw the smaller Suzuki sideways, slewing across the mouth of the side road. The shriek of tyres and the roar of a powerful V8 filled their ears as the Land Cruiser pushed them hard across the road.

Archer felt the jeep tipping and dropped the rifle, grabbing for a hold.

'Jump!' he yelled, trying to get his feet under him as the jeep lifted and started to go over. Izzy was still in the driver's seat as it went over the side of the road into a ditch. Archer propelled himself out in the most graceless jump he'd ever made, arms and legs everywhere as he fell through the air. He crashed into the undergrowth and landed with a thump that knocked the wind from him.

His ears were ringing and he couldn't breathe. He struggled to get up, knowing he had to get away fast. He got to all fours and was feeling for the Glock when he heard someone arrive. A boot slammed into his ribs, knocking him down, and he looked up to see a rifle butt coming at his face.

No time to move, just an explosion of pain and the Earth spun. He hit the deck and best his best to cover up.

14

———

Archer was aware of being picked up and dumped in the back of a vehicle, shoved hard across a metal floor, and the slam of doors.

The balaclava over his head blocked his vision and muffled his hearing, and smelled like sweaty socks. His head ached and he could feel blood dribbling down his face. He was lying on his side and could feel the vehicle moving. The engine sound told him it was a V8, probably the one that had rammed them off the road.

Back of a truck, being driven somewhere. Not good.

His hands were bound behind his back and his feet were trussed together. His body hurt and his mouth was dry.

He didn't know if Izzy was alive or dead. Maybe they just wanted him. He rolled over onto his other side and bumped into something soft. It groaned.

'Izzy?' he croaked.

'Uh-huh.'

'You okay?'

She cleared her throat. 'Depends. Nothing broken, I think.'

Archer did a check of himself, as best he could with limited movement. He couldn't feel anything obviously broken either. 'Me too.'

The vehicle started to slow, turned and the surface turned bumpy.

'I don't know where they're taking us,' Archer said, trying to prep her as fast as he could. He knew the CSIS would give training to prepare their officers for being bumped in a foreign state, but this was probably beyond what they prepared for. He could only hope she would hold up to whatever was coming. 'It's me they'll want. They were supposed to kill me; I doubt you guys were in the equation.'

'Good to know,' she said drily. 'Just collateral damage then.'

Archer struggled to get his thoughts together. His head throbbed and he wondered if he had concussion. He was also aware that they might not be alone, so he had to choose his words carefully

'You can claim innocence, you were obviously sent to spy on the same target I was, nothing more. It's just coincidence that we happened to cross paths.'

'What's that asshole Capstick got to do with these guys?' she said.

'I don't know. He's a pacifist lefty, these guys aren't. Maybe nothing.'

He knew in his gut that wasn't true. The chances of them all being in the same place at the same for different reasons were so remote as to be farcical. He thought he heard movement somewhere behind him, the opposite side to Izzy, just the scrape of a boot against a hard surface.

Cunning bastards. They'd stuck one of their guys in the back to monitor them. Good move. He stayed silent now, deciding the less information they gave to the enemy the better.

Izzy followed suit and soon the truck came to a stop. The rear was opened and they were dragged out and dumped on the ground. Hands grabbed Archer by the arms and dragged him backwards across rough ground. His shoulders ached and he felt every bump in the ground, but he kept his mouth shut. He could smell sea air and hear birds above him. A light breeze brushed his skin.

Somewhere by the sea. Hopefully not going for an impromptu swim.

The ground beneath his feet changed from dirt to wooden slats and he heard the gentle slap of waves. They stopped, the two guys dragging him pausing to catch their breath. A chain rattled, a door creaked open, and he was dragged again. They shoved him hard and he fell against a wall and went down, unable to stop himself.

He lay there, sucking in mouthfuls of warm, dirty air, automatically running an inventory of himself again. A few more bruises, no doubt about that, but he'd live. He heard more movement, a grunt of exertion, then Izzy landed heavily on top of him. She came down hard, her shoulder slamming into his face, and he heard her cry out with pain.

The door banged shut and the chain rattled then there was silence.

'Get off.'

Izzy twisted off him and he wriggled himself into a sitting position. The balaclava over his head wasn't tied on, and after a good minute of shaking and flicking his head he managed to throw it off.

The shed they were in was bare aside from the two of them. Izzy was lying on her side next to him, breathing hard and trussed up the same way he was. He could see blood soaking the makeshift bandage he'd put on her arm wound and fresh scratches on her arm, legs and neck.

'You look like you've been dragged through a blackberry bush,' he said.

'Feel like I've been hit by a goddamn snow plough, eh,' she said.

'Hold still.'

Archer shuffled on his backside and got in a position to pull her hood off. She got herself sitting up beside him and looked him over.

'You look like a bag of assholes,' she said.

'Thanks. You smell like one.'

They both grinned and the mood lightened immediately. Izzy actually laughed out loud, the absurdity of the situation not escaping her.

'You know we should be dead, right?' she said. 'I was stuck under that frickin' jeep and those bastards dragged me out by my hair. You're telling me to jump – great advice, by the way. If I'd've jumped the frickin' thing would've crushed me.'

'Seemed like a good idea at the time,' Archer said.

'Well if you get any other good ideas,' she grumbled, 'you can shove them up your ass.'

Archer waited for her to take a breath. She was way outside her comfort zone here.

'So why have they grabbed us?' she eventually said. 'If they're supposed to kill you, what's the point in kidnapping us? What, are they gonna hold us to ransom?'

'I don't think so.' Archer had been pondering the same thing. 'I don't know why, but I doubt it's a ransom thing. You ever heard of Black Star?'

She shook her head.

'They're a PMC, based in the States. They do work all over the world, including for the Agency. Well, they did anyway, not sure about now. I butted heads with them a few times over the years. We had a pretty big run in on an op and they came off second best.'

'A PMC? Like a security outfit?'

'Yeah, private military contractors. They're all ex-Army dudes, and not the cream of the crop either. They've been in the media a bit over the years, killing civilians in Iraq, that sort of stuff. They think they're the shit but they're really just a bunch of fuckin' cowboys. Big discipline problems.'

'When you say they come off second best,' she said, 'you mean you killed them?'

He looked her in the eye. 'Yep. I put them down like the dogs they were.'

She didn't flinch, just studied him, running a bullshit-o-meter over his face as she nodded carefully.

'Good,' she said quietly. 'These bastards killed Michael. I'm glad you killed those guys back there.'

'No issues with that then?' he said carefully.

Killing Porter in front of her had been a mistake, one that could easily land him in jail. The man was unarmed and no threat at the time. The legally correct thing to do would have been render him assistance, not finish him off. In Archer's experience with guys like that, the morally correct thing to do was sometimes quite different. Porter would have cut his throat if he'd had half a chance.

'No issues at all,' she said firmly. 'Those sons of bitches deserved everything they got, and some.'

'You knew him well? Michael, I mean?'

'Yeah.' She nodded, her expression shifting. She looked away. 'I did.'

'Were you...?'

She gave a wry smile. 'No, not like that. I think he would have wanted to, but no. We did our initial training together then ended up on the same team a few years later. He used to be in the Army too, like you.'

Archer wasn't surprised that they'd profiled him. He'd have done the same in their position.

'He tried out for Special Forces, missed out, and came to the Service instead.'

Archer nodded. He had worked with the JTF2 boys before, and rated them highly. They were an excellent SF unit with very high standards. He suspected that went some way to explaining Michael's attitude towards him; Archer had accomplished something he had failed at.

'He seemed like a good man,' he offered.

Izzy gave that small, wry smile again. 'He was. He thought you were a dick, though.'

Archer shrugged. 'I can live with it.'

'But thanks.'

They were silent for a few beats. Archer was relieved that she wasn't falling apart. He couldn't afford to carry a passenger if they were going to get out of here alive. He was aware that the shed could well be wired up, but there were things he needed to know and they needed to make plans.

'What was your brief on Capstick?' he said.

'Observation. We had the same int as you. He's supposed to be meeting someone, we don't know who.'

'So you've still got guys on him?'

'Yep.'

'Why bump me then?'

Izzy gave a chuckle. 'That was Michael's idea. I didn't think it was the greatest plan, but it was likely you'd spot us anyway so he wanted to speak to you directly. He also figured it would keep you on the back foot.'

'And give him the upper hand.'

'Exactly.'

Archer shook his head. The man's idea of getting the upper hand had put him and his partner directly in the line of fire and he'd lost his life as a result.

The shed got stifling hot in the afternoon sun and the slight airflow that came through the cracks did little to alleviate their discomfort. They ended up slumped shoulder to shoulder against the wall, shifting occasionally as their limbs went numb.

Archer found himself talking to her, slipping easily into a conversation as if they were two old friends. He told her a little about his childhood, how he'd spent his weekends eeling with mates, playing rugby and racing their bikes, exploring the bushwalks around the city, and always having a hankering to get out there and explore the world.

Izzy told him about her own childhood in Vancouver, a normal middle-class existence with normal middle class parents and an older sister who liked playing with dolls and dressing up.

'I'd rather climb trees and ride bikes,' Izzy said. 'Gymnastics was about the girliest thing I did as a kid. I was good too – age group rep teams, the whole works.'

'Did you carry on as an adult?'

'Not for long. I got busy doing other stuff.' She gave a low chuckle. 'I'm still very flexible though.'

Archer filed that away for future reference. If – or *when* – they got out of here, he might just follow that up a bit further, he decided.

'Do your parents know what you do?' he said.

'They know enough. Can't tell them everything, of course. Yours?'

He shook his head to himself. 'They think I'm still doing what I used to do,' he said.

She pressed against his shoulder. 'You kind of are, eh?'

He grunted. 'Didn't hang out much with girls back then, though.' He nudged her back. 'There's a downside to everything, I guess.'

15

Sometime in mid-afternoon the door opened and a pair of guards came in, covered by another at the door.

All three were standard-issue Black Star shooters in their fatigue pants and desert boots. The first two piled straight into Archer, booting him about the torso and legs in a frenzy that was only punctuated by grunts of exertion and the thud of impacts.

Izzy tried to move out of the way but copped some loose boots as well, one to the side of the head being enough to knock her flat.

Archer could do nothing but bring his knees up to protect his vitals and hope for the best. One of them overcame this by dragging him up by the hair and throwing him down again, allowing them a free reign. Archer closed his eyes and tried to curl into a ball to ride it out. He could hear Izzy screaming at them in the background but he blocked everything else out and focussed on absorbing the hits.

After a minute or so they seemed to have had enough and stepped back, both of them breathing hard. One of them crouched over Archer and grabbed his face, squeezing and twisting it round so they were eye to eye.

'Those were my buddies you killed, you motherfucker,' he hissed.

He was a big solid unit with angry blue eyes and his breath was hot in Archer's face. 'I get the chance, I'm gonna fuck you up myself.'

'Cool,' Archer wheezed. 'Can't wait.'

The two men replaced the balaclavas with rough sacks over the prisoners' heads and tied them off with cord, before leaving them alone again. Archer lay where he was, getting his breath back. He'd hurt enough before from the jeep crash, but this was a whole new level. It felt like every part of his body had felt the wrath.

'You okay?' Izzy called out.

'Wonderful,' he said. He forced himself into a sitting position and rolled his shoulders and neck, feeling and hearing the joints pop as they released. 'They're pussycats really.'

'I'm sure,' she said.

He shuffled back over to her and leaned there, taking stock. The touch of her shoulder against his was comforting. He had no idea what they were waiting for, and he could only presume it was for either orders or someone to come. The guards were also seriously pissed, so whatever the outcome was of their capture, it wasn't going to be pretty.

'You mentioned Viktor Kozlowski,' Izzy eventually said. 'You think he's behind this?'

'Chances are. He's an evil bastard.' Archer licked his dry lips with a rough tongue. 'He works in with whoever pays him, and it sounds like Capstick was getting int from him.'

'Remember the white supremacist bombing in Vancouver last year? The car bomb outside the mosque?'

'Yeah, I heard his name was mentioned in that.'

'We know he supplied the gear and we know he was in contact with the bomber. I was involved in the investigation.'

'Makes sense. The bomber blew himself up, didn't he?'

'Suicide by cop. He shot one cop but they dropped him.'

'One down,' Archer muttered.

Her hood rustled and he guessed she was trying to look at him. 'You're a hard bastard, Archer.'

'I prefer to think I'm realistic,' he said. 'So what's a nice girl like you doing in a dump like this?'

She let out a laugh. 'I was wondering that myself. It's not my usual holiday destination. The accommodation's pretty crap. This place was supposed to have a king bed and a spa bath.'

Archer chuckled. 'I can't say much for the food, either. The service is rubbish.'

16

———

Dusk was falling when the door next opened.

Izzy was asleep, her head on Archer's shoulder. He was still awake, having been dozing fitfully through the afternoon.

He heard the rattle of the chain, the creak of the door, and multiple footfalls. Someone stopped in front of him and he felt hands at his neck. The tie there was snipped and the hood was yanked off.

Archer looked at two sets of legs in front of him. One set wore dirty jeans and desert boots.

The other set were bare. Shapely, tanned and smooth, with jandals on the feet. The toenails were painted dark red and there was a silver ring on each big toe. He ran his eyes up. The legs ended in a pair of short khaki shorts. Above that was a smooth tanned belly with a diamante navel piercing, a white linen shirt knotted in the front, and a well-developed cleavage.

Hands on hips, Krystal Raines gave him an amused smile.

'Surprise,' she said. 'Didn't see this coming, did you?'

It was all Archer could do to keep his jaw from dropping.

The public face of a peace activist movement, dedicated to waving placards and chaining themselves to oil platforms, cosied up with a team of mercenaries? No, she was right. Not in a million years would he have guessed that.

He did his best to swallow his surprise and act cool.

'Really?' he said. 'You think you're that clever? You've been on the radar for years, Miss Raines. Why do you think we're here?' He gave a dismissive shake of his head. 'I'm surprised you haven't figured it out for yourself.'

A flicker of annoyance crossed her face, just a momentary lapse before she regained her composure.

'I didn't take you for an amateur, Mr Craig Archer. You can play all the silly mind games you like, but it won't work. I know who you are and why you're here, just like I know who your little friend is here.' She gestured towards Izzy, and one of the guards removed the hood from her head. 'Miss Isabella Priestley of the Canadian SIS. Shame.' She shook her head in mock sadness but the vicious smirk on her painted lips belied her true sentiments.

Archer felt a twist in his gut. This woman was evil, pure evil. And sitting there as her captives, he had the distinct feeling that he and Izzy were fucked.

'And poor Dee Dee.' More mock sadness. 'Such a shame. You obviously had something special going there.' She crouched in front of him, eye to eye, positioned over his feet. He could smell her sweet perfume. She lowered her voice to a whisper. 'I hope she suffered terribly.'

Archer fought back his natural instincts and held her gaze. He leaned forward slightly so they were almost nose to nose.

'Don't worry, sweetheart,' he said softly. 'She died quickly.' He paused a beat, holding her gaze. Her eyes were a very pale blue. 'But when I kill you, it will be slow. You'll feel it. I promise you that.'

The depth of venom in his voice surprised even him, but it barely seemed to register with Raines. She smirked again and leaned forward, her lips brushing his cheek. Her tongue touched his cheek and licked upwards, warm and wet.

She put her mouth to his ear.

'I like it slow,' she breathed.

She sat back, smirking that vicious smirk again, and gave a short, barking laugh. 'Enough games,' she said, rising to her feet. 'Put their hoods back on.'

Archer locked eyes with her until the hood came down, determined to let her know he was serious. Problem was, he realised as darkness descended, she did realise that but it didn't bother her. It was like a game to her.

The door closed behind them and silence returned. Archer sat, gathering his thoughts. It had certainly been an interesting turn of events.

'That bitch,' came Izzy's muffled voice from beside him, 'is fucking mental.'

Archer couldn't have said it better himself. He sat back and tried to get comfortable, preparing to wait. He knew that the balloon would not have gone up in Auckland just yet. He wasn't due to have contacted Ingoe until this evening, and even if he missed that contact it wouldn't result in a team of commandoes arriving five minutes later with guns blazing.

If the bodies had been discovered that would have set alarm bells ringing, but he had no idea whether that had happened. He could only hope, but it was unlikely. If not, they were on their own.

Night had fallen properly when the guards returned. Nobody said anything until Izzy was pulled to her feet. He heard her protesting and struggling, and he tried to kick out at the guards. A boot to the head knocked him onto his side and he saw stars, blood loudly hammering at his brain.

Before he could recover they were gone and he was left alone in the dark. Silence returned.

Archer gradually sat up again, breathing deeply and getting himself together. There was nothing to be scared of in being alone in the dark. People tended to freak out because they were scared of the unknown. Archer knew what it was like to be alone, *really* alone, just him and his thoughts.

Exercise Von Tempsky was an integral part of the Selection process for the SAS, named after a Major in the Land Wars, and involved 24 hours of pack marching through swamp and bush with a 35kg pack, weapon and your own mind. Mental strength and self belief were the keys to getting through it. Self belief had never been a big problem for Archer. It wasn't that he necessarily thought he was better than anyone else, although he knew his own abilities very well, but he wouldn't give up. He'd always had a feeling of being unsatisfied, restless, until he'd joined the SAS. That feeling had disappeared as he went through Selection. He knew what he was and he knew where he wanted to be.

The resistance to interrogation phase was known as the most difficult mental stage for all applicants. Over a day or so every soldier was broken down, stripped back to their bare bones. It forced them to look deep inside themselves, delve into the darkest recesses of their personality and acknowledge who they truly were. Some men broke. Those that didn't, came out stronger.

Archer sat in the darkness, comfortable in his own skin. It gave him time to plan.

17

———

Rarotonga, Cook Islands
Friday

It was well after dawn when they came for him.

Three men, one standing by the door, two coming straight in and grabbing him, yanking him up by his arms. A fist to the gut knocked the wind out of him and a voice sounded close to his ear.

'That's for starters, asshole. Gimme an excuse and I'll put you the fuck down, geddit?'

Archer was too breathless to respond, and hung limply while they dragged him out of the shed, being sure to bang him off the door-frame as they went. He felt the heat of the sun on his exposed skin and felt his feet bumping over wooden slats. The sound of water slapping at rocks. Sea birds calling. A diesel engine idling.

They paused, he heard muffled voices then he was pushed from behind and was falling through the air. Laughter behind him. Someone half caught him but he still hit with a thump, his left shoulder and hip taking the impact. He groaned and tried to suck a breath in.

More hands grabbed him and dragged him across a wooden deck, shoved him against something he knew was the side of a boat, and left him there.

More muffled voices then the sound of the engine changed. The boat began to move. It felt big, definitely bigger than a runabout but not a proper ship. Probably a fishing boat, he guessed.

Soon they were picking up speed and he could hear waves slapping at the hull beside him. The motion of the boat was somehow soothing and helped him to focus. No point sweating the small stuff; he couldn't control that. He focussed on what he could do which, right now, wasn't much.

The boat powered on through the gentle waves for what he sensed was maybe half an hour or so before the tone of the engine changed again and footsteps sounded.

Archer screwed his eyes up as the hood was yanked from his head. The sun was blinding overhead and he turned away from it, squinting as his eyes adjusted.

The man bending over him was a big islander with a bushy beard and thick, heavily tattooed arms hanging from wide shoulders. He said nothing, just grabbed Archer's arm and jerked him up.

The boat was rolling on the gentle blue swell, the engine idling easily. Gulls drifted on the air currents above them and the breeze was light and warm.

There was not another craft in sight and he could see land in the distance, several klicks at least. He knew he could swim that far, if he survived long enough to give it a go.

But that clearly wasn't the plan.

The other two men on the deck of the boat were busy preparing, and it was obvious what the goal was.

One was plucking fish from a bucket, chopping them in half with a machete, and tossing the pieces overboard. Blood covered the filleting station he stood at and his arms were streaked with it. He was a tall, lanky islander, maybe thirty. Like his companions he wore a dirty singlet and shorts.

It seemed obvious to Archer that they were actually fishermen by trade, but about to become killers by choice – if they weren't already. In all likelihood they were three of the criminals deported from Australia that Steve had mentioned.

The second man, younger and chunkier, was lifting the lid off a large bucket. He dropped the lid and lifted the bucket to the side of the boat, steadied it, and dumped the contents over the side. Blood and bits flowed into the ocean, a chunky red swill that would act as a magnet for sharks.

Archer felt his own blood run cold.

The bastards weren't just going to kill him and dump him; they were going to feed him to the sharks.

Already he could see the surface starting to boil as the big beasts raced to the blood in the water, keen to feed on whatever it was that had fallen overboard. If they found nothing they would inevitably feed on each other.

He knew that as soon as he hit the water he was as good as dead. The sharks would tear him apart and the best he could hope for would be that it was fast.

He glanced over at the lanky guy cutting the fish. The guy was grinning to himself, and Archer knew then that these guys were no rookies. They'd done this before and they liked it.

'Hold.' The big man held tight to Archer's arm while he leaned down and sliced through the cable ties around his ankles, using a filleting knife that Archer eyed eagerly. If he could get his hands on that it could be a game changer. Of course, it wouldn't help having his hands behind his back.

'How much do you want?' Archer said. His tongue felt thick in his parched mouth as he spoke.

'Huh?' The big man squinted at him.

'How much money do you want to let me go? A hundred thousand?'

The big man squinted a bit more, then his brow furrowed and he gave a harsh laugh. He turned to his two mates and grunted something Archer didn't understand. They both laughed and carried on doing what they were doing. They were like machines, the three of them steadily working through a process that would ultimately bring them to the goal they had been set.

Archer could see there was no point trying to negotiate with them; they had a task and they would do it. A hundred thousand dollars was a lot of money in anyone's book, but it was huge to people like this. The fact they hadn't even entertained the idea told Archer that whoever they answered to had far more sway than he did.

Still, it may delay things, and delays were good. Delays brought options.

'A million,' he said.

The big man looked at him again and Archer could see the pause in his demeanour.

'Million bucks?' the big man said.

'Yup,' Archer nodded. 'A million US. Just let me go. Drop me back on land somewhere and I'll get it.'

'You don' gotta million bucks,' the big man growled. Up close, he stunk of body odour, unwashed teeth and fish. 'You full o' shit, bro.'

'I've got it,' Archer insisted. 'Come with me and get it. The three of you will be the only ones who know.'

'Bullshit,' the big man said. He tugged on Archer's arm, pulling him towards the chunkier guy at the side of the boat. 'You gonna go swim, bro.'

The three of them laughed and Archer was unable to resist being dragged towards his death.

As they reached the side and the big man pushed him up against the railing, Archer looked down. The water was a metre or so away, frothing white as the beasts below surged about, snapping at the chunks of meat floating in blood. One broke the surface, its dorsal fin grey-blue and terrifying.

Twisting back towards his captors, determined that he wasn't going over the edge without a fight, Archer saw the tiniest of windows present itself.

The lanky man chopped the last fish in half and tossed the pieces overboard. He was a metre away from Archer, side on at the filleting station. The short machete he was using was held casually in his right hand, closest to Archer, tip up.

The big man still held Archer by the upper arm, his fingers tight. The chunkier man was a couple of paces away.

It was now or never.

Archer leaned into the big man, pushing him ever so slightly off balance, and lashed out with his right foot. He connected with the hand holding the short machete and kicked up and back, sweeping it straight up at the lanky man's face.

The rounded tip of the blade connected somewhere on the guy's cheek and opened it up, bringing a shriek of surprise and pain and causing the lanky man to stagger back.

The other two were momentarily caught by surprise and Archer attacked.

He pulled away then slammed back into the big man, shoulder first into his chest, pulled back again and drove in a second time.

The big man tightened his grip and yanked at him, giving Archer more momentum. He carried through, crashing his forehead into the big man's face, missing the nose but surprising him enough that the guy let go of him.

The lanky guy was yelping and holding his face, distracting the chunkier guy enough to allow Archer to focus on the big man, who he gauged was the bigger threat anyway. He drew his head back and went for another butt to the face but the big man saw it coming and weaved back, creating space between them but latching onto Archer's arm again.

Archer pushed off the side of the boat and drove into the guy, pushing him backwards across the deck. The big man swung at him, his mitt big enough to knock Archer on his arse if it connected.

Fortunately he stumbled as he swung and the punch sailed past Archer's nose rather than breaking it. Archer pushed up on him, using his body weight to keep the guy off balance, twisting at the same time and managing to get his arm free as the big man went down.

As soon as the guy hit the deck Archer was on him, stomping a heel down into his balls then his guts, his ribs, moving up to try for a kill shot.

This was no time for niceties; he had to be more brutal than the enemy to have a hope of surviving this. The big man grabbed at Archer's foot, clamped it between both huge mitts and wrenched, throwing him off balance.

Archer staggered, caught himself, and saw the big man rising up. He sensed movement behind him and ducked instinctively, weaving to the side a nano-second before a bucket whooshed over his head.

He spun, still low, seeing the chunkier guy right behind him, his arm fully extended with the bucket. He'd gone for the big swing and missed, leaving himself horribly exposed.

Archer drove his heel into the front of the guy's knee, buckling it back at an unnatural angle. The chunky guy screeched and dropped the bucket, bending to grab his injured knee.

Archer's own knee came up like a haymaker, smashing straight into the guy's nose and flattening it across his face with a loud crunch and a spray of blood.

Leaving the chunkier guy to it, Archer turned back towards the big man, who was on his knees and trying to push up. A squashed scrotum wasn't helping him at all.

There was a blur of movement from the side and Archer was crashed sideways by the lanky guy. They both fell to the deck, the lanky guy swinging wildly from on top.

Archer rolled, managing to get halfway free before the guy landed a couple of good punches to his head.

The big man reached out a paw and grabbed at Archer's foot again, but he was too slow to seize his chance. The foot slipped free and the heel smashed into his jaw, knocking him back down.

The lanky guy was getting his aim in, landing solid punches that were enough to rattle teeth. He was straddling Archer's torso and grinning as he threw punches, feeling this was all under control now that he was on top.

He didn't account for either the desperation of a condemned man or the skill and brutality of a trained killer.

Archer bucked hard, throwing the lanky guy up a few inches at a time, either buck more determined than the last. He wriggled at the same time, moving down until the lanky guy was almost sitting on his head. His enemy realised what he was doing and locked his knees against Archer's head, trying to choke him.

Archer twisted his head and bit down hard on the soft inner thigh, clamping his jaws shut and tearing like a rabid dog.

The lanky guy screeched in pain and lifted off, allowing Archer to wriggle free and scramble awkwardly to his feet.

Before the lanky guy knew it, he was being stomped from behind, a foot slamming him to the deck and trying to drive him through it.

Archer focussed on the guy's spine, hammering it again and again until there was a cracking crunch. The guy went limp and silent and Archer left him, stepping away and steadying himself against the rocking of the boat as he scanned around him.

The chunkier guy was on the deck, cradling his shattered nose and knee, out of the game but conscious.

The big man was also on the deck, holding his face while blood flowed from his nose. He was making a half-hearted attempt to get up, his eyes fixed on the lanky guy who was not moving. Archer presumed he was dead, so at least for now put him down the order of priorities.

He spotted the discarded machete and manoeuvred awkwardly to pick it up behind him. He got it in his hands and began slicing at the cable ties binding his wrists.

'Bro.' The big man's voice was muffled as he tried to get the chunkier guy's attention. 'Bro.'

The chunkier guy had no interest in anything but his injuries, so the big man pushed up, deciding he would have to sort things out himself. This had not played out like it should have.

Archer felt the ties break and pulled his hands apart, feeling the tingle of blood rushing back into his cramped arms and hands.

The big man saw he was free and started to move. Too late.

Archer took two steps forward, cocked the machete and swung. The short blade arced down and chopped into the big man's left shoulder, through the collar bone, a deep red wound opening up immediately. He bellowed with pain and snatched at the shoulder, staggering back, his eyes wide. Archer pressed forward, hacking him in the same area again. The big man stumbled, let out a shriek, and went backwards over the side of the boat.

There was a big splash as he hit the water then silence for a long, drawn out second. Then the ocean erupted. Archer saw a leg kick up above the surface then the water went pink and frothy and he saw a shark tail flick up into the air and down again. He left the sharks to their feeding frenzy and turned back to the other two men.

The chunkier guy had realised what was happening and was trying to drag himself away, as if he had somewhere to escape to.

Archer bore down on him like the grim reaper and he could the fear in the guy's eyes as he stood over him. Blood dripped from the blade of the machete.

'Who sent you?'

'Bro, I don't...'

'Who sent you?' Archer's tone was flat and calm, but full of menace.

'I don't...just a job, boss. I swear.'

'You want to go for a swim with your mate?' Archer gestured with the machete. 'Or do you want to tell me and live?'

'I don't know, boss.' The guy was crying now. If he hadn't tried to kill him, Archer might have felt sorry for him. 'I just get paid, I don't know who's the boss, bro.'

'You've done this before? Dumped people out here?'

The guy dropped his head and stared at the deck, tears running down his brown cheeks. 'Yeah.'

'How many?'

He shrugged weakly. 'Three...four.'

'Uh huh.' Archer knew in his heart the guy was telling he truth about not being the shot-caller, and that he was downplaying the extent of his murderous activities. 'Get up.'

The guy looked at him, a glimmer of hope in his eyes, and took a few moments to get painfully to his feet.

'You sure you don't know who's behind this? Last chance.'

'I don' boss, I swear.'

'Thanks.'

'For what?'

'Making it easier.'

Archer kicked him hard in the midriff, propelling him backwards. His arms flailed wildly but he couldn't stop himself. He went over the side backwards, screaming all the way.

The sea boiled with frenzied thrashing, foaming pink, the bodies of sharks leaping and diving and tearing at their meal. The guy was thrown waist-high out of the water, screaming inhumanely, and Archer could see that a shark had seized him around the legs and was trying to carry him away from the other beasts.

One hand grabbed helplessly at the sky before he plunged beneath the surface again.

Archer turned away, his stomach churning at the brutality of the man's end. He was no stranger to violent death but to see this up close was something else.

He grabbed the feet of the lanky man who lay face down on the deck, unmoving, and dragged him to the side. The guys eyes were open and he was breathing fast.

He heaved the limp form up under the arms and flopped it over the side. It splashed into the dirty red water and bobbed for a few seconds. Archer turned away and put his hands on his hips, sucking in the clean sea air. The burst of activity and splashing behind him told him the lanky man had joined his two murderous mates.

Archer rummaged about until he found a bottle of water and used it to wash his hands and face – he daren't dip his hands overboard in case they were ripped off by the beasts that lurked beneath.

Feeling as refreshed as he could be, given the circumstances, he moved to the wheelhouse. It had been a while since he'd piloted a boat, but there was no time to muck round.

He needed to get the fuck out of there before any other bastard – man or mammal – tried to kill him. He got the vessel moving, fixed a point on the nearest land mass he could see – some kind of island, he guessed – and set about getting back to civilisation. A further rummage through the wheel house found another bottle of water and one of Coke. He drained both of them as he made his way towards shore, gradually rehydrating himself – the soft drink wasn't great but at least it had plenty of sugar, which gave his energy a boost.

As he got closer to land it became clear that he was heading into the main port at Avatiu. Hopefully there wasn't a welcoming committee waiting for him.

As he steered with one hand and drank with the other, Archer got to thinking. And the more he thought, the more things fell into place.

Problem was, he didn't want to believe it.

18

Rarotonga, Cook Islands
Friday, 1900 hours

The small parking area outside the bar was nearly empty, but the music was pumping inside.

The large pink neon sign on the front wall identified it as Pukeko's Nest.

Archer watched and listened for a few minutes from outside, the early evening birdsong struggling to do battle with the reggae mix coming from inside.

Archer had never been a fan of reggae.

He walked through the front doors into the open drinking area. The bar itself was to the right, another open area beyond that. A few of the leaners inside were occupied, but all of the tables were empty. The pair of pool tables down the back were playing host to several burly, tattooed thugs. Archer guessed they were more of the deported criminals from Aussie that Steve had told him about.

He scanned again but couldn't see Steve anywhere.

The barman was a very tall islander with a mohawk cut and a moustache. He was wiping up a spill on the bar top when he saw Archer approaching.

'Bro,' he said, 'you look like shit.'

Archer caught his reflection in the mirrored wall behind the bar. The barman was right. His clothes were filthy, he had dried blood on his face and his hair was wild.

Right now, that was his last concern.

'Where's Steve?' he said.

The barman looked wary, wiped his hands on the cloth he'd been using and glanced sideways towards the thugs around the pool tables.

'He's not here, bro.'

'Where is he?'

The sound system was thumping and he could barely hear himself think.

The barman's eyes shifted. 'I dunno, bro. Maybe he'll be in tomorrow, you could try then.'

'Bullshit,' Archer said. 'Tell me where he is or I'll tear this fuckin' place apart.'

The barman mad a scoffing noise and half-grinned. 'Bro, I don't think...'

'And that's the fuckin' problem.' Archer leaned over the bar in an instant and dragged the guy down by his shirtfront, face to face. 'If he's here, I'll see him and that'll be the end of it. If not...'

Archer saw movement in the mirror behind the bar and side-stepped, just in time to avoid a pool cue chopping down at his head. It hit the bar instead and bounced into the face of the barman, surprising both him and the thug who was holding it.

Archer swept an empty beer handle off the bar and smashed it across the side of the thug's face, opening up a large gash and sending shards everywhere.

The guy recoiled back, dropping the cue which Archer snatched up.

A second thug was close behind him, also carrying a pool cue. He ignored his injured mate and came straight in, swinging like he was going for a home run.

Archer ducked, the cue arced above his head, and the thug was left wide open. It was a rookie mistake that the guy would forever regret.

Archer reversed the cue in his hand so the thicker end was available, whipped it across the guy's kidneys from behind, and drove his heel into the back of the guy's closest knee. The leg buckled and dropped him to his knee.

Archer shifted his grip again and hammered the thick end of the cue into the guy's skull. The soft part behind and below the ear took the full impact and the guy dropped like a stone, lights out.

The other five big thugs were moving towards him but the first one stopped in his tracks when he saw his two mates taken out so quickly.

The one with the cut cheek was holding onto the bar and trying to stop the flow of blood, but he was leaking like a broken pipe. The second one was face down, out cold.

'What the fuck?' the third man demanded. 'You know who the fuck we are?'

He was a big guy, Archer's height but easily 30kg heavier. He had a goatee, plenty of ink, and sharkies pushed up on his cropped hair.

Archer eyed him. His blood was up and these fuckers were just wasting time.

'The real question,' he said, 'is do you know who I am?'

The guy sneered. 'I dunno who the fuck you *think* you are, cunt,' he said, glancing at his mates for support, 'but you're a dead cunt.'

He turned back towards Archer, reaching for an empty bottle on a nearby table. He was still turning when Archer took two steps forward and front kicked him in the balls. The guy's eyes bugged and he let out a gasp as he started to fold forward.

The pool cue whipped over his head, clocking the man to the right across the face. The next guy tried to grab it as it swung past, and managed to get a hand to it. Archer yanked the cue back then slammed it forward into the man's face.

The thick end smashed out his front teeth and knocked him backwards into the guy behind him, blood and broken teeth spraying out as he fell.

The front man was still folding forwards and trying to cradle his damaged jewels. Archer slapped a hand to the back of the guy's skull and jerked it downwards, driving it into the knee he was bringing up.

The guy's nose flattened and he sagged, still not quite going down. He was a very big unit and looked like he'd taken a few hits in his time, as well as dishing plenty out. The problem with guys like this, though, was that they were usually dishing it out to much smaller, scared and less skilled victims.

Archer was definitely smaller, but he was far from scared of these guys and his skills had been learned the hard way.

He gave the guy a second knee to the face, pushed him aside, and sidestepped away. The two guys at the back of the group were splitting up, moving around the tables and chairs to outflank Archer on each side.

The other patrons were hanging far back, not wanting a bar of it. Archer didn't blame them; he had better things to do than fight these idiots.

Seeing the guy to his left lunging forward around a table, Archer stepped back, keeping another table between them. The guy shadowed him, the last guy closing in on the right. Each of them had picked up a bottle and had it cocked, ready to rock and roll.

'Well come on,' Archer said, glancing between them. He had the pool cue cocked like a batsman on the mound. 'Would one of you please get your balls out of your handbag?'

His dig worked and they charged at the same time. Archer leaped onto the table in front of him, side kicked the guy on his right in the face, planted his foot again, and slammed the other guy across the side of the head with the pool cue.

The guy on the right had bloodied hands up at his face and didn't even try to defend himself as Archer kicked him again, stomping hard this time on the guy's collarbone. He heard a loud snap and a crunch, the guy screeched in agony and staggered away, and Archer turned to the last guy.

He saw a low grab coming at his legs, jumped it, retained his footing on the circular table, and kicked the guy hard under the jaw.

The thug's teeth slammed like a vault door and his head snapped back. He fell across a chair, rolled onto a table, and went down in a heap with the furniture falling around him.

Katrina and the Waves were belting out "Walking on Sunshine" over the sound system. Archer scanned the seven thugs.

The only one still standing was the guy who had only received a single blow to the face with the pool cue. He had a hand to his face but no obvious injuries. His face registered total shock as he looked around at his fallen mates.

It wasn't supposed to have gone like this. These guys were used to dishing out the beatings, not taking them.

The guy turned his gaze to Archer. His lips moved but nothing came out.

Archer could see the other patrons behind him against the far wall, cowering in fear. The barman was standing with them. Nobody said a word, but Archer was well aware of the sort of fear thugs like this instilled in law-abiding citizens.

For those citizens to see the tables turned on the bullies was a watershed moment.

He locked eyes with the thug.

'So what are you gunna do now?' he said.

The thug blinked. Decision making wasn't his strongpoint, so Archer did it for him.

He took one step forward and brought his right hand up fast, the heel of the palm slamming up under the thug's chin.

His head snapped back, his eyes rolled into his skull, and he collapsed against a table. The table legs snapped under his weight and he landed flat on his back, out for the count.

Katrina was still walking on sunshine, and as Archer surveyed the damage he'd caused, he had to admit that it *did* feel good.

He moved away from the fallen thugs and caught the eye of the barman.

'Where's Steve?' he said as he came closer.

'Out the back,' the barman said reluctantly. He gave Archer an odd look. 'Don't go back there.' His eyes flicked towards the bar and then across to the opposite wall. 'Serious, bro. Just walk away.'

Archer gave him a thin smile, devoid of any humour. He had a pretty good idea what was going on, and who was responsible for the tragedy that had befallen Dee Dee. And that person was going to pay.

He jerked a thumb towards the gangsters he'd put down. 'Get someone to take out the trash, will you? The place is a mess.'

He crossed the floor to the short corridor to the toilets. It was a narrow, dark passageway with band posters on the walls. He passed the toilets and reached the door marked Private.

He pushed it open, ready to confront the traitorous bastard who had sent his sister to her death. What he saw instead caused him to take a step back as if he'd taken a body shot.

Steve was tied to a solid wooden chair with immovable arms and legs. He slumped back in it as if he were asleep, his head lolling back. He was bound with zip ties at the wrists and ankles, and by rope around the waist and neck.

If he were able to reach sleep it would be a blessing. Steve had been worked over good and proper.

Even from where he stood, Archer could see a lot of damage.

The fingers on his right hand were all twisted and buckled, either dislocated or broken. The fingertips on his left hand were bloodied and swollen.

His shirt was ripped open to the waist and his torso was streaked with sweat and blood. There were marks on his chest where it appeared a knife had been dug in, not far enough to damage any organs but certainly enough to draw blood and cause pain.

His face was covered in blood, some of it already dried. His lips were split. His nose was fat and clogged with dark clots.

But it was his eyes that caused bile to rise in Archer's throat. The right eye was swollen like a balloon, black and purple and grotesque. But it would heal.

The left eye was gone. What remained was a bloody socket of red flesh that oozed fluid down the cheek below.

The empty socket stared blankly at the wall. The other eye creaked open slowly, painfully, and tried to focus on the newcomer.

Archer doubted that Steve would be able to focus at all, and the sight of the empty socket made him want to vomit. At the same time he felt a terrible wave of guilt hit him.

He had come here for revenge, convinced that Steve had sold out his sister and determined to avenge her death.

What he was faced with told a different story entirely. Steve was not the traitorous sell-out that Archer had presumed him to be, not even close.

He had, in fact, endured horrendous torture at the hands of some person, or perhaps persons, who was so twisted that they could happily inflict such barbaric brutality on another. Archer was not averse to using force himself, as a means to an end.

But this was something else.

He needed to get Steve out of here and quickly. Who knew what internal damage he had suffered.

He crossed the floor, drawing the multi-tool from his pocket, and sliced through Steve's bonds in seconds.

'Bro.' The voice was raspy, forced through sand from deep below. 'You...made it.'

'Sssshh.' Archer stood, putting away the multi-tool and drawing the Kel-Tec instead. He thanked his lucky stars for the foresight of stopping by his room on the way here from the port. Although it had been searched and trashed, whoever had done it had missed the security package he had stashed in the garden outside. It allowed him to have a weapon, a tool, his passport and money.

He checked the hallway for any sign of enemy. Nothing.

He went back to Steve and paused, a thought niggling at him. The barman had scanned around when he was warning Archer not to come out the back. Scanning for what.

Archer's gaze fell on the split-screen monitor against the wall by Steve's desk. CCTV. The barman had been checking the CCTV cameras.

Someone was watching. Someone was just here, and the barman knew it. The fucker.

Archer left Steve where he was and hurried back out to the bar, the pistol low at his side. The thugs were gone, the patrons were gone, and the barman was gone. The place was completely empty.

The Rolling Stones were rocking out Brown Sugar over the sound system. Archer went behind the bar and turned it off, letting a sudden silence fall over the room. He could hear a vehicle somewhere outside, going away. No voices.

Everybody had gone for a reason, which meant only one thing to Archer.

Someone else was coming.

He went to the front doors and locked them, trotted back to the office and moved to the CCTV system. He found the hard drive and unhooked it. No time to download or view footage right now; they needed to move fast.

He tucked it under one arm, got the other arm around Steve and lifted him. The other man cried out in pain and put his damaged hand to his stomach, grimacing and bending at the waist.

'Steve, listen to me,' Archer said. 'We need to go and I need to help you. It's gunna hurt like a bastard but if I don't get you out of here you're fucked. We're *both* fucked, okay?'

Steve nodded weakly, his remaining eye closed again and his split, bloodied lips set firmly. He nodded again, more definite this time, and his lips barely moved when he spoke.

'Do it,' he croaked. 'I tr...trust you.' He reached out and gripped Archer's arm, surprisingly hard. 'They got...got my daughter...fuckers.'

Archer nodded to himself, putting that aside for now. He would do something about that later. He secured his grip around Steve's waist, and moved for the door.

Steve made animal sounds in his throat with every step but he didn't cry out again, not once as they took the fire door at the rear out to the parking area behind the bar. Steve's vehicle was there, a seen-better-days Nissan Navara double cab ute.

With Steve secured in the passenger seat, Archer raced back inside. He went to the bar and grabbed two bottles of water from the fridge, a rag, the first aid kit from under the till and a bottle of cold lemonade for himself.

They were bumping out onto the road within seconds, both belted in securely in anticipation of the ambush Archer was looking for.

He had the tiny Kel-Tec tucked under his thigh, ready to grab. If he'd been the enemy, he would have at least left a spotter nearby, watching the bar, if not a full ambush of some sort. Whoever these guys were – and he was guessing it was still Black Star, rather than a third party – they weren't amateurs.

Sure enough, they had gone only a hundred metres from the bar when he caught a glint of light in the darkness off the side of the road. Up ahead on the right was a narrow lay-by, midway between streetlamps, just a narrow clearing from the road into the bush.

As Archer got closer he became more certain. He was almost there when he hit the high beams and swerved to the right. The beams lit up a man sitting on a dirtbike, a radio in one hand and a smoke in the other. He was white, bearded and wearing a tight T-shirt. A rifle sling crossed his muscular chest.

He instinctively threw up a hand when the beams lit him up but it was too little too late.

The Navara hit him head on, the bumper lifting the front wheel of the dirtbike and the momentum of the truck carrying through. The truck slammed into him, throwing the man and his bike up and back.

Archer hit the brakes and cut left again, not stopping. Darkness fell back over the layby as the truck raced away.

19

'I need an urgent exfil,' Archer said, the phone pressed against his ear. 'I've been burned, my contact is wounded, a local contact and a CSIS officer are KIA and another CSIS officer has been abducted.'

Ingoe was as cool as a cucumber. Archer may as well have just given him the cricket score. 'No problem. Are you okay?'

Archer considered the question for a moment. He'd taken a reasonable beating, he'd been kidnapped, and he'd killed several men. But he had lived to fight another day.

'I'm fine,' he said.

'We've got contacts in Apia who can zip over and get you if they're available, but it's fifteen hundred clicks,' Ingoe said, thinking aloud. 'No direct commercial flights; it'd have to be military or charter. Auckland's twice the distance but more flights. Stand by.'

Archer heard the Ops Manager call out to an underling in the background, directing someone to find him a plane. He rubbed his jaw and glanced around the empty hospital room. Steve was in emergency surgery next door, being attended to by a team who were surprised to say the least.

He knew the two Aussie pilots based in Samoa, a pair of pirates if ever he'd met them. He'd be quite happy for them to come and pick him up, but chances were he'd be on a Jetstar flight back to Auckland instead.

Ingoe came back on the line. 'Your contact need a medevac?'

'He's in surgery but he's not safe to stay here.'

'Roger.'

More waiting and he paced impatiently, eager to get a plan together to move. When Ingoe came back on the line, his solution wasn't one that Archer had seen coming.

'We have an Orion in the air diverting to you, it's currently doing an anti-smuggling op not far away. ETA in Raro is three hours, got that?'

'Got it.'

'Your contact will stay where he is for now, the aircrew will leave a couple of men with him until we can organise a proper medevac, probably tomorrow.'

'Got that.'

'The Orion will bring you to Auckland and we'll go from there. All clear so far?'

'Yep.' Archer sensed something coming, and Ingoe didn't let him down.

'Our friends from Ottawa have been onto the boss, they're aware of what happened there and as you can imagine they have a lot of questions.'

'Fair enough.' Archer nodded to himself, a memory clicking in as he spoke. Izzy had told him the Canadians had had another team at the resort, watching Capstick. *Where the hell were they now?* 'Have they grabbed Capstick?'

'Who?'

'The Canadians.'

There was silence for a long moment. 'If they have then they haven't told us.'

Archer heard a door bang down the corridor, followed by a commotion of excited voices.

'Don't worry,' he said, 'I think they might have just arrived.'

He opened the door to find two very agitated men in shorts and loose shirts arguing with the nurse at the nurse's station halfway down the hall. Both sounded Canadian and angry, and as soon as they saw Archer appear they came towards him. The lead guy was slightly built and dark haired, late thirties. The second guy was more athletic, also dark haired, unshaven and tired looking.

'What the fuck's going on, Archer?' the first guy demanded. 'It sounds like half the island's been shot to shit and our people are missing. What the fuck?'

He was so wound up he had dry spit flecking his lips. He stopped a metre short of Archer, locking eyes with him. The second guy stood off to the side, watching their backs.

'Izzy's been kidnapped,' Archer said bluntly, 'and your guy Michael's dead.'

The first guy visibly flinched.

'I'm sorry,' Archer said. 'We got ambushed by some Black Star guys, Michael and a local contact got hit, Izzy and I made a run for it but they got us and held us for a day or so. I don't know where they've taken her.'

'You son of a bitch.' The first guy threw a wild swing at him and Archer pulled back, letting it fly past. He brushed away the follow up swing and gave the guy a firm push in the chest.

'Get a grip, mate.' The guy was clearly not a fighter and Archer resisted the urge to sit him on his arse. For now, at least. 'Maybe if you dickheads had told us you were here we could have worked in together, rather than charging round like a bunch of cowboys.'

'You fuckin'…' the first guy started and Archer cut him off.

'Shut up. I don't have time for schoolyard bullshit. Your officer has been taken and we need to find her. What've you done with Capstick?'

The first guy paused. The second guy maintained his silence. Clearly he was the muscle, not the mouth.

'We have him,' the first guy said eventually. 'You could call it protective custody.'

'I don't care what you call it,' Archer said. 'I need to talk to him.'

The guy gave a condescending chuckle. 'Yeah, that's not gonna happen, pal.'

'Then you won't get Izzy back.' He returned the guy's stare. 'Capstick's the lead. Krystal Raines has her; she's working with the Black Star guys. Or they're working for her, by the looks of it.'

'That hairy-legged activist bitch? Working with private military guys? Gimme a break, Archer. This is bullshit.'

'No,' said Archer, 'what's bullshit is the fact that you guys had a whole fuckin' team over here yet you still missed the Black Star guys.'

'So did you.' The guy was defensive now.

'But I'm just one guy. And I still managed to put some of them down.'

They held a silent stare down for a few moments.

'I've heard about you,' the first guy finally said. 'They reckon you're pretty shit hot.' He cocked his head. 'But not as shit hot as you think you are.'

Archer let it go. He didn't give a shit what this guy thought, and he wasn't in the mood for a pissing contest.

'Right,' he said. 'I'm not here to fuck ducks.'

'What does that even mean, eh?' The first guy looked to the second guy, acting incredulous.

Archer ignored him and looked to the second guy as well. If his assessment was right, this guy was the muscle, probably ex-JTF2. Ideal for what he had in mind.

'We need to get shit done. A little girl's being held by these pricks as well. What's your background?' he said.

The second guy glanced to the first guy, as if uncertain whether to reply.

'Come on mate,' Archer pushed, 'the clock's ticking.'

'I used to be on ERT, RCMP,' the guy said.

Archer nodded. The Mounties' Emergency Response Team was a well-trained tactical unit, not as good as a military unit but better than nothing.

'Good,' he said. 'Got a weapon?'

The guy nodded.

'Right,' he said, 'you're with me. You,' he looked to the first guy, 'can stay here. My contact Steve is in surgery. These bastards tortured him and ripped out his eye.'

The guy looked like he was going to throw up. 'His eye.'

'His eye. You guard him with your life. They may come back for him, or some pretty nasty gangsters might too.'

The guy swallowed hard. This was way outside his comfort zone.

'Let your bosses know and see if they can get you some help. There's a plane landing in three hours and I intend to be on it, so we need to get this girl back before that happens. Everybody understand what's going on?'

They both nodded. The second guy had a definite glint in his eye which gave Archer some confidence.

'Let's go.'

20

Steve had been half conscious while Archer was racing him to the hospital, and it had taken all his effort to tell Archer what had happened.

While Archer and Dee Dee had been out sightseeing, he was on deck surveilling Capstick at the resort. He took a phone call from a man he didn't know, telling him to check his messages.

The photo he'd been sent showed his daughter, Cobie, being held in her bedroom with a gun to her head. The four year old girl was clutching her teddy bear and crying. The next call he took a few seconds later told him to come to the bar. He'd done as he was told, was tied up and tortured by two thugs in ski masks, who he could only describe as white guys with American accents.

They had grilled him as to what he knew of Archer's mission, what the Canadians were doing there and whether they were all working together, and what he knew of Archer's plans for Capstick.

That last had confused Archer. His was simply a surveillance op; he had no plans for Capstick but to watch him. Did they think he was there to take the guy out?

The two kidnappers had given Steve no indication of what they thought the plan might have been, which didn't help.

They had clearly kidnapped Cobie to force Steve to talk, which made sense to Archer; it was a faster way to the heart of the matter than simply trying to persuade, trick or beat him. Problem was, he didn't know a lot to tell them.

Naturally they hadn't believed him and it had taken some time to get to the point where any reasonable man would spill his guts, which Steve admitted, with great shame, he had done.

Archer didn't blame him at all. Nobody could hold out forever, and Steve lacked the training to even give it a decent nudge. The little he knew, he had given up.

As to why they had ripped out Steve's eye, they had told him the answer and it was chillingly simple.

'Fun,' Steve had said quietly, bouncing with the motion of the Navara on the rough road. 'The bastards...they did it for fun.'

It was at that point that Archer had decided, with no uncertainty, that he would kill the bastards who had done it.

The two men had remained until shortly before Archer had got there. Steve suspected his barman may have been involved somehow, because he had continued to run the bar while his boss was tortured in the back office. He didn't know whether the Aussie deportees were involved at all, but admitted they sometimes came to the bar.

Now, travelling through the darkness in Steve's Navara, Archer had a very loose plan in his head. He shared with the ex-Mountie, who had introduced himself as Don.

'I don't know if the girl will still be at his place. If she isn't, then I have no idea where she is. If she is, we'll go in and get her.'

'You realise it's probably an ambush?' Don said.

'Yep. But what are our options?'

Don ticked off points on his fingers. 'Do nothing; can't do that. Get the local cops involved; ain't got the training. Wait for a proper tactical unit; delay too long and she's dead. Go in; she may die anyway.'

Archer checked a letterbox as he cruised past. 'So when the only option available is a shit one, it's still the only option available. So that's what we do.'

21

T he house was a simple three-room bungalow set back from the road, occupied by Steve, his wife Mo, and little Cobie. There were chooks loose in the yard and a pig asleep in a muddy enclosure out the back.

They had no idea whether Mo was present or even alive. She had a cell phone which Ingoe was working on getting tracked. Archer rang him one last time before they executed their plan.

'It's pinging at the house,' Ingoe said without preamble. 'Just got it now. Looks like another cell there as well, working on getting some int on that but it could be a while.'

'Roger,' Archer said. 'We're going in.'

'Good luck.' Ingoe cut the connection. The Navara was silent aside from the ticking of the engine.

Archer didn't know why the bad guys would still be sitting on the girl. Maybe they needed her for something else. Maybe they didn't know Steve had been rescued. Too many maybes and not enough answers, but it didn't change what they needed to do.

He checked the Kel-Tec. He had a full magazine in it, and two full spares. Don had two full mags for his Sig.

Hopefully it would be enough. Ideally they would be going in each with an MP5 or an M4, flashbangs, and full tactical kit. Today was a different day at the office and they had to adjust.

He gave Don a nod. 'Let's do it.'

The approach down the road was quick and quiet. A dog barked somewhere in a yard. There was a streetlight a hundred metres away, but the front of Steve's property was in darkness. The curtains were drawn but there were lights on inside.

Don cut away to the right, angling to get round the back to the "black" side. Archer moved to the closest side of the property, the right or green side. The front was white, the left side red, the roof was blue.

He crouched in the darkness to look and listen. He could hear music faintly on the night air, from somewhere further down the road. The light breeze rustled through the trees around them.

He crossed fast to the side of the house, going firm beneath a window. No sounds came from inside. He ran through the plan in his head one last time before making the final step. Get in fast, take out the X-Rays, rescue the Yankees. It wasn't much of a plan, but it was the best he had.

Time to get on with it.

He edged around to the back corner, green/black. Waited thirty more seconds until there was a light rattle on the roof. The stone that Don had thrown was too small and barely seemed to make a whisper.

A few seconds later there was a better hit, a much more distinct thump. Archer heard footsteps inside the house, a shift in the light spilling across the back yard as someone moved a curtain.

That was good; bad tactics meant they weren't trained. It was likely that whoever the X-Rays were they were thugs, not Black Star guys. Still dangerous though.

He waited a few more seconds, heard a door opening at the back.

More light spilled out into the yard. At the same time he heard the creak of a hinge at the front of the house. Someone was coming out the front and would be approaching his rear.

Archer left Don to deal with whatever threat presented itself at the back and hurried towards the front. He got to the green/white corner at the same time as a large silhouette loomed around it towards him. The guy had shades pushed up on his head, shoulders wider than most doorways and a sawn-off single barrelled weapon in his hands.

Archer didn't hesitate. He was so close he could smell the guy's bubble gum breath. He raised the Kel-Tec in both hands, the muzzle barely six inches from the guy's forehead, and stroked the trigger twice. Both rounds went through the guy's temple and bounced around inside his skull. He dropped without uttering a word but the gunshots were deafeningly loud in the still night.

Archer was past him already, moving to the front door. He heard a shout of alarm from the back of the house, a curse from inside some-where and heavy footfalls through the house heading towards the back.

A double-tap sounded, followed by the crack of a .22 rifle, then another double tap.

Archer risked a glance around the edge of the front door, saw a lighted hallway through the middle of the house to the back door with a guy lying slumped there, propped up on one elbow with a rifle on the floor beside him.

Another big guy was tucked behind a doorway half way down the hall, looking towards the rear with a pistol in his hand. He fired a shot as Archer watched then ducked back. A return shot sounded and Archer hoped that Don's aim was good. He didn't want loose rounds flying about to take out either him or a hostage.

The big guy leaned out and fired another shot, not aiming, then another and another. He was such a bad shot that he blew a chunk off the wall above his wounded mate, who called out to him in a panic.

'Bro, bro! Stop it bro, you almost hit me!'

'Where's Aleki? Leki! Hurry up bro, he's out the back!'

The big guy turned to look towards the front door where he'd last seen Aleki. Archer and Don both fired as he exposed himself from behind his cover. Archer's two shots punched through his neck and the base of his skull. Don fired a single shot that took him high in the chest and spun him like a top. He fell out into the hallway, crashed into the opposite wall and fell backwards, hitting the wooden floor with a thump.

'Moving!'

Archer was up and into the hallway in a flash, ducking into the first room on the left and sweeping it in a second. Clear. Through the ringing in his ears he could hear sobbing from the next room over.

'That's me on black,' Don called. 'Clear here.'

Archer heard a shot and glanced into the hallway. Don was stepping over the first guy he'd shot, now lying dead on the floor.

'He went for his gun,' the Canadian said, checking Archer for a reaction.

'So did he.' Archer put a round through the other guy's forehead. The smell of cordite was strong in the hallway, a familiar and welcome smell to him.

Together they cleared the last two rooms, finding the two hostages in the master bedroom. Mo was huddled on the floor by the bed with little Cobie wrapped in her arms. They both looked up at the two men, trying unsuccessfully to stifle their sobbing.

'You're okay now,' Archer said, 'you're safe. The bad men can't hurt you anymore.'

Mo wiped a hand across her eyes and took a shuddering breath. 'Where's Steve?'

'He's safe too,' Archer said, carefully deflecting the question. 'But you need to come with us now, so we can make sure you're all safe together.'

Mo looked at him fearfully. Cobie buried her head into Mo's breast, avoiding looking at the men.

'You won't hurt us?' Mo said.

'No Mo, we're the good guys. But we need to go now, we need to move fast.'

'Come on sweetheart,' Don said, his voice tender. He helped them to their feet while Archer covered their backs. 'Stick with me.'

He grabbed a stuffed bear from the bed and gave it to Cobie. The little girl clutched it to her chest and peeked at him before hiding her face again. Archer hated to think what might have happened to the two of them in the time they'd been held by these thugs.

He killed the lights and led the way outside, seeing and hearing people moving about out on the road. Some called out, wanting to know what was going on. He ignored them and led the small party at a trot down the road to the Navara.

Leaving the interior light off, he fired it up and drove away at a brisk pace. He doubted that the local cops were much chop and certainly wouldn't be used to dealing with an incident like this, so he was reasonably confident they would be able to escape unhindered.

A police truck blasted the other way a couple of minutes later, followed closely by a second one. None of the cops in either vehicle seemed to give them a second glance.

By the time they got to the airport they hadn't seen a police vehicle in ten minutes.

Archer pulled into a layby and dug out his phone. Ingoe answered on the first ring.

'Sit-rep,' he said brusquely.

'Three X-Rays down, both Yankees recovered unharmed, no casualties for us.'

'Bloody good work. I've been in touch with Ottawa and they're getting a team out there ASAP too, coming from Canberra. Should be there in the morning. I'm also sending over some others. Your flight will be landing shortly, updated ETA is about half an hour away.'

'Got that.'

Ingoe checked on the wellbeing of the rescued hostages and of Steve before ringing off, and Archer sat in the darkness for a few moments, thinking it all over. The whole mission was seeming to get more and more bizarre and dangerous with each step.

Rarotonga was a sleepy little tropical paradise; shit like this didn't happen there.

Yet here he was in the middle of a battle between foreign intelligence agencies, biker thugs and supposed peace activists backed by a ruthless PMC. He couldn't actually remember how many men he had killed in the last day or so.

The whole thing had international headlines written all over it, and that was even without a hostage rescue job thrown into the mix.

He shook his head and started the Navara. In the glow of the dashboard lights he caught Don staring at him.

'What?'

'We all good?' the other man said.

Archer realised that Don found himself in the same position that Archer had found himself in the previous day with Izzy. Putting down a bad guy like that in front of someone you didn't know was a huge risk, the sort of thing that could easily end up in court and bring down an agency.

'Of course.' Archer looked him in the eye. 'We're in the same boat, remember?'

Don nodded and looked away.

'First time?'

Don nodded, studiously looking out the window.

Archer knew he would be going through a range of new emotions that would take some time to process. Nothing he did right now would be of much help; Don just needed to get his head around it in his own time.

Forty five minutes later an Orion had landed and two of its crew were climbing into the Navara. Both were armed with MARS-L rifles and looked competent – or as competent as aircrew looked on land, Archer thought to himself.

He went round to the driver's side and shook hands with Don through the window. 'You did good mate,' he said. 'Thanks.' He indicated the two quiet dark shapes in the back seat, huddled under a blanket. 'You saved their lives tonight.'

Don nodded his thanks. 'See ya round, buddy.' He gave a tight smile. 'And watch your back.'

Archer watched them go and hustled through the side gate behind another crew member. The big Orion P-3K2 was waiting on the tarmac for them, its props turning. With there being no commercial flights at this time of night, Archer wondered if they had woken an air traffic controller or just landed themselves. It didn't matter to him either way; he just needed to get out of there before the inevitable shitstorm blew up the next day.

The Orion normally had a crew of 12, so he copped plenty of curious looks when he climbed aboard. A grizzly-looking crewman parked him in a seat out of the way, gave him a spare set of overalls and a flask of tea, and told him to sit tight. Moments later the captain came to see him. He was young and unusually tall for a pilot, and introduced himself as Williams.

'I don't know what the game is, mate,' he said, leaning down to speak into Archer's ear, 'but you pulled us off the tail of a bunch of Indonesian people smugglers, so it better be fucking important.'

'Thanks,' Archer said blandly, 'I appreciate it.'

Williams straightened up with a scowl and turned away, muttering 'Dickhead' under his breath.

Within a few minutes they were airborne and heading home. Archer was asleep before the front wheels had lifted off the ground.

22

———

From where she stood in in the shadows of the private hangar, Krystal Raines watched the activity across the airfield.

It hadn't surprised her that Archer had escaped, but by Christ it pissed her off. And if she was pissed off then Kozlowski would all of that and some. It was not a phone call she was looking forward to.

'The coconuts are all dead,' the man beside her said, breaking the silence. 'Him and one of the Canadian fucks smoked 'em all.'

'Is there an opportunity at the hospital?' She kept her gaze straight ahead, watching the Orion lifting into the dark sky.

'Whaddaya mean?'

Raines felt the rage rise in her chest. This guy had to be kidding. She turned slowly to look at him. 'An opportunity to kill the other fucking coconut,' she said, slowly and clearly, as if speaking to a child of limited intellect.

He got the inference, and his jaw tightened. Rick. He was a big man, from Denver apparently, as if she gave a shit about that. For the last few days his blue eyes had barely left her tits, but that was okay; bone a guy once and he would come back for more. Do it right and he was feeding from your hand forever. And Krystal Raines knew how to do it right.

'Could be,' he grated, 'but they got two guys there with automatic weapons, so it'll be messy.' He hiked his thick shoulders and his teeth showed through his black beard. 'Gimme the word and we'll hit it.' It was he who had threatened Archer back in the shed, and she knew he was keen to get some payback for the comrades he had lost.

Raines felt a thrill of excitement run from her gut to her crotch. Violence was such a fucking turn on. If they were out of here tonight then Rick was going to get the boning of his life.

Unless of course Viktor wanted a message sent; then she'd have to kill him, and she knew she'd do it without a second thought. He was the leader of his crew of mercs, and there were no second chances in this game.

'Stand by,' she said. She took out her phone and dialled a number from memory.

Viktor Kozlowski answered immediately. 'You have good news, I hope.' His tone was quiet but full of menace. If anybody in this world scared Raines more than herself, it was Kozlowski.

'We still have the Canadian bitch,' she told him. 'Archer got away and is on an RNZAF plane right now.'

There was a long silence, broken only by his breathing. Raines could feel her heart slamming in her chest as she waited. Kozlowski was not a man who looked favourably on failure.

'Get her to Switzerland,' Kozlowski eventually said. 'Have a team on her.'

'Got it.'

'Think you can do that, Krystal?' His words were bland but the feeling behind them was unmistakable.

'Yes sir,' she said, her throat dry. 'We're on it, leaving any minute.'

A long, slow breath sounded in her ear. 'Good. And your friend Mr Capstick? Where is he now?'

'They have him,' she said. 'The Canadians lifted him...'

'I know that,' he said coldly. 'Where exactly is he now?'

Raines took the chastisement like a naughty child. Of course he knew that. 'GPS says he's en-route to Europe, looks like Poland.'

'So the Canadians will be using a US black site. That figures.'

The Canadians weren't as free and easy with advanced interrogation techniques as their neighbours, but they were willing to share. That worked for Kozlowski. Inserting the tiny tracking chip under Capstick's skin was paying off, not that the slimy little so-called journalist had appreciated it at the time.

Raines's skin crawled at the thought of him against her. He had been a means to an end, but not one she was willing to repeat in a hurry. She subconsciously ran an eye over Rick's muscular figure. Now that was a man.

'Yes sir.'

'Good. Carry on, Krystal.' There was a pause and she waited, knowing better than to jump the gun. Rudeness like that was one thing Kozlowski would not tolerate. 'Oh, and Krystal?'

'Sir?'

'There is no room for more errors, do you understand?'

'Yes sir.'

The line went dead and Raines lowered it from her ear. She let out her breath, feeling a rush of relief. At least for now, they lived another day.

She turned to Rick. 'Let's go. Wheel's up straight away.'

He barked an order over his shoulder at the flight crew who were waiting in the hangar. The private jet was a loaner from a wealthy businessman with dubious connections to certain ex-Soviet states, and the crew were his guys. Discretion was their lifeline.

Rick turned back to her. He was a brute of a man and he knew it. Watching him gouge out Steve's eyeball had been an education in sadism for her, and it was one she had relished.

'Are we good?' he said softly.

Raines felt a cold smile flick across her face. She clapped her hand to his crotch and gave him a squeeze through his fatigues, causing him to flinch. The power of having a man by the balls was incomparable.

'We're good,' she said with a smirk. 'Let's move.'

23

———————

Auckland, New Zealand
Saturday, 1300 hours

'The Canadians are bloody furious,' the Director snapped. 'The Cook Island Government is demanding answers, and so are the fish heads in Wellington. The Australians are poking their noses in and everybody's pretty pissed off.'

Archer pursed his lips. 'Probably not as pissed off as Dee Dee's family,' he said with some feeling.

The Director looked at him sharply. 'I'm well aware of that, thank you,' he said. There was real ice in his tone. 'The question is, what to do from here?'

Archer was fairly sure the Director wasn't actually asking for his opinion, so he kept his trap shut. He didn't trust himself not to erupt just yet anyway.

The Director stared at him across the desk. Archer could feel himself being examined with cold detachment.

The man was ruthless all right, and it made Archer wonder what exactly was going on inside that old head. They were a different breed, these career intelligence types. Nothing was ever what it seemed, and just when you thought you had a handle on them they took a different turn.

'The CSIS are working on finding their officer,' the Director said. 'Our contact from the islands is back here with his wife and his daughter, and they'll stay here while he gets his medical treatment. The media are all over it, of course. Bloody vultures.'

Archer said nothing. It was good to know that Steve would be getting top notch care.

'The story being leaked to the media is that it was a clash between these criminals deported from Australia and some locals. The local girl was killed by one of the kidnappers, and they were in turn killed by unidentified locals. We're supplying some assistance to the officials there, and they're very grateful of course, considering they have very limited means.'

Archer nodded.

'So for now, you need to get yourself back to London and wait for any developments. If we can assist the Canadians in any way we will. The issues with Five Eyes are getting more complicated and it's turning into something of a pissing contest, which is rather unhelpful. Mr Capstick has an awful lot to answer for.'

'Is he still in Raro?'

'No, he's on his way to an, ahh, an *interview* location. Hopefully he didn't get any sort of bulletin sent off to anyone before he got lifted. That's all we bloody need.' The Director peered at Archer over the top of his glasses. 'Unfortunately that seems quite likely, considering the very public nature of everything that happened over there.'

Archer had had enough. He was tired, sore and pissed off. 'Well perhaps if the int we'd had was worth more than a pinch of shit we'd have known exactly what the hell was going on.' He felt his cheeks getting hot, and forced himself to stop. The Director was eyeballing him coldly and Archer had a sudden urge to slap the old bastard. He clenched his fists and held fast.

There was a long pause. '*Sir*,' he finally grated.

The Director laced his fingers together as if praying and leaned forward with his elbows on the desk. 'Captain Archer,' he said quietly. 'You may think me an old fool, some relic who sits in an office and moves pieces round a chessboard with no concept of the humanity involved. But make no mistake.'

His gaze was heavy on Archer's face. 'I know bloody well what it's like out in the field. I cut my teeth as a young intelligence officer during the Cold War, working in stations all around the world. I worked Russian agents, real hard KGB bastards who had killed more men than you've had hot dinners. I was captured in Bosnia and hung out to dry until an exchange took place some weeks later. I debriefed one of our men who had been deployed in East Berlin for years in the early eighties. The poor bastard was so strung out he'd taken to sucking his thumb and wetting the bed. I found him hanging in a Christchurch hotel room the day after the debrief ended.'

The Director's lips pinched and he paused at the memory. The office was dead silent. 'So make no mistake, Captain Archer.' His voice was almost a whisper now. 'I know what it's like at the sharp end. And don't ever be so bloody conceited as to think that I don't.'

Archer could hear a faint rattle in the Director's chest as he breathed in and out. A cold, or an infection? Something worse? He was probably one of those men that was riddled with cancer but would work until the last minute then collapse, at his desk, disappointed in himself that he hadn't completed some task for the firm before he went toes-up.

Archer gave a short nod. 'Fair enough, sir. My apologies.'

The Director slowly sat back. 'Then we'll move on. You sent images of the meet between Capstick, the Raines woman and another man. We put Blues on him and they've managed to identify him.'

That was a good move. There were two highly-trained teams based in Auckland known as the Blues. One was the underachieving Super Rugby team, who had all the talent but few results to show for it. The other was the SIS surveillance team whos abilities and dedication brought results every time they went out.

'So who is he?' Archer said. 'He looks like an IT geek who spends his weekends gaming and binge-eating.'

The Director gave a grunt which could have meant anything. 'Well you're at least half right. His name is Lee Sweetman and he's a world-class hacker.'

Two things fell into place in Archer's head right away.

Firstly, "Sweets" was not a term of endearment from Ethan Capstick; it was the man's nickname. Therefore he and Capstick probably weren't lovers as Archer had thought, and the int on Capstick and Raines being lovers instead was probably right. He mentally checked himself for allowing a prejudice to colour his judgement.

Secondly, Sweets was now a very important factor in this mission. A hacker was a key player for any terrorist organisation, and it made sense. How did Capstick get vital int leaked to him? It had to be either an inside man or a hacker. Lee Sweetman could well be the answer.

'What else do we know about him?' he said.

'He's highly intelligent but socially stunted. He lives alone in an apartment in the city. He hasn't held a steady, legal job since leaving university, but he has a net worth of close to two million dollars. He likes to work with crypto-currencies and hasn't had a girlfriend he hasn't paid by the hour, ever.'

The Director cocked an eyebrow at Archer when he said that last, and Archer wondered if there was some hidden meaning behind it. Perhaps the Director was subtly hinting at Archer's own hedonistic lifestyle.

'He's thirty four years old,' the Director continued. 'Never been in trouble with the law, aside from being questioned a couple of times in relation to low level hacking a decade or so ago. Never got charged. And ahh,' the Director said it almost causally, 'he's Canadian.'

Archer did a double take. Canadian. The cunning bastards had kept that to themselves. It explained why they, out of the other four partners in Five Eyes, were so keen to get involved. It was information that could have come in handy earlier.

He turned his focus back to the Director.

'So what do we do about him, sir?' he said.

24

———

Auckland, New Zealand
Sunday, 0330 hours

The Pinnacle Apartments were supposed to be the top shelf of apartment buildings in downtown Auckland, but as far as Archer could see, the needle-like building looked no different to any of the others poking up towards him.

Mind you, he was free-falling towards the city roofs and the leased Beechcraft that he had jumped from was several kilometres away by now.

The wind was screaming past him and he was keeping a close eye on his wrist-mounted GPS. To overshoot the roof would spell disaster. The moon was partially obscured by clouds and for some reason the street lights in the block around the Pinnacle Apartments had cut out just a few minutes ago.

Archer checked his altimeter, realising he was getting close. 500m. It was time.

He pulled the ripcord and a second later was jerked upwards as the black sports parachute he was using unfurled and caught air. He checked his ropes – all good. GPS – all good. Wind – no problem.

The city roofs were just below him now and it felt like he could touch them. Despite the ungodly hour there were still lights on in most of the office buildings, maybe cleaners or company slaves working late, maybe a night shift keeping the ball rolling while their bosses slept.

He couldn't see any lights on in the penthouse apartment owned by Lee Sweetman. The Blues had him at the casino, donkey-deep in a game with a bunch of Asians.

A casual glance out the window would be unlikely to catch the black-clad figure arcing through the night sky, but Archer knew it was a risky move dropping in like this. Due to the high security at the Pinnacle, there were few options that didn't require substantial planning and resourcing to get in there, so he and Ingoe had gone with the parachute jump.

It had been a while since he'd done a city jump to a target like this, but the skills had been well drilled in during his time in Air Troop, and the adrenaline was pumping.

200 now and he could almost spit on his target.

The Pinnacle had a narrow roof with air conditioning units, vents, aerials and other obstructions dotted about. There was a small open area around the roof access door and this was what Archer was aiming for. Skewering himself on an aerial held little appeal.

100. He turned into the wind, fixing his aim on the open roof area, the Pinnacle dead ahead now. Dropping, a tweak to correct his line, dropping, 50 out, another tweak to the right, 30 out and looking good.

Crossing the street far below, 15 out, almost there, over the lip of the building now, right on target, and he flared, the final move to drop himself neatly onto the square of dirty concrete below.

And then Mother Nature intervened.

The gust of wind hit him from the left, filling the 'chute and plucking Archer into the air just as his boots were about to hit the roof.

He bit back a curse as he was yanked sideways, grabbing at the release to drop the 'chute and free himself, but too late. He slammed his leg against some obstruction, unseen in the dark, then he could see car lights below him.

Fuck fuck fuck!

He swung out over the lip of the Pinnacle Apartments, disregarding the release now – whatever was going to happen now had to be better than trying his emergency 'chute and potentially just dropping to his death on the city streets below. Base jumping had never appealed to him.

There was a sudden jerk on his harness and he was flung sideways and back, slamming against the side of the building. He grunted and hung there, sucking in a breath, waiting for the next move.

Nothing happened.

The 'chute must have caught on something above him, leaving him dangling in space. Craning his neck to look, he guessed he was about five metres down from the lip of the roof. With his back against the wall, Archer hung in place and assessed his situation.

He figured he had two options – go up or go down.

Assuming that the chute had ripped, or would rip if it came free, it was not of much use to him. There was a balcony below but it was narrow and probably three floors away. The chances of landing on it if he dropped were pretty slim, let alone surviving.

There were no footholds to his left.

He looked to the right and realised he was almost at the corner of the building, maybe three metres away. He could see an outlet pipe of some sort a metre or so in from the edge which he could use as a handhold, but he quickly realised it was the only one.

Fuck it. He should have been in by now. The streetlights would be coming on in a few minutes and he'd be lit up like a sideshow for all to see.

He tugged on the 'chute, testing its grip. It seemed to hold. Perhaps that was the way up.

Archer turned so that he was face against the wall, held on for a moment to catch his breath and decide whether his plan was actually viable or whether it was suicidal.

With no other options on the table, there was only one way to find out.

He quickly gathered the lines in until he had them bunched in his right fist. He carefully hit the release with his left hand and detached himself from the safety of the 'chute harness. He felt himself drop slightly and his stomach lurched, making him grip the bunched lines tighter with both gloved hands.

He was now hanging by his own weight, praying the damaged 'chute would hold, eighteen stories above street level. It wasn't quite how he'd seen the night playing out.

He moved his right hand up, secured a grip and pulled, snagging the next hold with his left. He had no issue with free-climbing up a rope, but this was a different ballgame altogether.

Hand by hand Archer moved his way up the lines, using his feet where he could for extra purchase against the side of the building. Sweat was pouring down his neck and soaking him inside the jumpsuit.

Seeing he was maybe halfway there, he upped his effort, pushing out a way from the building so he could use his feet properly. That made it easier and he gained a quick metre, but he could also feel the parachute beginning to tear.

His body weight was dropping him further out from the building and increasing the pressure on the 'chute. He could feel it starting to give way and he knew that he was only seconds away from it giving up completely. Falling from this height would leave him as a splat of jelly on the concrete.

The lip of the building was only a metre or so above him. Archer leaned in closer to the building, maintaining a grip with just the toes of both boots, and redoubled his efforts. Hand up, grip and pull, next hand up, grip and pull, and again, and again, until he could see the sky at the top of his vision.

He had run out of lines and was now holding onto the 'chute itself, which was never designed to be used as a climbing rope, and the fabric was moving, pulling towards him like a conveyor belt that he was trying to get along to the safety of the ground beyond it.

Less than a metre to go. Sweat stung his eyes and his breathing was tight, every fibre focussed on getting himself up that last little stretch to safety. The 'chute was still tearing but he was almost within reach now.

One more hand up, grip and pull, then he pushed up with his toes and lunged. Right hand up and slapping over the edge, fingers gripping hard, pulling up. Letting go of the parachute with his left hand, Archer got that up too, holding securely, pushed with his toes against the side of the building and heaved with all his strength.

One last effort heaved him over the edge and he rolled onto the roof, moving away from the lip and lying flat on his back, staring up at the night sky.

Jesus Christ that was fucking close.

He sucked down air, got himself together, and gathered up the 'chute. It had snagged on an air conditioning vent and was damaged far beyond repair.

He bundled it up, rammed into his pack, and slung the pack back on. The street lights below came back on then, casting ambient light even this high.

Time check – six minutes over time. He needed to move. He took a minute to put his earwig in and do a radio check. Ingoe was on the other end, listening from an OP in a nearby street.

'Loud and clear, Nighthawk. What's your delay?'

Nighthawk – he knew Ingoe was taking the piss out of him with his callsign. He began moving towards the access door. 'I was just hanging around,' he said. 'Things got a bit ropey. On target now at the top door.'

'Roger.'

25

———

He knew that Ingoe would know something had gone wrong, but now was not the time for long explanations.

The electric door picker he carried was shaped like a small drill but with picks instead of bits. It was almost silent and made short work of the lock on the access door. He secured it behind him and pulled on his night vision goggles. The interior of the dark stairwell lit up in luminescent green.

The door at the bottom opened outwards and the service corridor beyond was empty. Archer moved down it quickly, his boots silent on the scarred lino floor. Part way down was the last access door he would use and he paused there, listening intently before gently turning the handle.

The door opened inwards and he took his time, checking the foyer on the other side was empty. The lighting removed the need for the NVGs, so he stashed them away again. Security at the Pinnacle Apartments was very high at ground level with cameras, a guard, and access control ensuring the occupants were protected from unwanted visitors and the general riff-raff.

However the measures in place at that level lulled them into a false sense of security, the thought of anyone being able to drop in from above so remote as to be absurd. That flaw in the system was Archer's advantage. Access control limited the visitors to the penthouse floor, and the level of privacy expected up here meant there were no cameras.

He wasn't concerned about any standalone cameras that Sweetman may have installed in the penthouse suite either; the thin balaclava and gloves he wore would make it impossible to identify him even if he was seen.

He closed the door behind him, crossed the thick pile carpet to the penthouse door, and set to work. The door lock was a more robust affair than the one on the roof, but the lock pick Archer carried was one of the best available, and within a minute he was in.

He let Ingoe know and got a quiet "Roger" back.

The penthouse apartment was in almost darkness, just a couple of sidelights casting a pale yellow glow over the plush interior. Archer secured the door and paused, looking and listening. There should be nobody home but he didn't want to leave it to chance and get a nasty surprise.

After sweeping the rooms for a physical check to confirm he was alone, he began to methodically search the apartment.

It was decorated with a mix of mid-market and chain-hotel furnishings. Archer didn't see anything about the place that screamed "wow factor", and if anything it was all a bit sad. It was like an adult living in a faceless hotel room but thinking he'd made it. Sure, the views would be killer, but it didn't seem like Sweetman would be taking much advantage of them. Archer suspected his days were filled with screen time, sleeping and going out to meet his loser associates.

Archer wondered for a moment what people would think if they were to search his flat in London. With Eva now gone, did it scream bachelor? Sad loner? Or was it just a comfortable city pad with even a touch of homeliness about it?

He wasn't sure. He wasn't sure about much to do with home anymore. Best he just focus on work instead – at least he knew what he was doing there.

As expected, Sweetman had several electronic devices dotted

about. His desktop set up was in the spare room and this appeared to be his main base of operations.

Archer wondered how much crime had been committed from this room, how many people had been victimised and how many criminal or terrorist groups had been supported.

Sweetman may have outwardly appeared to be just another geek, but without the likes of him the foot soldiers' job was much harder. As far as Archer was concerned the supporting geeks were just as liable as those that pulled the trigger.

He plugged a device into the USB port of the desktop and watched as a green light on the device flickered a few times then went solid. It looked like an external hard drive, and did have a large storage capacity, but the device was much more than that. Archer didn't really get the techo side of it – as long as it did its thing, he was happy.

The technical staff assured him the device was state of the art and would defeat any protections Sweetman had installed.

Sure enough, within four minutes the device had accessed the hard drive of the machine and was unleashing a virus that would sit dormant until the computer fired up. Once it did that apparently the virus would glean data and send it to the geeks who would interpret it into something that the laymen who ran the int services could understand. Apparently.

Archer didn't care, as long as he didn't get caught doing his bit.

He waited impatiently, eager to crack on. He only had the one device and needed to get as much done as he could before Sweetman got back.

'Sitrep,' Ingoe said in his ear, and Archer jumped involuntarily.

'First one.'

'Roger.'

Silence again for another few minutes until the green light turned red. Archer unplugged and went to the laptop under the bed in the master bedroom. He repeated the process there, wondering if the geeks would be receiving a whole bunch of Sweetman's favourite porn rather than national secrets, and did the same with another laptop on the lounge coffee table.

Within half an hour he had done all three machines and checked the time. All okay. He checked the apartment again and confirmed there were no other electronic devices he should be accessing.

He hit the pressel switch on his belt and spoke softly into his throat mic.

'All three done, ready to exfil.'

'Roger. Standby.'

Archer waited by the door, knowing that Ingoe was checking in with the surveillance team. He came back on the air a few moments later.

'Blues are good, still eyes on. Go exfil.'

'Roger, moving.'

The plan was to exfil via the stairs, or if necessary in the elevator itself – either in the car or the shaft, whichever option was available. Once he was in the basement garage he could use his swipe card to exit. As with most buildings it was far easier to get out than in.

Archer carefully cracked the door and held there, listening and scanning the foyer before stepping out and securing it behind him.

The building was silent and unaware of the intruder, and it remained that way until he had gone.

26

———

New Zealand High Commission
Haymarket, London
Monday, 1200 hours

'This bloody Sweetman guy has one of the highest levels of security I've seen in a while,' Ari said, 'but between us we cracked into his system.' He smiled nervously. 'Shall I run you through how we did it?'

Archer looked at him flatly. 'Do you know how to fieldstrip and reassemble a Sig 228 in less than a minute while blindfolded?'

Ari looked surprised. 'No, I've never really needed to know that.'

Archer spread his hands and raised his eyebrows.

'Ahh, I see.' Ari nodded his understanding. 'You don't need to know, do you?'

'Even less than that,' Archer agreed, 'I don't really give a rat's arse how it works mate. What'd you get from it?'

'The question isn't what did we get from it,' Ingoe interjected, 'the question is what *didn't* we get from it.' He turned towards the projector screen on the wall and tapped his tablet. A list of names accompanied by passport-style photos appeared on the screen. Male and female, Caucasian, Indian, Asian, Maori. A wide range of ages. 'This is the first list.'

Archer scanned it but none of the names meant anything to him. He glanced at the Ops Manager. 'Who are they?'

'Nobody you would know. These are all employees of GCSB, all different levels and all different roles.'

Ingoe brought up the next page, showing what looked like account numbers and names. Archer recognised some of the names from the previous page and guessed where this was going.

'Sweetman was bribing GCSB staff?' he said. 'To leak intelligence that he could on-sell?'

Ingoe nodded. 'We believe that was his intention, yeah. Not sure yet whether it actually happened, and initial investigations haven't brought anything up, but it's early days yet. Anything's possible.' He looked Archer in the eye. 'This is potentially the biggest breach of national security that we've ever had, even if it hasn't been pulled off.'

Archer nodded. The implications were huge. 'So this is linked to Capstick and Raines and on to Kozlowski, or the other way around?'

'Not sure which way the information flows,' Ingoe said, 'could be both ways. We had thought that Kozlowski was feeding intelligence to the other two, but it could have been Sweetman feeding them instead. Or it could have been both.'

'Too early yet to confirm whether these people have received any payments?'

'An initial recce hasn't shown anything obvious,' Ingoe said, 'but that's just their normal bank accounts. They'd be pretty stupid to put anything in the bank. It's more likely to be via Bitcoin or offshore accounts or something like that.'

Archer nodded. The presence of Capstick and Raines in the Cook Islands, a known secrecy jurisdiction, took on new meaning now.

'Others will be looking into that,' Ingoe said. 'In the meantime, we still have the issue of the missing Canadian woman.' He brought up Izzy's picture on the screen. 'We're in regular contact with Ottawa and needless to say, they're pretty pissed. They're also eager to talk to you to get anything from you they can.'

'No problem,' Archer said.

'It's not happening,' Ingoe said sharply. 'I've got a job for you. What with this and the issues within Five Eyes, the only way we can fix our relationship with the Canadians is to get their girl back.'

Archer raised his eyebrows but said nothing.

'You're going after her,' Ingoe said. 'You're going to get her back.'

THE INTELLIGENCE that was held on Krystal Raines came from many sources, as you would expect for someone who had lived much of her life in the public eye.

Put together and analysed by boffins who knew a good widget when they saw one, it all helped to build a picture that was shared far and wide in the right circles.

One thing that wasn't shared, however, was one little titbit of information that had only recently come to light for the GCSB.

A single phone call made four days ago from a burner phone that was confirmed by a human source as being in Raines's possession at the time. The call originated in a hotel room in Rome, and was received by a similar burner phone in Switzerland.

The call lasted eleven minutes and was tracked by a US satellite which the GCSB had access to. The call itself was of no importance to any other partner in the Five Eyes network, since Raines was just a local activist, but it had taken on incredible importance since it was identified in the last twelve hours.

The intelligence had not been shared with the Canadians yet, but Archer knew it would have to be. Failure to do so would only lead to more distrust between the partners.

What he had, at least for now, was a slim lead. But a slim lead was better than nothing.

A fast drive from Haymarket to Luton airport had left him just enough time to get to the departure gate before the doors closed.

That was okay; the less time spent in Luton, the better. The Easyjet flight was crammed and he took the opportunity to spend the bulk of the hundred minutes in the air with his eyes closed and his earbuds in.

The pair of chavs beside him were sprayed an unusual orange, the colour of urine when you were severely dehydrated. They competed for the volume of both the hair product they used and their voices, both of which were far too excessive for Archer's liking.

He gritted his teeth and did his best to ignore them as they told the world about what they had planned for their trip to Zermatt and their later trip to Ibiza.

By the time the pilot had practically slammed the plane into the tarmac at Zurich and they'd disembarked, it was after four and Archer's stomach was growling. He hurried through the Arrivals hall with his carry-on bag in hand, pleased that he had travelled light.

There had been no time to race home and grab his cold weather gear, so the first stop was a clothing outlet. Thermals, a couple of sets of clothes, a down jacket and a bag to carry it all in.

The rental company desk was clear and the lady behind it gave him a practiced smile when he stepped up. She was close to fifty and losing the battle against the greys. But in true European style, it didn't seem to matter. Back home it would have been an issue that bothered her; here, she was aging gracefully and looked classy.

'That is booked for three days, Mister Archer,' the lady said in flawless English, 'and of course you have full insurance on that.'

'Of course.' Probably a good thing, he figured.

27

———

Zermatt, Switzerland
Monday, 1745 hours

The silver BMW 320i was warm and comfortable and ate up the A4 as he headed towards Zermatt in the Klein Matterhorn area, with some of the highest pistes in the legendary skiing grounds of the Swiss Alps.

The mountains loomed high and sparkly white and Archer could see why they were so popular with the ski bunnies. They were breathtakingly beautiful. He'd spent time in Norway in the Army but had only ever passed through Switzerland, never taking the time to enjoy all that it had to offer.

The actual ski fields weren't open for another couple of months yet, but that didn't matter to him. He wasn't here to ski or sightsee.

With Zermatt being car-free, drivers had to leave their vehicles at Tasch and grab the mountain cog railway from there for the final leg, making the BMW redundant for much of Archer's mission. He could have caught a direct train from the airport to Tasch instead, but without knowing exactly what he was going into, it made sense to have a car available. And if everything went well, he didn't want to be relying on public transport.

It was gone nine by the time Archer pulled into the curb outside the hotel he'd been booked into. It was a simple affair that looked as cosy and homely as a bog standard traveller's hotel could be. The owner was the same, a portly woman with a huge bosom that strained at her well-worn grey cardigan.

She booked him in efficiently, appreciated his use of German and left him with a handful of tourist brochures plus a local map.

With a steaming mug of tea beside him, Archer sat on the bed and opened the map in front of him. He found the hotel he was looking for half a klick away in town. According to Google's street view it was surrounded by other hotels, eateries and shops. Easy enough to surveil if he needed to do that and probably easy enough to break into for a close target recce.

He sipped his tea and mentally plotted his plan for the next day. Nothing was written down; no point leaving a trail that could bite him in the arse if things went tits-up.

As he sat and let the day drain away his mind wandered and soon enough, inevitably, it turned to Eva.

She would have loved it here. Skiing during the day, a romantic dinner somewhere with an open fire, some good wine and back to a cosy hotel to make love and fall asleep in each others' arms. They'd done that often enough, although not always for skiing. Their long distance situation of him in London and her in Germany had meant city breaks became the norm for them.

Still, it had its upsides. They'd been to plenty of different places and had some great adventures, and the passion when they did see each other was far beyond anything he had experienced before.

And then it had all died. Archer knew, when he was brutally honest with himself, that ultimately it was always going to end. She was committed to her career with the BfV, and there was no way she was going to leave Germany.

He was no different. He was a service man, whether it was the military or the SIS, and he was more than happy doing what he was doing.

He considered that for a moment. Perhaps it was more accurate to say that he was happy when he was on operations. The down time between jobs was boring and he hated it. Constant operations were what he wanted, maybe what he needed.

The hunt for Viktor Kozlowski had given him that, and now he was on the trail again. It felt good. Even without Eva by his side, like she had been for so long, it felt good. The activities of the last few days had stimulated him, jerked him from his depressive stupor and thrown him back into the fray.

The fling with Dee Dee had been fun, the action in Rarotonga – aside from the innocent deaths, of course – had been a welcome return. Hell, even falling off the side of a building had been exhilarating.

He wondered what Eva would think of that. She had always said he lived too close to the edge, that he relished the danger. She was right about that, as she was about most things.

Maybe he had been fooling himself, and not for the first time, that the normal life of suburbia – the picket fence, the cookie cutter house, the family station wagon and 2.4 kids – was for him.

Why did he keep trying to grasp it? He didn't know. But what he did know was himself, and Craig Archer was not the man for that life, no matter how appealing the theory of it might seem. He knew within himself that the reality was very different.

But knowing that did little to ease the hurt inside, the deep-seated ache that was the loss of Eva.

Archer sighed to himself and pushed the map aside. He took a swig of tea. It had gone cold. He sighed again.

Fuck it, he decided. Tomorrow was another day.

28

Auckland, New Zealand
Tuesday, 1530 hours

The inside of Lee Sweetman's mouth felt drier than a desert rock.

It had been six minutes since he had logged on. Five minutes forty-five since the alert message had flashed up on the screen. He had only ever seen the alert when he had built the programme. Really, he should never have seen it again, because to see it put into practice meant that something had gone terribly wrong.

The message window didn't even have any text, it was just a simple red box. Flashing constantly, but saying nothing. He didn't need a written warning to tell him someone had tampered with his system.

Someone had tampered with his system.

The same system that moved money around the globe. The same system that communicated with terrorists and criminals. The same system that hacked some of the supposedly most secure networks in the world.

Someone had tampered with it.

Sweetman had no idea how this could have happened, but he had a very good idea of what the consequences would be.

Forcing himself to take a breath, he stood up from his swivel chair and paced a half circle around it. He pressed his face into his hands, closed his eyes and sucked in air. When he looked back at the screen the red warning alert was still there, flashing hard.

'OhmyGod,' he muttered to himself, 'ohmygod, ohmygod, ohmygod.'

His knees felt weak and he desperately needed to pee. He forced down another breath, took his seat again, and stared at the screen. This was not good, not good at all. But maybe, just maybe, there was a glimmer of hope. Maybe there was a fault. Maybe it was a foiled attack.

Maybe.

He quickly checked for faults. Nothing. On a normal day his clogged arteries worked hard to service his heart, but right now they were slaves to the grindstone. He could almost feel the organ bouncing in his chest.

Cold sweat trickled down his temples, his neck, his back.

To do a full diagnostic on the system would take hours, but he already knew the answer. Deep in his over-worked, deep-fried heart, he knew the answer.

He was fucked.

He had no choice but to raise the alarm. If he didn't then he was a dead man, no doubt about it. If he did, well, it wasn't going to be pretty but maybe he would get through it. He was a valuable asset, after all. World class hackers weren't exactly a dime a dozen, and Kozlowski was a smart man.

He picked up the phone and, with trembling fingers, he composed a text. One word.

Poseidon.

He hit send, sat back and stared at the wall while he waited.

Goddamn, but this was a nice apartment. It would suck to have to leave it, but he was pretty sure that would be the answer.

He forced himself to his feet, clutching the phone in his slippery paw, and made his way to the bathroom. He realised he'd already let go a dribble in his underpants but he didn't care. The relief was immense.

The incoming text bleeped. A one word reply.

Kentucky.

Sweetman let out his breath in a whoosh, not realising he'd been holding it in. Kentucky was good. Kentucky he could work with. Kentucky meant he had to get to the airport and make contact by a clean phone for further instructions. If the message had been Lollipop, he'd have been shitting himself. Lollipop meant he had to wait there. Considering Poseidon meant he'd suffered a potentially-severe technical attack, Lollipop would probably spell death for him. At least Kentucky meant they wanted him to get clear.

Getting clear was good. He could do that.

Sweetman pulled the phone apart, snapped the SIM card into pieces and flushed it, and put the broken pieces of the phone in the bathroom sink. A small bottle of acid from the vanity cabinet took care of it from there.

He quickly grabbed an overnight bag from the bedroom wardrobe, tossed in a change of clothes, his toiletries and his medications, and zipped it closed. He grabbed his passport from the drawer, five grand in cash from the envelope taped to the back of the bedside table, and was good to go.

Almost.

The last thing he did was open a new file on his desktop. There was no need to follow suit on the laptops as they were clean, aside from a shit-ton of porn, but none of that illegal. It was a virus he had created himself, a virus that would destroy everything in its path and leave no trace behind for even the best forensic investigators.

He hit Upload and watched as a slithering snake image appeared. It rolled around and around itself in a never-ending circle as the virus unleashed, before stopping, opening its mouth wide and vomiting a stream of green bile that cascaded across the screen, wider and wider until the whole screen was puke green and the snake had disappeared.

The screen went blank and Sweetman powered it off. He stood and looked around. There was nothing more to do here, and nothing he needed. He paused for a moment, reconsidering his plan. He was putting a lot of trust in some very bad people, he knew that.

He could always sidestep and hop a flight to a destination of his own choice. Somewhere he could connect with his own sort of people. Copenhagen maybe, or Amsterdam. There was a huge community of hackers out there, conspiracy theorists, anarchists, social activists. People with their ears to the ground and their noses where they shouldn't be. People he knew would look after him and use his skills.

But the people he worked with would always find him, he knew that too.

No, he would be okay. Getting him out of the country was a sign of good faith. No hard feelings. He was a valuable asset, that was the thing. They knew what he could do for them.

He moved to the door. He would grab a cab to the airport and be gone before anyone here in this shitty little country knew better.

Feeling positive, Sweetman closed the door behind him. It was time to start a new adventure.

29

Zermatt, Switzerland
Tuesday, 0830 hours

The call from Krystal Raines had been made to Room 211 at the Alpine View Hotel. It was a mid-sized hotel in a narrow back street in central Zermatt. The name was deceiving but the location was handy.

Archer had left the car and caught the railway, getting there early to allow himself time to get his bearings and do a walk-by recce. The trains ran every 20 minutes from Tasch and he blended in with the other passengers.

The day was shaping up nicely, the sun making a solid appearance and little breeze. The climate here was dry and clear, the cold mountain air invigorating enough to make you feel healthy even when you were sitting still.

The pistes above were more than 3000m high and picture perfect. Archer was pleased of his warm socks and thermals underneath his clothing, with a beanie pulled down over his ears. He had a mental shopping list of extras he needed to buy later that day, both to keep warm and also to fit into the skiing scene.

Archer completed his walk by, noting the side exit down a service alley, the general layout of the hotel and the buildings on either side. If needed he was sure he could gain access via the rooftop – but not by parachute this time.

The doorman looked alert and physically capable. The reception area inside was busy as tourists emerged for the day.

The serious skiers would already be up on the slopes, he figured, although it was only the glacier open at this time of the year, more suited to the less-skilled intermediate skiers than the hard core.

There was a café across the road from the hotel and two doors down, already doing a good trade. Archer completed a circuit of his target and ducked into the café. He ordered a coffee and managed to squeeze into a table at the window, angling himself to maintain a view of the hotel's frontage.

The coffee came, strong and frothy and comforting. Chatter hummed around him but he didn't understand most of it aside from the German.

He sat and watched casually, as if waiting for a friend or getting himself up for the day, sipping his coffee and debating whether to order food. People came and went outside, some bundled up in all the gear, others just dressed to get to work.

He was draining the coffee when movement caught his eye in the street. He didn't see a person; he saw form.

Special forces operators had a particular way about them the world over. Just as a cop could spot another cop a mile off, Archer pinged the guy walking past without even trying.

It wasn't the desert boots or the chunky divers watch or the beard that first caught his eye. It was the intangible form, the way the man moved. Athletic but not staunch, confident but watchful. The way he held himself when he moved.

He was almost past the café before Archer even looked, being careful not to turn his head and make it obvious. A black outer shell, a woollen skull cap pulled down tight, jeans and dessies. Dark hair. Mid sized. Didn't see his face to pick the age.

Archer knew without a doubt that the guy was an operator, which begged the question; what was he doing here?

Archer slid off his seat and stepped out into the cold again, the man a good twenty paces ahead by now, moving with purpose but not hurrying. He hit the main drag and took a left, heading away from the Alpine View Hotel.

Not to worry. Archer had two options now; hold the hotel or take the man. One-man surveillance was fraught with difficulties, but he followed his gut and proceeded on foot.

The man was definitely aware, his body language giving away the little signs that told Archer his eyes were constantly on the move. He maintained a steady pace, staying in the middle of the street and weaving through the pedestrians, giving no indication of his destination.

At the last second he cut away to the right into a small grocery store, the bell above the door tinkling when he entered. Archer calmly continued on past, appearing to check the map in his hand. Just another tourist on the way somewhere.

He went a few doors past and stopped outside a clothing store, pausing to look in the front window at the ski jackets and pants on display there. He knew that Ingoe would baulk at the prices, but he would probably be stopping back here later for some gear. Travelling light to a ski destination was never a great idea, but time had been the enemy, as it had been for the whole operation so far.

He felt like he was constantly chasing, always behind the eight ball. He didn't mind as long as there was light at the end of the tunnel, but he knew that Izzy's fate was in his hands and that of her colleagues at CSIS. He didn't care who got to her first, as long as someone did.

Although he had been accused in the past of being a glory-hunter, he didn't give a damn about recognition. The fact that his medals were tucked away in a safety deposit box spoke to that.

He gave the window display a couple of minutes before moving across the road and checking out another store window, this one giving him a good reflective view of the grocery store door.

Two minutes later he saw the door open and the man in the desert boots emerged with a shopping bag in one hand and a phone at his ear in the other.

He turned back the way he had come and strode off without a backward glance, seemingly engrossed in his phone call.

Archer gave him a few seconds before peeling off and tagging along. He stayed on his side of the road and maintained contact with the man in his peripheral vision. He was confident enough that there was sufficient cover from other pedestrians for him to melt into the background but he was wary of pushing his luck. He didn't want to come this far and fuck it up by being overeager.

But something was nagging at the back of his brain, trying to break through. Maybe he was tired, or too focussed on the task at hand, but it stayed there for now, dancing just out of reach. Something about the man he was following.

They reached the side street back towards the Alpine View Hotel and the man entered it without hesitation, the phone still glued to his ear. He was moving slightly faster than when Archer had first spotted him. The pedestrian crowd thinned out on the side street and Archer dropped back, keeping the map in his hand and his appearance relaxed.

The hotel was coming up on the left and Archer watched as the man ducked into a side alley beside it, disappearing from view. Archer stayed wide, not wanting to be jumped as he rounded the corner, and had a quick visual check first.

He spotted the man taking a side entrance to the hotel. The alley was a service lane, dotted with dumpsters and discarded boxes.

Archer gave the man a head start before entering the alley, his senses jumping up a notch. The nagging thought in his head was still dancing around there, teasing him, and he broke his stride. He'd missed something and he knew it. He slowed his pace, keeping his eyes on the side entrance but scanning his surroundings. He felt his senses pinging.

The man he was following was an operator. Situationally aware. But he never looked around when he left the shop. Head down and away he went, not looking.

No operator did that.

At the same time as the realisation floated to the surface, Archer detected movement to his left. A man, close up, hand raised, coming from behind a dumpster.

Archer stepped sideways and back, throwing the map at the man's face with his left hand. The guy was moving fast but steady on his feet. Dark jacket, no hat, brown beard. Fit, mid-thirties, capable. He brushed the map aside and continued forward, a knife in his right hand, zeroed in on Archer.

The ice beneath Archer's feet was slippery and he felt his grip slide as he backed away, going for space. He didn't want to be up close with this guy just yet, not on the back foot. He caught himself, steadied, feinting a left jab at the guy to test him.

His reactions were quick but impulsive, swiping at the jab with his knife, hoping for an easy connection that never happened.

Archer continued to move on his feet, constantly shifting, keeping the guy on the move too. His biggest worry right now was a second guy coming in as backup, and he kept his eyes and ears open, wary of the tunnel vision that usually came with close quarters combat.

The guy continued to jab with the knife, his focus totally on Archer. Neither man had said a word.

Archer had options available and he ran through them in his head in a split second.

Run away and get distance, maybe risk being chased. Stay and fight, and risk being killed.

He figured that running away probably wasn't an option.

Obviously these guys, whoever they were, knew who or what he was. They would hunt him and find him, so he would only be delaying the inevitable.

By staying and fighting, he knew he was making a life and death decision. This guy wasn't here to take prisoners; one of them would not be walking away today. But Archer knew something that this guy did not. He knew his own limitations.

The guy had made two fatal mistakes when he attacked Archer with a knife. One, he telegraphed his intention to kill. Two, he didn't put his target down fast.

It opened the door for Archer, and he stepped right through.

'Aaaaagghhh!' Archer let out a bellow of sudden fury and lunged at the guy like a madman, wind milling his arms.

The guy was momentarily stunned by the bizarre change of behaviour and hesitated, distracted by the roar and the swinging arms.

Archer kicked him hard in the shin and swung both arms at his face. The knife came up to slash at his arms but Archer was faster.

He avoided the knife swipe, snatched the wrist that held the weapon, and grabbed the guy's face with his right hand. He clawed at the eyes, ripping at the skin, booting him in the shin again as he did so.

He twisted the wrist he held, kicked again, the guy pulling his head back to escape the clawing fingers that were trying to gouge his eyes.

Archer held fast to the wrist, pushing it down and away from him, and got a finger into the guy's nostril. He rammed it in as hard as he could, forcing the head back and hearing a squeal of pain.

The guy pulled his head as far back as he could, scrabbling awkwardly at Archer with his left hand, trying to get his face, but his hesitation had left him vulnerable.

Archer withdrew his hand and smashed his knee up into the guy's groin. As the guy came forward Archer hit him in the throat, bent knuckles straight into the Adam's apple. It didn't take much to disable a person with a throat punch and Archer gave it the full noise.

The guy doubled up, instinctively reaching for his throat, gasping breathlessly. Archer twisted the knife free from his limp hand, gripped the guy by the back of his collar, and rammed the knife up into the side of his neck. He twisted, ripped and released.

The guy fell face forward to the ground, the snow and ice already turning red beneath him before he hit it.

Archer dragged him to the side by the dumpster he'd been hiding behind, wiped his hands and the knife on the guy's jacket, and sucked in a breath. Sweat beaded his face despite the cold air and his armpits and back felt wet.

At least it wasn't blood.

He quickly frisked the guy, finding nothing but a cheap burner phone. He pocketed it, stood, and looked around. The altercation seemed to have gone unnoticed. He couldn't see any CCTV cameras anywhere, so that was something.

He sucked in more air, feeling his heart slamming in his chest. It wasn't quite how he'd envisioned his intro to Switzerland.

30

———

Archer took out his own phone, snapped a shot of the guy's face, and pocketed it again. He would send it to Ingoe later with the hopes of getting an ID. That done, he shucked off his jacket and dropped it. Still nobody had come into sight. He hefted the dead man on to his shoulder, lifted the lid of the dumpster, and heaved him in. He tossed in a few flattened boxes and left him there. It wouldn't keep the secret forever but it was the best he could do right now.

He put his jacket back on, covering up the bloodstains on his top, and kicked some loose snow over the blood on the ground. The side entrance of the hotel took him into a lobby with a door in front and a stairwell to the left. The door was swipe-controlled and led to a service corridor.

Archer took the stairs to the first floor and found another access control point at the door to the accommodation. He backtracked to the street and made his way round to the front doors. A family of tourists were loudly trying to organise themselves, two small kids chasing each other around the parents, who were arguing over a brochure of attractions.

Archer skirted round them to the check-in desk where a young man was busy on the computer, the phone jammed between his shoulder and ear, while a middle-aged man waited, impatiently drumming his fingers on the countertop.

Archer could see the young guy was flustered, so took advantage. He leaned over the desk and caught the young guy's eye. He ignored the signal to wait and spoke in German, hoping that his attempt at an American accent would do the trick.

'Excuse me friend, which room number are my friends in?'

'One moment please sir.' The young guy gave him a frown and tapped at the keyboard.

Archer pressed forward. He had the room number from the GCSB of course, but there was always the chance the target had moved. There was no point busting into the wrong room and blowing the slim lead he had. 'I'm sorry, but it's kinda urgent.'

The man beside him harrumphed and sighed.

The young guy's frown turned to a scowl. 'Excuse me sir, but I am busy.'

Archer smiled understandingly. 'Sorry my friend, the room number?'

The young guy sighed and covered the mouthpiece of the phone. 'The Americans?' he said with a sneer. 'Two-one-one.'

'Thank you.' Archer smiled and turned to the middle-aged man beside him, who was still harrumphing and drumming his fingers. Archer gave him a wink. 'You have a nice day now,' he said, and headed to the stairs.

31

'Joel's on it,' the man said. 'We're moving now.'

Izzy was used to the man's voice but had no idea what he looked like. She imagined he was rough but smart. He sounded and acted like a soldier, which meant he was a merc, because real American soldiers wouldn't have kidnapped her for a terrorist group. His accent was from somewhere in the Midwest. Probably a farmboy from Bumfuck, Idaho. Joined the Army to better himself, saw action overseas and went private for better money, like so many of them did.

'I'll give a sit-rep when we're clear.'

In the days she'd been with these guys – it seemed like frickin' weeks already – she'd got used to the darkness of the hood. It had only come off sporadically – when they fed her and once when they'd gone through some public space.

They'd given her a shot of something first and she was mostly out of it, so had no idea where it was, except that they had acted like she was a patient being transported. She knew she'd been on a plane and in vehicles, but still had only a vague idea where she was now.

Last night there had been a drunk outside shouting in German, and she knew that it was cold outside because the men always put coats and hats on when they left and took them off again when they came in. She'd heard one of them joke about going skiing.

She was picking that were somewhere in Germany, Bavaria maybe. Unless the guy shouting hadn't been a local; then they could be anywhere and she was no better off.

Not that she was at any advantage anyway.

She'd been hog-tied at the wrists and ankles almost the whole time they'd had her and she was certain that she'd be suffering permanent ligament and muscle damage when they eventually freed her.

That was unless they put a bullet in her head and dropped her in a hole. But then why would they have kept her for so long?

She wondered what had happened to Archer, the New Zealander. Up until ten minutes ago she had thought he was dead like Michael. Then the phone calls had started just a few minutes after two of the men had left the room to get some supplies.

Hushed conversations then another one of the men had left the room.

By her calculations that left just one still here with her. She was pretty sure his name was Jack. The bed was soft beneath her but still she wanted to roll over. She began to move when she heard a footstep and the man grabbed her by the arm.

'Up,' he said, 'feet over the side.'

He helped her into position and she felt a wave of wooziness from sitting up so suddenly.

The hood was jerked from her head and she found herself confronted by a set of very nice green eyes. There was a hardness behind them though and the man's face was weathered despite his relative youth.

'We need to move,' he said quietly. 'We've been compromised. That means I don't have much to lose, understand me?'

Izzy nodded.

'I'm gonna cut your feet free and move your hands to the front.

We're gonna walk outta here like normal people. Nobody'll know any different, right?' His eyes hardened more. 'But if you try anything stupid, I'll drop you like a fuckin' stone, you understand?'

Izzy nodded again. She had no doubt that he was telling the truth. These were men of violence; they didn't make idle threats.

'You keep your mouth shut and your head down and everything'll be okay, right?'

'Got it.'

He quickly did as he had said and slung a jacket over her bound hands before moving her to the door. He paused and listened, checking the peep hole. Apparently satisfied, he cracked it, checked again and led her out into the hall.

They moved to the stairs, paused to check again and started down. Izzy was unsteady after lying prone for so long but her captor hustled her along, gripping her arm tightly.

They hit the second floor landing and turned to start down when the door behind them burst open. Izzy turned just in time to see Archer rushing her captor.

Archer pushed her aside and slammed an elbow strike across the side of the man's head as he started to turn, knocking the guy off balance. He went straight for the gun, knowing it was there even though he couldn't see it, reaching round to lock his hand onto the guy's gun hand.

The guy twisted and tried for a head butt but Archer was moving fast, getting his fingers onto the slide of the pistol and wrenching at it, stepping back outside the guy and applying pressure to the guy's grip on the pistol. He slammed a knee into the back of the guy's own knee, half-dropping him, cracked him an elbow across the temple as he reached over the shoulder and got both hands on the pistol.

The guy was fighting hard against him now, Izzy no longer being the focus, and he threw a loose fist at Archer's face. Archer took it, drove a forearm across the guy's elbow and wrenched hard on the pistol.

A finger snapped as the gun came free but the guy didn't even grunt, just focussed on trying to retain his weapon, but it was too late.

Archer yanked it free then rammed it straight up into the guy's Adams apple, stepped back and kicked him hard across the back of the knee.

As his leg buckled the guy started to drop and catch his breath at the same time, Archer jerked him back and down then drove him forward.

The combined power of Archer's drive and the guy's own body-weight hurtled him off the top step into empty space. His legs kicked and his arms wind milled and he let out a gasping cry.

A second later the guy hit the wall with a loud thud and fell backwards. His head collected the handrail on the way down and there was an ugly crunch before he collapsed on the landing like a rag doll.

Archer breathed hard. The man moaned and twitched.

'Come on.' Archer sliced through Izzy's bonds and led her by the arm down the stairs. He paused beside the man, whose eyes were flickering without focus.

He quickly went through his pockets, recovering another burner phone, a spare magazine, some cash and a US passport. He pocketed them all and pried the guy's pistol from his hand. It was a Sig Sauer P229, a handy weapon.

The guy moaned again. Peering closer, Archer recognised him as one of the guys who had dealt to him in the shed back in Rarotonga. He should have taken his chance when he had it. Karma was a bitch.

Archer could tell from the stillness of the guy's body that he was fucked from the impact, probably paralysed from the neck down. If he survived this at all he'd be slurping his meals through a straw.

He was tempted to leave the prick as he was. Let him suffer. He hesitated, then placed the guy's own limp arm over his mouth and nose. The thick sleeve of the puffer jacket covered both openings and in seconds the guy's eyes were rolling frantically as he snorted and struggled to breathe. Archer looked away and maintained the pressure.

'Oh my god,' Izzy whispered behind him.

The snorting soon stopped and nothing more came from the guy.

Archer dropped the arm and stood up. He took out his phone, snapped a shot of the guy's face and put it away again.

'Let's go,' he said.

He hurried Izzy down to the ground level and out to the street. Her pale face told him all he needed to know just now.

They needed to get the hell out of there and fast.

32

Archer headed through the town centre towards the railway. He needed to get distance from the Alpine View Hotel and the dead bodies, which surely would be discovered soon. There was nothing to be gained by hanging around, and getting arrested for murder was certainly not part of the game plan.

The train station looked like an overgrown alpine villa and was bustling with disembarking passengers.

Archer guided Izzy to a bench seat out of the way and told her to stay put. He was back within three minutes with a bottle of water each and tickets.

'Where are we going?' she asked as they climbed aboard. The train was a sleek red and silver machine and amazingly clean for public transport. Archer was constantly surprised by the quality of services in Europe compared to back home.

'We'll get to Tasch and get on the road from there,' he said, sliding into the aisle seat beside her. He had a good view of the closest door from where they were. 'I'll make a call on the way and with any luck either your people or mine will get us out of here sharpish.'

Izzy cracked a bottle of water and took a long drink. She watched

Archer while she drank. She wiped her mouth on her sleeve when she was finished. 'My people will get us out,' she said.

Archer stayed silent, watching people come and go out on the platform. His adrenaline was still pumping and he was eager to get going. He presumed there were more bad guys out there somewhere, but he had no way of knowing how many or where.

His hand rested on the Sig in his waistband, ready to react as soon as a threat appeared. With so many people around any such action would likely result in a bloodbath, so he would need to get in first. Hit hard and put the bastards down, otherwise they were fucked.

The doors closed and they began to move. Archer felt his pulse ease off a notch. It was only a twelve minute ride to Tasch. He checked around them, noting again every passenger he could see. None jumped out at him as a possible threat.

He opened his water and drank. Izzy sat silently beside him, staring out the window at the stunning scenery passing by. There was nowhere quite like the Swiss Alps.

He wondered what had happened to her during the time she'd been held captive. He would need to get rid of her as soon as he could; there was no room for a passenger on this mission. The CSIS would be gagging to grab her up and debrief her, so there should be no problem there.

Archer got his phone out and sent the photos of the two dead men to the secure inbox. Then he put a call through to Auckland. The duty officer who answered had the personality of a headstone salesman, but took the message.

The iPhone encryption negated the need for code talk.

'I have the package,' Archer said, 'we are unharmed but two enemy are down in Zermatt, the Alpine View Hotel. We're on the train to Tasch and will go north from there. We need an urgent exfil. Got that?'

'Got that,' the duty officer droned. 'And the photos.' Archer could hear keys tapping in the background and knew an urgent sit-rep was being sent to Ingoe and whoever else needed to know. 'Are you being followed?'

'Don't believe so.'

'And your intended destination from Tasch?'

'The second ERV.' Archer rolled his eyes to himself. A stupid question from a desk jockey.

'Roger.' More tapping. 'Keep your phone on and stand by.'

The line went dead. Archer scowled and put the phone away. As if he was going to turn it off. *Dickhead.*

There was no reception committee waiting for them at the Tasch station and it was only a five minute walk to Archer's hotel. He put Izzy in the car outside and grabbed his bag from his room, dropping the room key on the bed and ensuring he'd left nothing behind.

Within five minutes they were on the road. The second emergency rendezvous point was Interlaken, a town about two hours' drive north. Ingoe rang back a few minutes later. His tone was unhurried but to the point.

'I have an exfil team en-route,' he said. 'ETA probably three hours. You'll need to hold somewhere nearby until you get the word. Got it?'

'Yep.' Archer held the phone in his lap as he drove. 'You're on speaker.'

'Confirming you're both okay? No medical attention?'

'We're okay.'

'I've seen the photos, we'll try and get them ID'd. Any ideas?'

'If I were a betting man I'd suggest Black Star.'

'My thoughts too. Talk me through it.'

Archer did so, keeping it short and to the point. When he was finished he passed the phone over to Izzy, who gave Ingoe a rundown on what she could tell him. Having been bound and blindfolded most of the time, it wasn't much.

'Have you spoken to my firm?' she asked at last.

'I have, and Pierre is very much looking forward to getting you back. He knows that you're safe and where you are, and as soon as we get you out of there you'll be going home.'

'No.' Izzy's tone was sharp. 'This isn't over.' She glanced sideways at Archer. 'These bastards kidnapped me and killed my friend, and I'm not getting invalided out. I'll spend days being debriefed while your man here chases these sons of bitches down, and I'll have no part of it. Tell Pierre that's not happening. He needs to come up with an alternative plan.'

Archer was sure he heard a chuckle down the line. He concentrated on driving the windy mountain road and said nothing.

'I'll pass that on,' Ingoe said, 'and I admire your spirit, young lady. But that's a decision for your boss, not me.'

'Fine. Just make sure you tell him.' Archer noticed that Izzy had regained some fire in her belly since they'd left Zermatt. Maybe she wouldn't be such a passenger after all.

'What about Capstick?' Archer called out. 'Any word from our friends on him?'

'He's talking, took all of five minutes to break him. Unfortunately it doesn't sound like he knows much of real worth.'

Archer nodded silently to himself. It made sense in a way. It had always felt like Capstick was just a pawn in the game.

'The Raines woman?'

'Gone. We've got people on it, trying to track her, but she's probably gone by private plane. And Lee Sweetman?'

'The hacker, yeah?'

'Also gone. Caught a flight to Dublin a short time ago.'

'Do we have eyes on him there?'

'We're in contact with the Gardai.'

Archer digested all this info for a few moments. It wasn't a good sign, some of the main players flying the coop. Something was happening and they didn't know what it was. A spectacular perhaps, some significant terrorist event gunning for maximum exposure? Or simply circling the wagons, knowing they'd been rumbled and shit was going down? They still didn't have enough pieces of the puzzle to put it together yet.

'What about Steve?' His throat tightened even just saying it, and he knew he was dreading the answer.

'Lost his eye,' Ingoe said bluntly. 'That's not gunna change. Everything else is either repairable or at least he can live with it.' There was a pause down the line. 'He's a lucky man, all told.'

'He wasn't meant to die. If they'd wanted him to be, he'd be dead.'

'Why kidnap his family then?'

'Leverage over him.'

'Why not kill them? They had the opportunity, and they were no use once he'd given up whatever he could.'

'They didn't have time.'

'Bullshit. The bad guys were gone before you got there. All they needed to do was make a phone call. Hell, they could've driven over and delivered the message themselves.'

Archer mulled on that for a few moments, realising that Ingoe was right. It didn't make sense.

'They used us to tidy up their loose ends,' he said, and he heard the grunt of agreement through the speaker. 'Those guys were never gunna get out of there alive. They were never meant to.'

'Exactly. All trace to the bad guys is wiped; dead men tell no tales. Steve moves in some fairly dubious circles at times, part of why he's of use to us. All that happened over there could be written off as gangland shit, criminals hitting criminals. The only person who would know would be Steve himself, and he's not gunna say anything is he? The Service would never come out and publicly back any claims he made, so he'd be left to suffer in silence.'

'Maybe that's the point,' Izzy said. 'The suffering. If Kozlowski really is that vindictive, maybe that's him making his point.'

'"Cross me and suffer the consequences"?' Archer nodded. 'Could be. Makes sense. He *is* a vindictive bastard.'

'He used you to do his dirty work for him.'

'People do,' Archer said with more feeling than he'd intended.

'You made your choices a long time ago, Arch,' Ingoe said. 'Don't cry about it now. I'll be in touch.'

Ingoe rang off and Izzy handed the phone back. She looked at Archer until he took his eyes off the road for a moment to meet her gaze.

'Not big on emotion is he, eh?'

Archer grunted. 'No.'

'Thank you,' she said sincerely. 'I was really in the shit there.'

'No problem.' He nodded and looked back to the road. 'Those guys knew the rules of the game.'

She was silent for a moment. 'It doesn't bother you, does it?'

He sensed what was coming and stayed focussed on the road.

'Killing.'

He gave a small shrug. 'If killing bad guys bothered me, I'd be in the wrong job. I didn't train to be a storeman counting blankets.' He glanced at her. 'Does it bother you?'

'Ha. I've never killed anyone before. But it doesn't bother me that you did.' She paused and seemed to reconsider for a second. 'Although...that guy on the stairs. That was pretty...'

'Cold?'

She nodded, seemingly aware she was probably entering dangerous territory.

'Yeah it was. But it was necessary. He was dying anyway.' He took his eyes off the road long enough to give her a firm look. 'He was the enemy, but I don't see the humanity in leaving him to die painfully like that.'

Izzy nodded cautiously. 'I wasn't questioning your motives,' she said quietly. 'I'm just not used to it, that's all.'

Archer nodded and focussed on the road ahead. He had nothing else to say.

33

Leeds, England
Tuesday, 0912 hours

The phone on the bedside table was on silent, but Krystal was alerted by the vibrations as it went off. She reached for it in the darkness, pulling the covers away from Rick as she did so. He grunted behind her.

She knew who it would be even before she heard his voice.

'We have a problem,' he said as soon as she answered.

Krystal pulled herself up against the headboard, the sheet falling away from her naked body.

'Sweetman has been compromised, a cyber attack. He's heading for Dublin.'

Krystal felt her heart sink. That wasn't good at all. She knew what was coming next.

'Contact Mei Kim. She needs to deal with him when he gets there. He cannot be scooped up, understand?'

'Got it.' Krystal felt Rick moving beside her, rolling his big bulk over and putting a hand on her bare thigh. She swatted it away.

'Make sure she is very clear on that, Krystal. It needs to be done fast and it needs to look like an accident. I don't want a murder investigation by the cops.' He paused to let that sink in. 'Questions?'

'None.' Krystal took a swallow of water from the bottle beside the bed. 'I'm on it.'

He disconnected and she sat there for a few seconds, her mind working. She hadn't much sleep, not with Rick alongside her. She put the phone down. She had a few hours to spare before needing to get Mei Kim organised.

She scooted back down and Rick's hand came back to her thigh. This time she didn't swat it away. The man was insatiable.

34

Auckland, New Zealand
Tuesday, 2015 hours

Izzy was right; Jed Ingoe was not a man given to emotional responses.

A lifetime in Tier 1 Special Forces and black ops had beaten that out of him long ago. But knowing that Archer had got through another scrape unscathed, and rescued the Canadian girl to boot, brought a wave of relief.

He would never tell Archer so, but the former troop commander was one of the best he'd ever served with. By rights he should have gone on to greater things than simply Captain, but Ingoe knew that Archer wasn't the type to spend his time driving a desk and attending cocktail parties with dignitaries.

In that regard, he probably would have been better off joining as an NCO and staying in the Group. But Ingoe was bloody glad he hadn't.

He rubbed a hand over his face and considered his next move. He and the duty officer, a young guy named Murray, were the only occupants of the ops room. Murray sat at his workstation, dutifully updating some details on the operation, his back to Ingoe's desk. Auckland was ten hours ahead of Switzerland, so it was just gone seven pm. The city was alive outside, workers heading home and night owls emerging. He knew he would probably be kipping on the couch in his office tonight. Again.

'What's the update on the exfil team?' Ingoe said.

'Last update was two hours forty five,' Murray said, spinning in his chair to face Ingoe. 'You want me to check again?'

'No.' Ingoe shook his head. 'They'll tell us if it changes.' He stood and headed towards the door. 'I'll be back shortly.'

He swiped out of the room and made his way down the hallway towards the Director's office. The floor was quiet and when he reached the reception area he noticed that the boss' EA was gone. He knocked on the office door and received a curt "Yes" from inside.

He went in to find the Director at his desk, a tumbler of whiskey to one side, furiously stabbing at his keyboard.

'What is it, Jed?' The Director didn't look up, just continued thrashing the keys. 'I'm just sending this off to those bloody halfwits in Wellington. I don't know when I started having to make my own travel arrangements but apparently I do. Bloody useless.'

Ingoe smiled to himself. The boss must be really pissed to have said "bloody" twice in quick succession.

'Archer has recovered the Canadian officer,' he said. 'He killed two guys to get her and is now on the move to the ERV, should be with the exfil team in just under three hours.'

The Director stopped torturing his keyboard and looked up. 'Excellent work,' he said. 'That should keep our friends happy. For a while, at least.' He paused to take a belt of his drink, putting the tumbler back down with a clunk. 'I've been called to an emergency meeting with the Five Eyes partners,' he said. 'The Director and myself. Flying out in the morning.'

Ingoe raised an eyebrow. It was the first he knew of it. 'Where to?'

'London.' The Director gave him an appraising look. 'I know; bad timing while we have a live op going on. Can't be helped, I'm afraid. This whole network is on the verge of falling apart and we need it.' He frowned. 'We really need it, Jed. Five Eyes keeps us in the game, you know that.'

Ingoe gave a small nod. He did know that. Small nations had to find their niche to be of value to the big boys of the intelligence playground. The spy satellite stations at Tangimoana and Waihopai provided that for New Zealand.

'So all five partners are attending?' he said. 'Or is it just us and the Brits?'

'All of us. Bloody inconvenient, but we have to go. The DG was given a pretty blunt message, as I understand it.'

It always seemed odd to Ingoe when his boss referred to the Director-General, who had so little to do with their branch of the Service. In their world, *he* was the boss. The actual head of the Security Intelligence Service was far enough removed from the activities of the Division that she was rarely seen or talked about.

'I take it that security is all in hand? You'll be taking your usual team?'

The Director looked at him with a hint of amusement. 'Not worried about me are you Jed?'

Ingoe didn't smile. 'It would be a great target,' he said. 'The top ten chiefs of the Five Eyes network all in one place. Hell of a coup for an enterprising terrorist.'

'It had crossed my mind.' The Director knocked back the last of his whiskey and licked his lips in appreciation. 'Not to worry, RSM. You keep the ship afloat here and we'll all be fine.'

Ingoe gave a nod of agreement, but he still wasn't convinced.

35

———————

Zermatt, Switzerland
Tuesday, 1130 hours

A service centre stop had given Archer and Izzy the opportunity to freshen up and refuel.

They'd used the toilets, stocked up on food and water, and bought extra clothes for her. Archer changed his own outfit both to clean up and alter his appearance.

With the aroma of freshly ground beans filling the car, they continued on their way. Izzy had donned a black baseball cap and sunglasses, and remained silent through most of the drive.

Archer's mind wandered to Eva. He wondered what she was doing right now, and who she was with. Had she met someone else? If not, then how long until she did? How long until he was just a ghost, closed off in a locked box in the far reaches of her memory? How long until that happened for him and he stopped thinking about her?

He had no answer for any of the questions but the surprising thing was that it didn't bother him now as much as he had thought it would.

Instead, he found his focus shifted to the mission at hand, what had happened and where it was going. The affects of the adrenaline had eased off and he felt normal again after the action of the morning. He thought dispassionately of the two men he had killed. He had no doubt they were guns for hire, American, likely Black Star killers. Kozlowski was behind all this; he could feel it in his bones. The evil bastard was pulling strings from afar and once again making people dance to his psychotic tune.

And the activist woman, Raines? How did she figure in all this? It hardly made any sense that someone like her would be involved with Kozlowski, exactly the sort of warmonger she had always rallied against.

No, there were far more questions than answers right now, Archer decided. He needed to take one step at a time and not get distracted by the things he couldn't control.

He took a comforting hit of his coffee, feeling its heat slide down to warm his insides. Outside was crisp and cold and beautiful. Izzy was dozing beside him, her head nodding as she drifted off.

Archer focussed on the road ahead.

36

───────

The ERV was a haybarn on a small farm well off the main road. It had been picked because it was unoccupied, the farmhouse having fallen into disrepair after the last occupants left.

Archer and Izzy pulled up with more than an hour to spare. He cleared the barn before swinging open the wide front doors and tucking the BMW inside. Light filtered through the numerous cracks and holes in the structure, and dust motes danced in the musty air.

The last of the hay was long gone and droppings on the floor showed the barn had been shelter for both animals and humans in the recent past.

They got out and stretched their legs, taking a few minutes to assess their surroundings and select escape routes. It was what Archer did every time he went somewhere new, whether it was a restaurant, a holiday destination, or an abandoned barn. In his world it was how the smart survived.

That done, he sent a short message to the Duty Officer to say they were in place.

He put the phone away and turned to Izzy, who was draining the cold dregs of her coffee. She licked her lips and dropped the cup into the rubbish bag they were using.

'I haven't had a decent coffee in a while,' she commented. She held up the last power bar they had bought. 'Do you want it?'

He shook his head. 'Fill your boots. We need to talk.'

She ripped open the wrapper and tucked in, getting half the bar down before leaning back against the car and looking at him expectantly.

He took the lead and for the next hour they debriefed, starting from when they had unintentionally parted ways in Rarotonga. Archer walked her through it step by step, probing with questions when he needed to, letting her go when she was on a roll. He listened intently, absorbing her body language as much as her words.

He could tell she was uncomfortable with the experience, probably embarrassed that she'd been kidnapped and feeling like she had failed. She got emotional when she talked about Michael and Archer wondered, not for the first time, if there had really been more to the relationship than just colleagues.

He didn't care if there was. There was no denying she was a beautiful girl and he found her accent enticing, and maybe in other circumstances things might have been different, but he was in no position to judge the romantic decisions of others.

When she was finished, Izzy gave a shrug and said, 'You know the rest from there.'

'What about the build up?' Archer pressed her. 'Prior to coming to Auckland, and from Auckland to Rarotonga; what happened in that time?'

Izzy gave him a doubtful look. 'I don't think I can really...'

'Oh, for fuck's sake.' Archer threw up his hands and stepped away from her, his eyes blazing. 'This is exactly why we're in this position now. No fucker's talking to anyone else. We're supposed to be on the same side but these pricks have got us all chasing our fuckin' tails and turning the whole network inside out.'

'Sorry, but...'

'This is bullshit.' Archer paced away from her, sucking in a deep breath to get a grip. He spun on his heel to face her again. 'If the fuckin' fish heads that run our outfits can't sort their shit out and get on the same page, then we need to do it ourselves. We're the grunts on the ground here, Izzy. It's our arses in a sling when it all goes tits up, not theirs.'

He could see the understanding in her eyes. 'You and I are in the hot seat right now. We don't have time to fuck about with niceties. I just killed two arseholes to save your life. So don't give me this confidentiality bullshit.' He was up close to her now, close enough to feel her breath on his skin. He took another breath and softened his tone. 'Okay?'

Izzy nodded. 'Sorry.'

He almost smiled. 'Why do you guys do that?'

'Do what?'

'Always apologise.'

She rolled her eyes. 'I'm Canadian. It's what we do.' She shrugged. 'Sorry.' A smile twitched at her lips. 'Why do you swear so much?'

'I'm Kiwi,' he retorted. 'It's what we do.' He gave a shrug of his own. 'Sorry.'

Izzy grinned and the ice was broken. 'Right then, sweary-man. Let's talk turkey.'

'I thought turkey was more of an American thing.'

Izzy pulled a face. 'Fuck the Americans,' she said.

37

Tuesday, 1340 hours

Archer saw the SUV approaching before he heard it, the glint of sunlight off the glass giving it away before it had reached the driveway entrance.

It was a plain white vehicle, maybe a Peugot or VW, and he couldn't tell how many occupants it had. The vehicle stopped short of the drive and his phone rang. He opened the line without speaking.

'Here we are,' a man said in his ear. 'Campfires and riverstones.'

'Marshmallows on a stick.' Archer never ceased to wonder who came up with the ridiculous code phrases they used on operations. Ingoe was probably pissing himself back there at his desk. 'Come on in.'

He watched through the gap in the barn wall as the SUV moved forward and started up the drive. He wondered who the extraction team were. The guy had a Kiwi accent but he didn't recognise the voice. Probably ex-Army or Service. Most of them were; retired or damaged guys, picking up extra cash to supplement their legal income or pension.

'Ready?' He glanced around at Izzy, who was draining the last water bottle. It reminded him that she would need a proper medical check up when they reached safety. She was probably dehydrated and hungry, and possibly had injuries she hadn't told him about.

She nodded, tossed the bottle into the car and straightened her cap. Tyres crunched on gravel and frozen ground, and the SUV pulled up outside the barn doors.

Archer gave Izzy a nod and she opened one door, stepping back into the shadows before two men entered. Entering the half-light of the barn, they didn't see Archer covering them until they were inside. Both raised their hands immediately and stopped, the barrel of the Sig an unwavering eye that watched them closely.

'Breakfast at Tiffany's,' the first man said without hesitation.

'Good.' Archer lowered the weapon, satisfied with the second security check. He stuck his hand out. 'Thanks for coming.'

The first man shook it, giving a brief nod. Like his colleague he was average sized, late forties, and dressed in standard jeans and ski jacket. He wore a beanie over greying hair and was clean shaven. The second man stepped forward and shook Archer's hand. He was balding and had a tidy beard.

'Ben,' the first man said, and jerked a thumb at his mate. 'Cam.'

Archer nodded. They knew who he and Izzy were, and even if they didn't, there was no need for names. From the look of them he guessed they were ex-military, but he didn't recognise them, so probably regular force rather than SF.

'What's the plan,' he said.

'We drive your car to Zurich airport and return it,' Ben said. 'You take ours and cross the border to Italy. You drive to Milan and hop a plane from there. It's about a two and a half hour drive, maybe three depending on any hold ups.'

Archer nodded. It was a good enough plan, although he knew that the more time they spent in country the more likely they were to get bumped.

'The keys are in it,' Ben said. 'Full tank and there's some food and drinks in the back. Didn't know if you'd eaten or not.' He removed a set of keys and a plain brown envelope from his jacket pocket.

'Cheers mate.' Archer exchanged keys with him, took the envelope and waited.

Ben looked at him quizzically before clicking. He got his phone out and cleared his call log, then showed Archer that he'd done it. Archer did likewise before moving towards the door.

'See ya next time,' he said, swinging the door open.

He stepped out into the cool air, fresh smelling after the mustiness of the barn, and glanced back to see if Izzy was coming after him. They could safely leave the BMW and their rubbish with the exfil team to take care of. It was time to hit the road. The envelope would contain a couple of grand in cash, minus whatever the exfil team may have skimmed if they'd been cheeky enough.

Izzy was still coming and he turned back towards the SUV. As he did so he caught a flash of fiery movement in his peripheral vision, and spun. A rocket was streaking through the sky towards them from a slight rise only a few hundred yards away, leaving a trail in the air behind it.

'Get down!'

Archer threw himself away from the SUV, hitting the ground and tumbling with his hands over his head, tucking in to protect himself as best he could.

The explosion of the rocket hitting the SUV was phenomenally loud so close in and the high explosive shock wave picked him up and sent him tumbling across the frozen ground, flailing like a rag doll in a hurricane as debris and smoke filled the air. Shrapnel rained down around him as he rolled to a stop and he covered his head again, hoping against hope that he didn't cop any of it.

No sooner had he stopped moving than he was up again, scrambling to his hands and feet to move from where the enemy might have last seen him. The SUV was a burning wreck, smoke pouring up to the heavens in thick black clouds. At least it gave some concealment from whoever had fired on them. The only other concealment was the barn itself, but that was clearly going to be a target too.

'Izzy!' He could barely hear his own voice over the humming in his ears. He ran to the front of the barn and saw her on the ground nearby, covering her head. The two guys were still inside the barn somewhere.

As he reached down and grabbed Izzy's shoulder, Cam came running out of the barn with a pistol in his hands, snapping off shots in the general direction of the enemy. It was pointless firing at this distance and Archer ignored him, getting Izzy to her feet and hustling her inside the barn.

Ben was there, down on one knee with a hand clamped to his chest. Dark blood was flowing freely through his fingers, soaking his front, and Archer guessed he'd taken some shrapnel.

'In the car!'

He shoved Izzy into the front passenger seat and went back to Ben, shouting at Cam to get back in there. Ben slumped down on his side, his hand falling away from his chest. He was deathly white and his eyes were unfocussed. As best as Archer could tell he'd be lucky if he had minutes to go.

Archer grabbed up the fallen BMW keys and was moving around the car when Cam appeared in the doorway. He was fumbling with a magazine change and paused, silhouetted perfectly. It was the last thing he did.

A high velocity round punched through his chest from behind, throwing him forward and snapping his head back with the impact.

Archer left him and got behind the wheel, starting the BMW up and slapping it into gear.

'Get on the floor,' he told Izzy, locking his belt into position.

Through the ringing in his ears he heard a round strike the rear of the car and he gassed it. Izzy was still climbing over into the back seat and he got her arse on his shoulder as she was thrown off balance. He gave her a shove and covered his face, ducking behind the steering wheel.

The BMW crashed through the end of the barn, splinters and

chunks of wood flying everywhere as he entered the field beyond. The bumpy surface was not ideal for a city car and the BMW growled as he gave it some juice, but nothing was going to stop them from getting away.

A second HE rocket impacted just behind them and the barn went up in a ball of fire, the shock wave lifting the back of the BMW enough to make it swerve and bounce.

Archer cursed as he was thrown about but kept his hands on the wheel, being careful not to overdo the acceleration and throw it into a spin.

'Motherfucker,' Izzy shouted from the back. At least she was alive.

In the far corner was a wooden gate that led to a track running from the road side over to the right away between the paddocks to the left. It was one of the escape routes Archer had sussed out on arrival – all they had to do was get to the track without being either sniped or blasted into oblivion, make it to the road and be away.

Easy.

Cows that had been grazing peacefully now stood and stared at the crazy man in the silver car that was bouncing across their paddock. Archer was throwing in swerves to keep the enemy guessing but the downside to that was that they were exposed for longer and the bouncing of the car on the uneven surface was enough to rattle the teeth in his head.

He figured the enemy were probably using an RPG-7, which were plentiful on the black market, as well as being reliable and easy to use. They also had an effective range of about 500 metres, so he needed to make space.

The driver's wing mirror disappeared in a burst of broken glass and plastic as a round came close. A few seconds later another round thumped into the roof just above him, came through and put a hole in the dashboard.

Whoever was shooting was damn good. It was only a matter of time before a bullet hit home.

The gate was coming up fast and he angled for it, getting low behind the wheel again and giving the gas pedal a kick in the guts.

The bonnet and bumper hit the gate, bursting through in a shower of shattered wood, and Archer flicked the wheel hard right. The car slid out, fish tailed then straightened and they were racing down the track towards the road two hundred yards or so distant.

A bullet cracked the driver's window a few inches from Archer's head but didn't penetrate and he instinctively pressed himself back into the seat, as if it was going to protect him.

The windscreen was cracked but he could still see well enough to drive.

Another round punched the bodywork, then another and another. The sniper was getting desperate to stop them before they got to the road.

Archer knew that a moving target was hard to hit and a driver in a speeding target was even harder, no matter how good the shooter was.

Bullets he could handle; hopefully they'd run out of rockets.

There was a tractor chugging down the road to his right, towing a trailer laden with haybales, the farmer staring across at the burning barn and vehicle. Archer hit the tarmac and swung a hard right, gassing it so hard that the tyres spun and poured out new clouds of smoke.

A round careened off the road just ahead of him and he floored it, not wanting the sniper to get his eye in. He flashed past the tractor, frightening the farmer so much that he swerved into the ditch and toppled the trailer over on its side.

'Are we clear?' Izzy shouted from the back, starting to lift her head. A bullet smashed through the window above her and she was showered with shards of glass. 'I guess not,' she muttered, and dropped back down again.

The BMW was screaming down the road, heading back towards the mountains, exactly where Archer didn't want to be going. He risked a glance to his right to assess whether they were out of range yet. There hadn't been any incoming fire for a few seconds, so maybe the fuckers couldn't see them now.

'Fuck!'

He slammed on the brakes and swerved to the right a nano-second before a rocket skimmed past them, millimetres from the headlights, and exploded in a fiery ball on the shoulder of the road.

The explosion lifted the BMW's rear wheels and pushed the car sideways, bouncing down hard and skidding across the road. He could vaguely make out Izzy screaming something behind him but he didn't have time to worry – it was all he could do to keep them on the road.

He cut left, fishtailed, corrected and gunned it. The car was dragging and making a horrible screeching sound and the rear wheels were throwing up showers of sparks. Both tyres had been shredded by the explosion and they were running on rims.

At this rate they wouldn't last long and he needed distance.

38

A village was coming up quickly and he started scanning it for any potential uses – ideally they needed to dump the car and get another, but that would be hard in such a small place.

People in villages tended to notice things like shot up cars running on rims. When they'd come through the village earlier he'd seen a cop car in the main drag, having stopped a motorist. If he was still there, hopefully he'd either deter the enemy – unlikely – or stay the hell out of the way.

Izzy popped her head up again, her eyes wide when she stared at him in the rear view mirror.

'Who the fuck are these guys?' she shouted. 'Was that a fucking rocket they were firing?'

Archer noticed that her swearing had suddenly increased, and he wondered if she would apologise for it.

'What the fuck are you smiling at?'

'Nothing,' he said. 'Yes it was a rocket. Are they behind us?'

She studied the road behind them. 'There's a vehicle coming but I can't see what kind it is. I don't know if it's them or not.' There was a pause for a second. 'Do you realise we don't have any tyres?'

'Really?'

She looked at him in shock then realised he was joking. She pulled a face. 'Of course you do.' She let out a short laugh, a sudden release of tension. 'Of course you fuckin' do.'

'We need to dump this and get some other wheels,' he said. They were right on the edge of the village now and he pulled into the car park of a small pub. There were only a couple of other cars there and he slotted the BMW between them. 'Let's go.'

In seconds they were out and moving. Archer slung his day pack on his back and kept the Sig P229 in his waistband under his jacket. A quick glance back down the road told him that a grey sedan was approaching at speed and his gut told him it was the enemy.

A siren sounded from the other side of the village and he spotted a cop car coming from that direction. Pedestrians were stopping to stare, some at the cop car with its flashing lights and others in the direction of the pall of smoke.

'Here.' He steered Izzy off the main road into a side alley. 'Run.'

They pumped their knees and got to the end just as the cop car went by, the siren deafening in the narrow street. No sooner had it gone by than the grey car entered the village and skidded to a stop at the top of the alley. A door opened and closed then the car took off.

Archer pushed Izzy ahead of him into an adjoining service lane that ran behind the main street shops, urging her on. The lane had a brick wall to their right, running all the way along, and a row of garages or sheds behind houses to their left.

The enemy were playing it smart by staying mobile but with someone on foot behind them. If they played it right they would corner their quarry in the small built up area, knowing that Archer and Izzy would not want innocent blood spilt. Archer ran through options in his head as they ran, and a loose plan quickly came together.

'Keep going,' he said, 'stop at the end.'

He gave her a push of encouragement and stepped off to the side through a doorway in the brick wall into the small yard behind a shop. It was home to rubbish bins and bags of crap, and a fat black cat who stopped, stared and hissed.

Archer heard running feet come around the corner, barely slowing before charging down the service lane. It was a good sign – not taking the corner tactically meant the guy was not thinking straight. It was something he could use to his advantage.

He eased the day pack off his shoulders and put it down, gripping the Sig in his left hand, waiting.

The running feet were right up there now and as they came level, Archer swung out from the doorway, fast and hard.

His right forearm came up straight and clotheslined the runner across the throat. The runner's upper body stopped dead and his legs kept going, kicking at the air as he went horizontal before hitting the ground on his back.

Archer dropped a knee onto his chest and rammed the barrel of the Sig into the guy's throat, pulled it back and repeated the action. The guy's eyes bugged and he immediately grabbed for his throat, gagging for air. Archer knew that he would have smashed the Adam's apple and the guy would be unconscious within a minute, dead not long after.

He pushed up, slung his bag back on and sprinted after Izzy.

He paused to check around the corner and spotted Izzy waiting for him, looking in all directions, jumpy.

'Let's go.' He grabbed her arm and they ran for the end of the service lane.

More sirens were filling the air now and he could hear engines racing. It would be too much to hope they were all just going to the fire, and he didn't fancy getting arrested.

They reached the end of the lane and found themselves on a secondary residential street, parked cars at the kerbs and people milling about, curious about the flurry of action in the normally sleepy village.

'Walk.'

They dropped into step side by side, moving with purpose but not hurrying. Archer wiped sweat from his face and hoped he didn't look like too much of a bag of shit that he stood out.

He worked to get his breathing under control and gave Izzy a big smile, muttering from the corner of his mouth, 'Be cool, we're just a couple of dumb tourists wondering what's going on. Nothing to see here.'

Izzy did her best to return the smile but looked more like she was constipated. 'That's right. Rocket attacks are pretty normal around here.'

Nobody seemed to pay them any mind as they made their way down the street and they were nearly at the crossroads that would take them back to the main drag when a grey Skoda came from the right, two heads in it. The two groups spotted each other at the same time and the Skoda's brake lights flared.

It was starting to turn as Archer pushed Izzy sideways into the front garden of the house they were passing and jumped after her. They crossed the front yard and ducked down the side of the house.

Tyres screeched behind them.

'Go left.' Archer turned and covered Izzy as she went over the fence into the neighbour's property, immediately bringing a volley of loud barking and a curse.

A man appeared at the front of the house Archer was beside with a pistol in his hands. He started to bring it up and Archer did likewise, hoping against hope it wasn't a cop. He hesitated a second and the other man got the first shot off.

It pinged off the brickwork of the house and Archer hesitated no longer. This was no cop. He stroked the trigger twice in quick succession, seeing both rounds impact the guy's torso.

Archer was halfway over the fence before the guy hit the ground. He dropped into the next yard and found Izzy face to face with a large German shepherd, eyeing each other and both poised to move.

'Archer?' Izzy's voice was tentative.

'No sudden moves,' he replied. The dog's big head shifted and it assessed him, determining who was the biggest threat. The growls coming from its throat were deep and menacing.

'No shit,' Izzy managed.

Running feet sounded from over the fence and he knew it was decision time. He had no desire to kill an innocent dog who was doing what it was supposed to do. He also had no desire to get shot.

'Come on you fucker,' he said loudly, and took a sudden step forward.

The dog bounded a few steps and leaped at him but Archer was already moving.

He cracked the dog across the head with the gun butt and gave it a hard shove in the side, sending it sprawling on the ground.

It gave its big head a shake and Archer booted it hard in the side, causing it to whimper and back away, suddenly wary of the intruder.

Archer didn't stick around to argue, but ran hard after Izzy who was already heading down the side of the house and back towards the road.

There was a shout behind them followed by the double crack of shots but they made it to the road and found more neighbours had come out.

'Polizei! Polizei!' Archer shouted in German, 'there's a man with a gun!'

People started to move and phones were coming out. He and Izzy ran to the right, where they had last seen the grey Skoda.

Archer was banking on the enemy driver having circled around towards the main street, intent on cutting them off that way. Coming up behind them was a calculated but dangerous move.

A siren was coming closer and a second later a police car careened around the corner, lights flashing and siren wailing.

Archer waved excitedly back the way they had come and the passenger gave him a wave of thanks. Both cops looked grim and focussed as they headed that way. He knew that they would be armed, so with any luck they would deal with the guy behind them.

'Come on.'

They ran on, stopping short of the main road to look and listen. No sooner had they stopped than there was an eruption of gunfire somewhere behind them, accompanied by shouts, a dog barking and screams.

Archer led the way into the main street, hoping to get his hands on a vehicle before the net really closed in on them. People were standing around rubber-necking and chattering. It was probably the most excitement the village had seen in years, he reflected.

'There.' Archer spotted a Toyota station wagon in a car park across the road. Easy to steal and inconspicuous; just what they needed. They stepped off the kerb between two parked cars to cross over at the same moment as the grey Skoda bore down on them from the left.

The driver swerved across the road, lining them up like skittles in a bowling alley, and gave it some juice.

Archer felt himself jerked backwards by a hand on his jacket and he tumbled to the ground awkwardly, crashing into Izzy as he went down. There was a crash as the Skoda smashed into the cars parked at the kerb and shoved one of them sideways. The engine roared and people shouted.

Archer rolled to his feet and snatched out the Sig, levelling it at the two enemy in the crashed Skoda. The Skoda was at an angle to him, nose in against a parked car, and steam was starting to waft from under the buckled bonnet.

The driver was trying to wrestle the car free around his deployed air bag, and past that Archer could see the front seat passenger starting to get out.

He fired a double tap through the driver's side window, seeing a splash of red, then leaped onto the boot of the car they had crashed into. The passenger was half out of the car with a sub machine gun in his hand.

Archer hit him with a double tap in the back, turned and gave the driver another two – popping the air bag in the process – then another two into the fallen passenger.

He jumped back down and grabbed Izzy's hand.

'Polizei!' he bellowed. 'Polizei!'

They raced across the road into the car park where he'd seen the

Toyota wagon. He ignored it now and ran on, cutting through a walkway to another residential street. They needed to get away fast and hopefully the confusion of multiple shootings, along with him identifying them as Police, would assist with that.

He spotted a tidy blue Renault Clio parked at the kerb. A compact hatchback was hardly his first choice but beggars couldn't be choosers. Finally the gods cut them some slack and he found the car unlocked. Clearly car crime wasn't an issue around here. Within two minutes he'd got it started and they were away.

Izzy stripped off her jacket as they headed out of town and tossed it in the back. She helped him shed his own top, buckled his seatbelt for him and looked at him.

'Sweet Jesus,' she said, 'these guys are pretty serious, aren't they?'

'Very.' Archer got the Clio up to speed and settled in for the drive. He glanced at her. 'Thanks.'

'For what?'

'For saving my life. If you hadn't pulled me back they would have bowled us both back there.'

She gave a snort. 'I think I still owe you a few, don't worry about it, eh.'

He shrugged. 'Thanks anyway. It's good to know I can rely on you.'

Izzy gave him the same look that many teachers had given him as a kid. 'I'm not stupid, Archer. I may not be as experienced as you with all this sort of thing, but I can think on my feet.'

'Fair call.' He turned back to the road, checked the mirrors again and took a breath. Sorted. Time to get on with it.

39

Benson Manor
Marlow, Buckinghamshire, England
Tuesday, 1500 hours

T he Director waited patiently while his PPO cleared the room, only entering when he got the nod and an "All clear, sir" from the copper.

It was a long-standing tradition that he was well used to, largely superfluous given the room had been cleared already by the Brits, but a necessity nonetheless. So much of what he did these days was like that, he reflected as he placed his attache case on the table.

The room was not as luxurious as many he had stayed in, but still more than adequate. No doubt the DG had the better digs; she tended to be more vocal about these things than he. The difference between a lawyer and a soldier, he supposed. Of course his soldiering days were now a long distant memory, cloaked in the mists of time.

'I'll be right next door, sir.'

'Thank you, Colin. Come and get me when we're ready.'

'Sir.' Colin nodded and shut the door behind him. Like many of the Protection Services people he was a trendy bastard, with a haircut that probably cost more than the Director's wife's did, and that was saying something. He reminded himself to call her later; she always worried when he was away, despite having been married for the better part of four decades.

The flight to London had been followed by a breakfast meeting at Haymarket with the High Commissioner, an old friend of the Director's. There he had picked up a security tail by two of the SIS staff based at the High Commission, a married couple that he knew from previous visits. Lunch with a contact at the Met's Anti-Terrorism branch, and then on the road to here.

The meeting place chosen was a former stately home in rural Buckinghamshire, a grand old dame that had been used during the war and later commissioned as a private hotel. The Brits used it regularly for conferences and the staff were well used to being descended upon by hordes of well-dressed people with earpieces and suspicious bulges under their jackets.

The main event was this evening, which would give him time to do some preparatory reading and, with any luck, perhaps a quick nap to carry him through.

The meeting was bound to be robust and heated, and he had already determined that he would need to keep the DG on a leash. She was prone to snarling when under pressure and that would be no good; their partners were already pissed off, the Canadians in particular.

The fact that one of their officers was now on the run somewhere in Europe with one of his own was not helping. At least she was alive, they could at least be bloody grateful for that.

According to their Five Eyes colleagues the whole shemozzle was the Kiwis' fault, and the Director was struggling to find a good defence for that.

He sighed and rolled his suitcase into the bedroom, deciding to unpack later. The bed looked lumpy and there was a noticeable sag in the middle. The Director harrumphed, tossed his overcoat onto the bed and turned away.

As if the meeting wasn't shaping up badly enough as it was, he would no doubt have a bad sleep to follow. Just what he needed.

With any luck Archer and the Canadian girl would surface unharmed and take the sting out of it. Right now, it was the best he could hope for.

40

———

United Kingdom airspace

Sitting in the back seat of a rented luxury white Cessna, Kozlowski swirled his tumbler, letting the ice cubes rattle together.

The Scotch was almost gone. They had levelled out and the seat-belts had come off.

Across the aisle from him sat Krystal Raines and her sidekick, the burly Rick. Both had drinks on their side trays, and were settling in for take-off. The only other people aboard were the two pilots and Kozlowski's personal bodyguard, a silent man named Constantine.

Craig Archer had killed his previous number two a year ago, but Constantine was a more than adequate replacement. Having grown up on the backstreets of Paris, he had spent time in the French Foreign Legion before being unceremoniously dumped out. Too violent, they had said. He was certainly that.

The left side of his face was horribly burned and twisted, the result of being too close to a phosphorous grenade. Plastic surgery hadn't been enough to repair the damage. He sat a row back, silently watching, listening, a lean shaven headed figure in a grey suit.

'Well this is a nice set of wings,' Rick said loudly, looking around him. He fixed his gaze on Kozlowski. 'Where we goin'?'

Kozlowski caught Krystal's eye roll in his peripheral vision. He kept his gaze on Rick, flat and calm. Unruffled by his guest's brashness.

'When we get there, you'll know,' he said smoothly. 'There are many things left to do. I need the both of you to step it up a notch and make sure we pull this off.'

'You can rely on us, boss.' Rick grinned and raised his tumbler in a toast. Krystal ignored him and Rick's face fell. 'What, I say somethin' wrong?'

'Just chill,' she said quietly. 'Show some respect.'

Rick's face darkened and his jaw clamped shut. He breathed through his nostrils, the hairs of his moustache dancing in the breeze. 'Sure,' he grated. 'I'll show some respect. That's what I get *paid* to do.'

She shot him an angry look and went to retort, but was cut off by Kozlowski.

'Money?' he said softly. 'Is money an issue for you, Rick?'

'I didn't say that.' Rick shifted uncomfortably, only now realising that he'd overstepped the mark. 'I'm good.'

'It seems to be an issue for you. Me?' Kozlowski's dark eyes glittered. 'I value money. It gets me a lot of things. But I value loyalty more.'

Rick squirmed and Krystal stayed silent. He'd made his bed and now he would have to lie in it.

'Do I have your loyalty, Rick?'

'Of course, Mr Kozlowski. Of course you do. I mean, I didn't mean...'

A thin smile formed on Kozlowski's lips. 'Money can't buy loyalty, can it?'

'No, sir.'

'Money is good for some things. For many things, actually. But it cannot buy loyalty.'

Rick was starting to lose his patience now. He didn't like playing games like this.

'Look, I didn't mean to offend anyone...'

'You're a blunt instrument, Rick,' Kozlowski said. 'And you're a boor.'

Rick scowled. He wasn't exactly sure what that meant, but he knew it was no compliment. He felt his muscles bunching. Nobody spoke to him like that. He locked eyes with Kozlowski across the narrow aisle. He wanted to hurt the man for speaking to him like that.

But looking into the eyes that met his, he knew without a shadow of a doubt, that he was looking into the soul of the devil. Two endless black pools of evil stared back at him, daring him to push it a step further. There was a beast in there, watching him, wanting him to come and play so it could rip his heart out.

Rick tore his gaze away, his cheeks burning with shame and a jolt going through him that, if he was honest with himself, he recognised as fear.

Kozlowski's voice was soft. 'That's what I thought,' he said. He glanced from the big mercenary to the beautiful woman beside him. An unspoken word passed between them and Krystal gave an almost imperceptible nod.

Kozlowski relaxed back into his seat. With things moving fast, there was no room for passengers.

And he would not stand for either insubordination or failure.

41

Bern, Switzerland
Tuesday, 1800 hours

They had made it to Bern in good time, dumping the Clio in a side street and walking from there for ten minutes until they hopped a bus for several stops.

Finding themselves in a shopping area they stopped at a sandwich shop and ate hungrily. Washing down the dregs of his second coffee, Archer sat back and looked across the small table at Izzy. She had some colour back in her cheeks now and looked as refreshed as she could be without proper rest.

'Right,' he said brusquely. 'What's your plan?'

She swallowed the last mouthful of a sandwich, drained her coffee and put the cup down with a clunk. Folded her hands in front of her and leaned in. 'First, we need to contact our people and get them to get us the hell out of here. Second, we get the hell out of here.' She raised her eyebrows. 'What d'you think?'

Archer gave a short nod. 'Pretty much sums it up.'

She started to rise but he stayed where he was. Izzy looked at him quizzically. 'Coming?'

Archer's gaze was intense. 'You get the feeling we're being played?'

Izzy paused, then sat again. 'In what way?'

'Think about it. If I'm seeing it the right way, whoever is behind the Five Eyes information leaks is trying to bring down the network, yeah?'

'Agreed.'

'And it's a fair bet that that person is Viktor Kozlowski, right?'

'Uh-huh.'

Archer leaned in close. 'So why kidnap you?'

Izzy frowned. 'What d'you mean?'

'Well what does he get out of it? No ransom demand. No prisoner exchange demand.' He spread his hands. 'So what did he want?'

'Well...an officer from a top level intelligence agency is a valuable commodity, right?'

He gave her non-committal. 'Depends on what the bad guys want though, doesn't it? If your purpose is to bring down an intelligence network, kidnapping an officer doesn't advance that at all. All it does is create a pain in the arse for one agency, or in our case, two. But realistically, neither of our firms are going to stop doing business just because we get killed or kidnapped.'

He saw realisation dawn on her face. 'It was a distraction.'

Archer nodded. 'It had to be. Either that or personal.'

'But even better if it was both, given your history with Kozlowski.'

'Exactly. This, us, we're not the main event. There's something else going on here, and we're just a side show. This is all just for entertainment and distraction.'

'So what's the main event?' Izzy pursed her lips thoughtfully. 'It's gotta be something huge, eh?'

Archer nodded. His face was pinched and serious now and his mind was racing. Pieces were starting to fall into place but although he could see the rough outline of the puzzle, he wasn't sure of the finer details yet.

He needed to make a phone call.

42

Auckland, New Zealand
Wednesday, 0500 hours

Murray swivelled in his chair and caught Ingoe's eye.

'I have the Consulate General in Geneva on the phone, sir,' he said. 'He says he's had a phone call from Captain Archer, requesting assistance.'

'Put him through.'

Ingoe snatched up the receiver as soon as it rang. The Consulate-General in Switzerland was currently a former liberal politician named Mitchell Crohn. He was known more for his junkets and taste in high-end prostitutes than anything that advanced trade relations between the two countries.

'It's been a long time, Mitchell,' Ingoe said. 'I understand you've heard from one of our people.'

'A Captain Archer, he tells me.' Mitchell's voice was like finger nails on a chalkboard. 'He's been quite demanding and I have him on hold. I told him I need to check with you first before I go authorising anything.'

'What's he after?' Ingoe had a fair idea anyway. He also had a fair idea that Archer wouldn't appreciate being put on hold by this pencil-necked arse wipe.

'He's requesting a private plane from Bern to London for he and a Canadian colleague. He clearly has no bloody idea how much that costs and I just don't have it in the budget to go financing flights of fancy like that. Who is this Canadian anyway, and why aren't they shelling out to cover it? Things are tight you know, Ingoe, and this sort of thing just isn't on.'

Ingoe waited until he'd run out of steam before speaking.

'A couple of things there, Mitchell,' he said calmly. 'Firstly, it's an urgent operational matter and you have the local contacts to get it done. That's the whole purpose of having consulates in foreign countries isn't it; to help our people in the field when they need help?'

Mitchell have a reluctant "Mmm" of acknowledgement.

'This is a matter of high priority for both us and the Canadian government,' Ingoe continued. 'I'm sure that both of our leaders will fully appreciate your co-operation. Of course, the reverse applies if the co-operation isn't extended.'

Silence in his ear.

'Secondly, there is a budget for this sort of thing, as we both well know.' Ingoe lowered his voice. 'If that budget has been spent elsewhere on other...*non-operational* matters, Mitchell, then that would present a problem, wouldn't it?' He could hear the Consulate-General's breathing pick up as the stress hormones kicked in. 'I suggest that you get him off hold and make those arrangements as quick as you can. I appreciate you checking in, but the reality is, lives depend on this and, dare I say it, so do careers.'

Ingoe paused, letting Mitchell churn that over in his head. As the Operations Manager for a unit of the SIS, which officially didn't exist, Ingoe didn't have the line authority on paper to speak to a diplomat like that.

But the reality was very different. Ingoe was known by many in the black-tie circles, and his reputation preceded him. Right about now, Mitchell Crohn would be shitting himself and reaching for a personal credit card to get it done. Immediately after that he would be doing some fast work on his budgets.

'Right, okay,' Mitchell said, grasping for some semblance of control. 'Well of course the funds are available, I just needed to check that this was all above board, right? I know what some of these people are like.'

Ingoe rolled his eyes to himself. The man really had no idea what the Archers of the world were really like at all.

'I'll get that organised and get them on their way. You might want to remind your man Archer to show a little respect when he rings and interrupts an important meeting wanting a favour. Respect goes a long way, Ingoe.'

The irony of the man calling him by his last name wasn't lost on Ingoe.

'Yeah,' he said. 'I'll be sure to tell him that, Mitchell. Thanks for squaring that away.'

They rang off and Ingoe sat for a moment, contemplating. There was no doubt in his mind that the Consulate-General would be getting some robust career advice in the very near future, but that was something for later.

He needed to speak to Archer, but would give him some breathing space to get himself sorted. Two things gave him confidence, despite not knowing exactly what his man on the ground was up to.

First, Archer had a plan and was executing it. When you were up against it, it was always better to do something than nothing. Second, Archer had taken charge. Obviously he wasn't relying on the Canadians to get them out of the shit, which told Ingoe that Archer was backing himself. Not only that, but it saved them from getting more egg on their face.

All told, things were going okay right now. As long as the emergency conference was all in hand, they would be okay. He rubbed his face and stifled a yawn. It had been yet another long day, and it wasn't over yet.

It was the evening in Switzerland, but being ten hours ahead in Auckland, it was nearly dawn and he was starting to feel it.

'Murray, it's time for a coffee.' He stood up, feeling a tingle in his stump. He subconsciously gave it a rub. At least a tingle was better than the ghost pains he'd had when he'd first lost the leg.

'Um....ahh...' Murray's eyes darted nervously.

'You don't drink actual coffee, do you.' Ingoe suppressed a groan. 'What would you like then? A trim soy decaf flat white with a caramel shot? Or is it an elderflower tea?'

Murray's face brightened. 'A chamomile would be fantastic, thanks boss.'

Ingoe couldn't suppress the second groan. 'For fuck's sake, I was kidding.'

Murray's face fell. 'Oh, sorry, um...'

'Don't worry about it.' Ingoe moved towards the door. 'Milk or sugar?'

Murray hesitated, unsure whether he was being kidded or not. 'Um, just water please...'

'Of course.' Ingoe swiped himself out the door. 'Water and chamomile. Just what a man needs.'

He closed the door behind him.

43

———

Bern, Switzerland
Tuesday, 2215 hours

Once the Consulate-General got a hurry up from Ingoe, things moved a lot smoother. As they got themselves organised, Archer reflected how amazing it was the difference one person could make.

Even though he had outranked Ingoe in the Army, the former Warrant Officer was one of those people who always carried influence, regardless of their position. The upshot of that was that Archer and Izzy were picked up by a driver from the embassy in a very nice late model Volvo S90.

After a stop for Izzy to purchase a change of clothes – which, Archer had to admit, she did very efficiently – they were dropped to a hotel near the airport to freshen up. The driver, a smiley older man who introduced himself as Liam, told them he would be back in the morning to pick them up, and get them to the airport, where a private plane would be waiting to get them to London.

The hotel was a bog-standard airport affair, but the room smelt fresh and airy and the décor looked like it had been recently updated.

Archer enjoyed travelling but he had always found hotels to be very hit and miss, and preferred smaller B&Bs or country pubs to the larger corporate affairs, especially when he was away with a girl. They didn't afford the same anonymity, however, and right now they needed to melt into the background.

Izzy waited by the door while he swept the room and closed the heavy drapes. She hit the lights and put the security chain in place on the door. It wasn't strong enough to keep out a determined attacker, but anything to slow them down was better than nothing.

Archer checked the mini bar and found tiny bottles of Johnny Walker Black Label and Absolut Vodka. He would send down for some mixers later, unless Izzy took it straight. He glanced over as she walked past him to the bedroom.

'I'll take the couch,' he told her. 'Help yourself in there.'

'I'm taking a bath,' she said. 'I guess we've got some time before we get the next phone call?'

'I'd say so.'

She sounded tired and he realised the constant running and fighting was taking its toll on her. He had to admit he could do with a rest himself. He tossed his jacket onto the sofa and moved a heavy wingback chair into a corner away from the window.

Should they be attacked in the room he needed to be ready and rearranging the furniture may give him some small advantage.

He could hear the bathwater running while he made his preparations.

That done, he boiled the jug and made a strong cup of coffee. It steamed on the table beside him while he used the dishcloth to wipe the Sig down. He unloaded it, removed the rounds from the magazine and checked them for any faults, then reloaded.

His own weapons were back in London, there having been no way for him to take them to Switzerland aside from through the diplomatic bag, which didn't work out well timing-wise. With all the shooting of the day, he felt underwhelmingly equipped. Their best defence right now would be avoidance.

He sat and waited, drinking coffee and thinking, letting a million thoughts run loosely through his head. The caffeine was helping to battle the fatigue but he knew he needed to rest soon. With any luck they would be extracted before too long, without anyone else being killed or anything blown up.

Izzy eventually emerged from the bathroom with wet hair, wrapped in a towel that barely covered her.

She paused in the doorway and sniffed.

'Do I smell coffee?'

Archer gestured towards his empty cup. 'Want some? Or there's some liquor there if you want something stronger.'

Izzy cocked an eyebrow and gave a small smile. 'Are you trying to get me drunk, Mr Archer?'

He gave a weary smile. 'Up to you if you'd like a drink or not.'

'Because it's okay if you wanted to.'

He could see the wanting in her eyes and felt a kick of excitement. Her intentions were clear. He ran his eyes the length of her toned body, and he liked what he saw.

She was a desirable girl, there was no denying that, and he was sorely tempted.

But there was also a vulnerability about her that hadn't been there before, a fragility that told him she was looking for protection as much as anything else.

Archer had never been one to say no to a pretty girl, vulnerable or not. Maybe it was the recent memories of Eva that were messing with his head. Maybe he was just too tired to think straight. Or maybe it was a nagging doubt in his mind that now was not the right time.

Whatever the reason, Archer gave a rueful smile and pushed up to his feet. 'I'll make you a coffee, eh?'

She blocked his way, putting her hands up to his chest. He could smell shampoo and soap and freshly brushed teeth. She was looking up at him with doleful eyes, and the top edge of the towel revealed a very inviting cleavage. He felt his resolve slip several notches.

He took a deep breath, his chest rising against the palms of her hands. He lifted her hands away and stepped around her. 'Do you want sugar?' he said.

Izzy's eyes flashed angrily then welled up, her lip trembled, and she spun on her heel. 'You can shove your coffee up your ass,' she cried as she stormed into the bedroom. The door slammed behind her and Archer stood in the silence, his head a jumble of thoughts. He couldn't quite believe what he'd just done. Any other time he would have been there in a flash.

He sighed, shook his head, and sat back down in the wingback chair. He drained the cold dregs of his coffee and settled in for the long haul.

44

Dublin, Ireland
Tuesday, 2310 hours

Lee Sweetman had two passions in life; one was hacking, the other was Asian hookers. Both gave him a rush he couldn't describe.

Naturally the first thing he did when he got to Dublin was book into a hotel. Nothing too swanky, but not cheap either. He always rated hotels on three things; the availability of room service, walking distance to the entertainment district, and discretion.

The Emirates flight had got him to Dublin, via a short stop in Dubai, just after eight pm. It was now close to eleven, which was about half way through Sweetman's normal work day, so he was perky and ready to go.

If he was going to fuck a hooker in a new town – which, to be fair, went without question – then he didn't want to have to travel far, he wanted a local recommendation (and hotel staff were always a gold-mine for this) and he wanted a goddamn cheeseburger and fries in his room afterwards.

The desk clerk at the hotel he'd chosen – Padraic or some such weird fuckin' name – had recommended Madame Woo's just off O'Connell Street. It was a small upstairs joint with a red dragon on the street level doorway, dim lights and those screen things everywhere, the ones that people always crashed through in kung fu movies.

The receptionist was older, maybe fifty, with a face that had seen it all and done it all and, for a fresh greenback, probably still would.

Her smile revealed a missing tooth but he didn't care. He paid her for an hour, full service, her fingers rough on his when she took the cash from him. She stashed it away beneath the counter. He followed her to a room off the hallway and she told him to wait there for his hostess.

Soft muzak was drifting through the speakers, not quite loud enough to drown out the squeaking springs from the next room. The double bed was stripped back to just a sheet and a couple of pillows. A stack of skin mags sat on a chair in case he was interested. The walls were decorated with cheap prints of scenery and alluring half-naked women.

Sweetman undressed down to his boxers, folding his clothes carefully and placing them on another chair. Hopefully some other dude's bare ass hadn't been on that chair too recently.

He rubbed his stomach and felt it wobble. He knew that most women found him repulsive; it was probably why the only sex he'd had in the last decade had been paid for.

He didn't care. He found women equal parts boring and intimidating. Far better that he just got to the point without the conversation or judgement.

The door opened behind him and the hooker entered. She was short and bony, with tiny tits and a waist narrower than his thigh. She wore a cheap nylon gown that opened at the front to show a hint of black lace and barely long enough to cover her ass cheeks.

The smile she gave him was supposed to be shy and seductive, and he let himself go with that. Of course she wanted him; he had money and a big cock. Well, he had money anyway.

'Hi baby,' she said, running a hand down his pale stomach and back up again. 'You want full service, hey?'

'Yeah, I do.' He reached out and placed a hand on her left tit through the gown. She didn't flinch. 'I wanna fuck you hard.'

It was his standard line with hookers. He had no idea if any of them ever believed it, but it didn't matter. It made him feel powerful. *He* was calling the shots here.

She smiled again and ushered him towards the bed, tugging at the waistband of his underwear.

'You don' need these baby. You go on bed and I give you massage first.' She expertly slid his underwear down and he stepped out of them, his back to her. She squeezed his shoulders surprisingly hard. 'Big strong man, so much tight up here.' She peeked around him at his flaccid penis, barely visible beneath the overhang of his gut. 'Oooh, nice cock baby. Lie down.'

He did as he was told and lay face down. He could tell she was going to be good and he would be getting his money's worth. If she played her cards right he might be back again, depending how many days Kozlowski wanted him in Dublin for. That guy was fuckin' weird, and Sweetman had never trusted him.

He paid well though, and the Kiwi chick, Krystal, had the finest set of tits he'd seen in a long time. Not that he had a shit's show in ever getting at them, especially with that little fag Capstick in the way. Sweetman had never got how a dick like Capstick got to bone a smoker like Krystal, it made no sense at all.

Sweetman had always thought Capstick would prefer sausage over muffins, but how wrong had he been. He nestled down into the lumpy bed, feeling the hooker straddle him and pour warm oil on his back. Her hands set to work on his knots and he let his mind drift.

The technical attack on his system had been highly efficient and almost undetectable. He still wasn't sure how deeply it had probed and how much, if any, information had been compromised.

Given sufficient time he could determine that, but Viktor

Kozlowski was not a man known for his patience. Knowing that Sweetman had been attacked left no option but to get him out of the country. They couldn't afford for him to be taken in by the security service – he would fall at the first hurdle under proper interrogation, and that was a risk Kozlowski wouldn't take.

The Republic of Ireland was a good option for him to get to, being so close to Europe but not part of the UK. By the time Sweetman got back to his hotel he should have instructions waiting. The next move was likely to be to an eastern European destination, somewhere with a strong organised crime presence and minimal interference from western forces.

Sweetman could see himself in Slovakia or Slovenia, maybe Poland or even Russia. Prague had always appealed. As long as there was somewhere to set himself up and there were Asian hookers on hand, he'd be fine.

He winced as the girl dug a thumb into a tight knot on his shoulder blade and she eased off. He felt the air move as the door opened, and he craned his head to look. The girl's long dark hair brushed his face as she leaned over him. He could feel her nipples brushing his back.

'Jus' relax baby,' she cooed in his ear. 'Jus' relax.'

He did as he was told, unaware of the second person entering the room. The girl stayed on his back, her hands pressing into the muscles there, as the second person crossed the floor and made eye contact with the girl.

It was the older woman from the reception desk.

Mei Kim had been in the game for years, which gave her unprecedented access to the smorgasbord of criminals, politicians, terrorists and businessmen that drifted through the vice scene. She was on the payroll of both the Gardai and the Real IRA as an informer, and the Chinese Mafia as a madame.

In her time she had seen many things and had killed two men. Both had been clean hits for her Mafia masters and she had no idea who the men were or why they needed to die.

Just as she had no clue who Lee Sweetman was or why he would be dying tonight. She didn't need to know and didn't care.

The syringe in her hand contained a dose of muscle relaxant that was substantial enough to put down a bull. She stepped up beside the girl on Sweetman's blindside, checked in the dim light that she had the right angle, and slipped the needle into the femoral artery of Sweetman's right thigh. He jolted when he felt the prick and he tried to turn, but the hammer came down on the syringe and muscle relaxant flooded into his artery.

The two women held him down easily as the drugs surged through his system, the panic reaction of his heart doing all the work for them.

In seconds he was melting into the mattress, unable to move his limbs or even speak. His sphincter relaxed and he shat himself, the girl on his back quickly dismounting and stepping back, covering her mouth and nose.

Mei Kim had no such revulsion.

She put the syringe aside and checked the pulse in his neck. Slowing rapidly. She took a second syringe from the bum bag around her waist, uncapped it, and lifted his limp left arm. She inserted the needle into a vein in his elbow, pressed the plunger and sent a hot load of high grade crack cocaine into his system.

The rush of the upper should have been enough to have a non-user like Sweetman bouncing off the walls, but the only reaction was a rapid fluttering of his eyelids. The crack wasn't enough to override the barbiturates that had turned his body into a useless lump of meat.

The track marks made by the extra puncture wounds Mei Kim was now making in his elbow would tell the tale when his body turned up in the Liffey in a few days. It wasn't uncommon for amateurs to experiment with the hard stuff here in Dublin, take a hot load and die. The Gardai wouldn't even bat an eyelid when they saw the track marks and any trace of the barbiturates would be gone by the time they fished him out of the water.

Mei Kim gave the girl the nod and sent her on her way. She would get a good bonus for her work tonight and would be relocated to a whorehouse in Sligo, where she would die within the month.

Such was the way of the world they lived in.

Mei Kim checked her watch. Perfect. Her man would be there within a few minutes to move the body, and she would let her boss know the job was done.

She had never heard the name Viktor Kozlowski before, and had no idea he was connected to many people higher up the food chain than her. It was of no consequence to her.

Her job here was done.

45

———

Benson Manor
Marlow, Buckinghamshire, England
Wednesday, 0400 hours

Getting close to the President of the United States was damn near impossible without a sniper rifle.

Getting close to a senior member of the CIA was almost as difficult, with highly-trained protection specialists everywhere and all the resources known to man available.

But there was more than one way to skin a cat.

With the Five Eyes network on the ropes and at risk of going down, Kozlowski had one more stroke which, if executed correctly, would be the master stroke that blew the network apart.

Benson Manor, the country hotel being used for the emergency conference, was well known to Kozlowski's organisation as it had been used a number of times before. Hotel staff were notoriously easy to bribe for information, so it was a simple matter of working through likely venues until they found the right one.

So far, so easy.

The hard part came when he considered the security in place. The Americans were staying at a separate venue that was five miles away and secured by a ring of steel and sunglass-wearing agents with automatic weapons. The risk in attacking such a place was too high.

The Brits themselves would be coming and going each day, so were also difficult to pin down to one place.

That left the Canadians, Australians and New Zealanders at Benson Manor. A small number of VIPs with a handful of their own protection officers between them, bolstered by a uniformed component of Thames Valley Police for external security. The manor was down a country lane a mile from the nearest town of Marlow, and close enough to the M40 motorway.

The hotel itself had a staff of fifteen allocated for the conference, from the manager down to the cleaners. One of them, a waiter, had supplied the information Kozlowski needed. In return he received a hundred quid cash, which he promptly spent on crack to smoke at the first available opportunity.

Under cover of the grey dawn, at the witching hour when the nightshift were on their last legs and the dayshift were nowhere near to replacing them, six black-clad figures emerged from the trees surrounding the southern side of the stately home.

A broad expanse of manicured lawn was between them and the house. Two uniformed officers patrolled on foot, doing a continual circuit of the house, deep in conversation about the state of the job and society in general, occasionally segueing into a debate of Tottenham versus Fulham.

Neither officer noticed the red dot appear on the side of their head, and both dropped without a sound as a suppressed 5.56mm round punched through their skulls.

The six figures were at the side of the house in seconds, dragging the two bodies with them into the shadows. In the parking circle at the front sat a patrol car with steamed windows.

The older cop behind the wheel was fast asleep, head back and snoring for Britain while his offsider was on stag. The younger passenger, Jacob Jones, was twenty five years old and still a probationer. Prior to joining the force he had served four years in the Royal Marines, with a tour of Afghanistan under his belt.

So far the cops had been a lot less exciting than he'd thought it would be. But compared to the military, it had a good pension, long term job security and he was far less likely to get blown up by a Tellytubby.

He glanced at his watch. Six minutes until he and Roy swapped with the other two for a stint on patrol. He sighed, barely able to hear it over Roy's chainsaw. Christ this was boring, and his feet were cold. Roy was hard work too. A fat old dude just counting the days to retirement, he hadn't exactly been thrilled about getting saddled with a young black guy from Peckham as his trainee.

Jacob shuffled in his seat, farted, and turned to look out his window. He looked straight into the muzzle of a suppressed M4 and the last thing he saw was a bright flash of light.

Roy woke with a start, gave a harrumph, and put a hand to the wetness on his left cheek. He didn't have time to realise it was blood before a round punched through his temple and he slumped sideways.

The six men in black moved into the building with smooth efficiency. They were well trained and had done this many times before, clearing buildings in the shit holes of the world. The only difference was that now they were better paid, weren't hampered by rules of engagement and swore no allegiance to a flag.

46

The Director woke suddenly, unsure of why.

He was normally a deep sleeper, especially after a nightcap like he'd sunk with the Aussie, Rod. He lay in the darkness silently, his ears straining.

Christ it had been a long time since he'd been in the field, but something had pricked his sixth sense and he had to listen to it. He heard the tiniest of sounds, a muffled slap like someone had dropped a wet towel on the floor. It could have been anything but he knew it wasn't.

None of the protection guys had suppressed weapons, which meant someone else was in the building.

The Director heaved himself out of bed, his feet cold on the floor, and crossed to the door. He quietly snibbed the lock and backed away to where his phone sat on the bedside table. He hit a number on speed dial, directly into the Ops Room back in Auckland.

The voice that answered was young and male.

'Papa One-One,' the Director whispered rapidly, 'code red, Sierra Sierra, code red, Sierra Sierra.' Ingoe had assigned him the callsign of Papa II, assuring him that it was not a veiled reference to him being the Division's father. The Director wasn't so sure.

'Got that sir.' Not a moment's hesitation. 'Keep the line open. How many?'

'Unknown.'

'Are you safe right now?'

The door handle turned quietly. 'No,' the Director said calmly. 'I'm about to be taken.'

The door crashed inwards at the same time as the door across the hall, where Rod slept. Weapon-mounted tactical lights swept the room and settled on the Director.

He immediately dropped to his knees, taking the phone with him. He managed to flick it face down on the rug before a boot slammed into his gut and took the wind from his lungs.

He hit the floor, all thoughts of the open line gone, and rough hands grabbed him.

47

Bern, Switzerland
Wednesday, 0530 hours

The room was in darkness aside from a floor level light that Archer had left on in the hallway.

It was enough for him to see Izzy exit the bedroom, her feet silent on the carpet. He stirred in the armchair and checked the time. 05:30. Probably a toilet stop for her. Almost time to get up anyway.

He took a draught of water from the glass on the table beside him and stretched. It was then he realised that she was not in the bathroom at all, but in front of him, watching him silently. She was clad in a T-shirt and panties and her legs were smooth and pale in the murky light. Her hair was mussed up from sleep and she ran a hand through to tousle it. He sat up, waiting for her to tell him what was on her mind.

'I'm a grown woman,' she said quietly. 'I make my own decisions.'

Aaahh.

Archer sat up straighter and she stepped forward, climbed onto the armchair and straddled his lap. He instinctively put his hands to her hips and she rested hers on his shoulders.

'I make my own decisions,' she repeated, looking him in the eye.

He nodded. 'Fair enough.'

He could feel himself responding as she pressed her heat against him, and he slid his hands up her sides, under the T-shirt. Izzy lifted the T-shirt over her head and dropped it. Her breasts were perfectly round and firm and he cupped them in his hands, feeling her nipples harden against his thumbs.

She leaned down and kissed him on the lips, softly at first, then with more hunger as he pushed back.

She had said what she wanted to say and Archer was not a man to argue with a strong-minded lady.

48

———

Auckland, New Zealand
Wednesday, 1407 hours

The call had come in via the ops room and Ingoe had hit the ground running. Murray was still on deck and reacted admirably, despite his fetish for ladies' tea.

'Mobilise Archer,' Ingoe said, barging into the ops room in sweaty gym gear. 'And get me Papakura on the line, we need Special Forces.'

They both knew that was a call he could not officially authorise, but that he would be making it regardless.

As Murray was hitting a speed dial number, Ingoe's mind was churning. Nowhere near panic, but a definite sense of urgency that would lead to efficient and accurate decision making. Panic led to confusion and mistakes.

'Get hold of Jack Travis and his team,' Ingoe said, crossing to his desk to grab the ringing extension. 'Get them in the air too. And as soon as this call is over I need you to get me Five on the line.'

He grabbed the phone. 'Ingoe here, who've I got?'

49

London, England
Wednesday, 0755 hours

The engine of the BMW patrol car was a throaty roar which, combined with the screaming siren, had Archer and Izzy well on edge. As if the news that their bosses had been kidnapped wasn't enough.

They sat in the back and held on for dear life as the young driver expertly threw the car about on their way from the hotel to the scene. Ingoe came back on the line and Archer kept the phone clamped to his ear, straining to hear. Izzy was doing the same beside him, an exact mirror image as she liaised with her own outfit.

'It's a hotel under construction,' Ingoe said. 'Getting stripped out and refurbished. The kidnappers have called again, they reckon it's wired to blow and they have cameras in place to ensure their instructions are followed.'

'What are they asking for?' Archer bumped his head against the window as the patrol car took a hard left at speed. At this rate they'd be lucky to make it to the scene at all.

Ingoe paused a second before replying. 'You,' he said.

Archer blinked with surprise. 'Me?'

'They've specifically said they want Captain Archer of the New Zealand SIS to enter the building. For what purpose, they haven't said. They have instructed you to speak to them when you get there. Oh, and you have a deadline. Three minutes to get there.'

'What's our ETA, fellas?'

The passenger checked the GPS in his hand. 'About four minutes, sir.'

'Make it three,' Archer said. 'I've got a deadline.'

He braced himself as the car accelerated harder still. 'We'll be there,' he told Ingoe.

THE DIRECTOR FELT himself floating to the surface.

His head was thumping and he felt he wanted to vomit. Whatever the kidnappers had doped him with wasn't chloroform, but it was nasty stuff. His mouth was taped shut.

He raised his head gingerly. His hands were locked in steel handcuffs, each arm extended out so he sat in a crucifix position. There was a wall against his back and a hard wood floor beneath him.

He saw Rod to his right, the Canadian Adam opposite him, Adam's 2i/c Lucy next then Rod's assistant Cameron to the Director's left. Five captives, chained together, sitting in a circle facing inwards. The Director was pleased he didn't have an assistant with him; at least that was one less captive.

He wondered what had happened to the bodyguards back at the hotel. Dead, he presumed. And the hotel staff. And the cops outside. Whoever had done this was bloody motivated and equipped, and he had a fair idea who it could be.

He forced himself to swallow, trying to moisten his throat. He worked his tongue around the inside of his mouth to create saliva. That bloody nightcap probably hadn't helped.

He took a deep breath and lifted his head properly. They were in an open space of what looked like an abandoned building. The walls were stripped and the floor was bare. The windows were exposed and sunlight was coming in.

He could see a skyline out there but couldn't see a landmark of any sort. He presumed they were in London, but it could just as well have been Birmingham or Manchester or Edinburgh. Or Paris or Berlin.

Looking around, the Director realised he had no idea where they were or why. His fellow captives all appeared to still be out of it.

He scanned the room again. It looked like maybe a ball room or a restaurant. He spotted a camera mounted on the wall opposite, a small fish eye lens. There was another on the other wall, another up above him, beside an electronic clock of some sort.

Whoever had them wanted to watch.

Kozlowski turned to Rick, standing beside him and looking over his shoulder at the laptop monitor.

'Time to do your thing, Rick,' he said. 'One job to prove your loyalty.'

Rick nodded. His jaw was set and he had his game face on. Krystal put a gentle hand on his shoulder.

'You're all clear on this?' she said.

He nodded.

'Archer will come up and try to defuse the device, thinking it's on a timer. I act like I'm going to blow myself up, only mine's a dud. I back out with the girl as a hostage, you activate the device and take out Archer and the hostages, and you pick me up on the roof. In the confusion we escape by helicopter and keep the girl as collateral just in case. When we reach our RV we dump the girl and go.' He grinned, a big dumb grin for a big dumb man. 'And Morocco, here we come.'

'Here we come, baby,' Krystal cooed. She reached up and kissed him firmly on the mouth. 'Good times ahead.'

'Good times,' he agreed.

'Now go. See you on the roof.'

Rick slapped her on the ass and headed to the door. The suicide vest he wore looked exactly like the sort of vest that bombers wore the world over.

Rick knew it wasn't real though, because he'd put it together himself. Krystal had helped him that, and if there was anyone he could trust, it was her, right?

He banged the door shut behind him.

Krystal turned to Kozlowski. He regarded her coolly, with just a flicker of smugness.

'No problems there,' he said.

'Think he knows?'

Kozlowski scoffed. 'Not a clue, the damn imbecile. He's perfect for what we need him for.'

Krystal gave a humourless smile. 'It's a shame. He's been a great ride.'

50

The safe forward point was organised chaos.

Archer had to give it to the Met, they were damn good at critical incidents. Experience counted.

A pair of men and a woman fronted Archer and Izzy as soon as they arrived. One of the men was a uniformed Superintendent, the other could only have been a spook. The woman was the only one he knew.

Sarah O'Loughlin from MI5. They had worked together before, a working relationship that had been clouded by a personal one. He hadn't seen her for several months and she looked good.

'You took your time,' the superintendent grumbled.

Archer ignored him. 'Hello Locky.'

Locky gave a nod and a brief smile, her game face on. He took the hint. She passed a black hardened plastic attache case to him. 'One of your embassy staff delivered this here for you.'

The superintendent looked at it and balked.

'I certainly hope that's not...'

'Clean underwear and a cut lunch,' Locky said smoothly, glancing at Archer up and down. 'He probably needs one more than the other.'

'You're Captain Archer, I take it?' The superintendent had the ruddy jowls of an enthusiastic drinker.

'Pleased to meet you.' Archer put out his hand and the man ignored it.

'Follow me.'

They hurried to a mobile command post where they found a negotiator waiting with a spare headset. People were bustling everywhere. Emergency tape was strung up, cones and barriers were set up and the whole thing had an air of efficiency about it.

Archer stepped into the truck and took a seat beside the negotiator, a thin man who smelled of cigarettes and tension.

'I have Captain Archer here,' the negotiator said into his mouthpiece.

'I'm here,' Archer added. 'Who am I speaking to?'

'An old friend.'

He hadn't heard Kozlowski's voice in a year, and he felt an instant chill run down his back.

'It's so good to see you again, Craig. And I see you brought your little Canadian friend too. That's great.'

'What is it you want, Kozlowski?'

'I heard you and Eva have gone your separate ways. Shame.'

Archer remained silent. He wasn't a trained negotiator, but he knew when he was being baited.

'And I have your boss here,' Kozlowski continued, unperturbed. 'And a bunch of his friends. They're not very happy about being here, I have to say.'

'You killed a bunch of people this morning, Kozlowski,' Archer said. 'Most of them unarmed. Is that how you play these days? I thought you'd be more of a man about it. It's clearly me you want, so why not come out and get me?'

There was a chuckle down the line. 'Oh Craig, I couldn't give a damn about you, I really couldn't. It's very arrogant of you to think so.' He tut-tutted. 'No no, we're not playing that game today. Today is just a test.'

'Of what?'

'Of your speed and skill, of course. I have five people here, all chained together, with a bomb set to a timer. You need to come and rescue them.'

Archer glanced at the superintendent, who was shaking his head vigorously.

'No problem,' Archer said, watching the superintendent's ruddy complexion lighten several shades. He was already breaking out in a sweat.

'I'll even let you bring your little friend with you for company, how's that?' Kozlowski had a chirpy tone to his voice.

'I won't need her,' Archer said, and Kozlowski cut him off.

'No no, she comes or they die. That's how this works. Understand?'

Archer raised an eyebrow at Izzy, who was leaning against his shoulder to listen. She gave him a quizzical look but nodded.

'Alright,' Archer said. 'Let's get this done.'

51

Krystal Raines flexed her fingers and rolled her shoulders as she paced the room.

It was an internal meeting room that afforded them privacy from the snipers who were undoubtedly set up outside.

The tension was unbelievable, a constant tremor running through her body as events unfolded. She'd never felt anything like it. This was it; this was the goal. The next twenty minutes or so would bring about change. Everything that she'd worked so hard for would now pay off.

She felt a twinge of regret about sending Rick downstairs to meet with Archer, but just a twinge. There was a greater goal here that needed to be achieved, and who better to help her reach it than an American war veteran and mercenary?

The United States and their warmongering ways, their extraordinary rendition of civilians who would never see the inside of a courtroom – kidnapping by any other name – their torture of innocents.

It would all come out.

The CIA and their use of Black Star contractors to do their dirty work, killing the supposed enemies of the West, judge, jury and executioner all rolled into one.

The support given to the US by their fawning minions, the UK, Canada, Australia and New Zealand. The Five Eyes network was nothing more than a snooping service for the US and it had been a great plan of Kozlowski's to attack that.

The fact that they still had undiscovered moles on the inside spoke to the man's brilliance.

Capstick's capture only added weight to the cause. The US and their Canadian puppets would be forced to either release him or kill him. If they released him they risked a hugely damaging expose, so damaging in fact that it could bring them to their knees. Kill him and the truth would come out anyway.

A video recorded statement from Rick would be released on the internet soon after she and Kozlowski made their escape, telling the world what had happened and why.

Poor Rick thought he was selling Archer a dummy and executing a perfect cover to allow their getaway.

The poor dumb fool.

Krystal trembled with anticipation, the sensation so strong that it was arousing. He was certainly assisting them in their escape, but really, he hadn't thought this through at all. If they had been so foolish as to place themselves right in the thick of the action and rely on a last-ditch helicopter pick up for their escape, when they were surrounded by cops and special forces, then they didn't deserve the credit they were about to get.

She glanced over to where Kozlowski was pulling on a pair of black pants. He had a white shirt, a hi-viz vest and a safety helmet on the floor beside him. A clipboard and ID tag completed the outfit of a council inspector.

A similar ensemble was ready for her too.

'Krystal.' Kozlowski tucked in his shirt and gestured towards her gear. 'You need to get ready.'

It was helluva risky being here, so close to the action, but it was also a move the enemy would never anticipate. Doing so was the action of either a madman or a genius, and there was a fine line between the two. Kozlowski wanted to be here – needed to be here – to ensure it all went to plan.

When it all went down they would simply walk out of the building amidst the chaos and lose themselves in the crowd. If that failed, they had a back-up plan, and a back-up to the back-up plan, but Kozlowski was confident. That bolstered her own confidence.

The two gunners at the door watched as she joined their leader. They were two of the team who had made the snatch this morning. The other four had dissipated, one to pick up the chopper and standby, three to mingle into the crowd ready to create further diversions to cover their escape.

All six of them were Chechens, battle hardened and with a deep hatred of the West. They knew they were unlikely to be walking away unscathed today, but that was of no consequence to men like this. They lived to fight and they lived to strike back. To have such an opportunity, right in the heart of London, was an honour.

Krystal stripped to her underwear, knowing that both gunners were watching her. She didn't care – she was the last semi-naked woman they would ever see. She dressed quickly, tucked in her shirt, and put on her safety hat.

She turned to Kozlowski. 'Let's do it.'

He gave a firm nod, his dark eyes glittering. 'We're making history here, Krystal.'

She trembled again and gave a nervous smile. 'People will remember us and what we did.'

52

The instructions from Kozlowski had been clear.

The tenth floor was where the hostages were being held. No time limit was given, but it was clear that there was no room for delay.

Twenty flights of stairs was a decent workout. Add in the expectation of being slotted or blown up, and it was enough to make an average person curl up in the corner and wet themselves.

Archer and Izzy didn't have that option. They had to get in there and deal with whatever they found.

Snipers were dotted about on neighbouring buildings, but the hotel had been well chosen. Not only was it higher than any other building in the block, but most of the windows were tinted, prohibiting any views in.

Reaching the ninth floor landing, Archer paused to listen and catch his breath. The building felt silent and empty. Outside was a cacophony of noise and activity, muffled somewhat by the double glazing and distance.

He couldn't shake the feeling that they were walking into the lions den.

'Okay?' he said.

Izzy was a couple of steps below him. 'Uh-huh.' She nodded and wiped sweat from her brow. 'So when were you screwing her?'

'Say what?'

'The MI5 woman. I take it that's all over?'

He hesitated, not quite knowing what to say. They were about to attempt a hostage rescue of some sort, and she wanted to know about a past conquest. Women – unbelievable.

'Long ago,' he said. 'Ancient history. And I think we have more important things to worry about right now, don't you?'

Izzy gave a nonchalant shrug. 'Just checking.'

Archer shook his head in amazement. 'Come on,' he said, 'and remember to follow my lead.'

They took the last two flights and paused again at the door. Izzy gave him a nod and Archer opened the door.

THE DIRECTOR HEARD the door open and looked up.

He saw Archer and the Canadian girl enter cautiously. The big meathead in the suicide vest grinned when he saw them. He lifted his right hand in the air, showing them the dead-man switch in his hand, the thumb firmly pressed down on the plunger. Releasing that grip would activate the explosives strapped to him, hence the name.

The Director made eye contact with Archer as his man swept the group of hostages. Archer gave him a small nod and a questioning look.

The Director nodded back and used his chin to indicate the bomb in front of him. Archer nodded again and turned his gaze to the man in the suicide vest.

A RADIO SKITTERED across the floor towards Archer. The man in the suicide vest gestured with his free hand for Archer to pick it up.

He bent and did so, keeping his eyes on the man at all times.

Normally radios were a no-no anywhere near explosive devices, but he could see that this was a completely rubberised military-grade secure unit. These guys knew what they were about alright.

'You have a choice, Mr Archer.' Kozlowski's voice was loud and clear over the radio, and Archer could almost hear the smile in his voice. 'You have two available options, but only enough time to complete one task.'

Archer's heart was pounding in his chest and, despite the man's resolve, he could see the apprehension in the Director's face as he struggled against his bonds. He knew there was no way he could break free.

'The man in front of you has a bomb strapped to him. No doubt you have seen the dead man's switch, so you know you cannot just shoot him. If that bomb detonates, you all die. If the bomb beside the VIPs detonates, you all die. Do you see where this is going, Mr Archer?'

'I'm getting the general idea.'

'Good. If you don't disarm the device, the man in the vest will detonate his. If you try to negotiate a surrender from him without attempting to disarm the other device, he will detonate his. Your only chance at saving everyone and being the hero that you always wanted to be, is to disarm the main device first. Do you understand?'

'I get it,' Archer transmitted. 'You want to see me try to do it and then blow it up anyway, is that it?'

There was a pause then a slight chuckle. 'So cynical, Mr Archer. Either way you're like a rat in a trap. You have to follow my orders whether you like it or not.' There was a definite chuckle in his voice now, and Archer knew he was loving every second of the torture he was inflicting. This was delicious nectar to a man like Kozlowski.

'What's it going to be, Mr Archer?'

Archer's eyes darted between the hostages and the man in the suicide vest. The Director was staring at him intently. The other dignitaries were still coming around but no doubt they would also be terrified out of their minds soon enough.

'You'll kill us all either way,' Archer said, playing for time. 'So what does it matter what I do?'

'It always matters, Mr Archer. But you're right, you are playing a game of chance. There's a chance you won't complete a task. There's a chance you will all die anyway. But you still have a choice to make. Back away now and you and your friend will be safe.'

'How about you come here to me and we do this man to man? Stop fucking around, hiding behind other people. Come and face me, Kozlowski.' He could feel the anger welling inside him, threatening to boil over. Maybe that was what Kozlowski wanted.

'No no no,' Kozlowski chided him. 'That's not how this works. And you're wasting time, Mr Archer.' His voice hardened. 'Make a decision. Your time starts now.'

Sure enough, the clock on the wall above the hostages flashed into life, big red numbers lighting up. The digits immediately clicked off from 3:00 to 2:59 and the race was on.

Archer made a snap decision and he knew he was fucked. Whatever decision he made right now, death was inevitable.

53

Archer scrambled across to the group of five VIPS, huddled together with their wrists handcuffed to each other. All of them had their mouths taped shut.

The device sat in the middle of their circle, connected to a length of detonation cord that entwined all five of them. Even activating the det cord alone would be enough to cause grievous injuries, if not actually kill them all.

Affixed to the device itself, which was a package wrapped in black electrical tape, was a digital timer. The red digits were counting down in unison with the clock on the wall.

The Director met his gaze again, his eyes steady and deadly serious. He gave Archer a short nod. Archer quickly glanced at the other VIPs, recognising them all.

All of them were in various states of grogginess but coming around, and must have been aware of what was going on.

Archer checked the timer. 02:48.

Fuck. He'd dealt with plenty of explosives in his time but this was a job for an EOD specialist. It wasn't simply a matter of cutting the red wire then the blue one; all the wires looked the same and it would take an age to dissect the damned thing. Time was something he didn't have, so this was going to have to be a far more robust operation than was ideal.

'Fuck it,' he muttered to himself, 'he's gunna kill us anyway.'

He saw the Director scowl and he mentally shrugged. If they lived long enough for the Director to chastise him, they'd both be happy.

Archer leaned between the two Canadians to the device, running his eye over it quickly to check for a mercury switch. Couldn't see it, so time to crack on.

It was highly likely that the timer had been rigged to blow if it was disconnected. The battery below it gave the power supply. Any messing with that and the thing would go up. Archer couldn't see how he could disable the device within the two and a half minutes that were remaining.

He felt the Director's gaze on him, and glanced up. The Director was scowling and jerking his head downwards, using it to point at the floor. Archer frowned, not wanting to get distracted. What the hell was he on about?

The Director was no operator, but one thing he was, was deadly serious. Something told Archer that whatever the man was on about, it was important. He leaned over and yanked the tape from the Director's mouth in one quick swipe. It must have stung like hell but the Director barely flinched.

'Under me,' he gasped. 'Pressure switch.'

Archer felt his guts drop. Of course. The clever bastard had rigged it so that it would blow as soon as the Director was moved. He would know Archer would try and move his boss. If all else failed, it was the safety net to make sure they went up in smoke.

Archer nodded and looked to Izzy.

'Pressure switch under him,' he said, his throat like sandpaper. 'Probably under all of them. See if you can see any.'

She physically recoiled but dropped to the floor to check.

'Careful,' he said. 'Don't lift them up to do it, but you need to check.'

'Okay.' She muttered something that he couldn't make out, but it sounded like she was praying. All told, he figured it wasn't a bad idea.

The red digits gleamed. 02:15.

None of the other hostages were conscious enough to be of any assistance to him. They wouldn't register what he was telling them, let alone be able to carry out instructions properly. The pressure of responsibility bore down on him like a ton weight and cold sweat looked down his temples and back.

02:09.

There was only one thing he could do, and that was to remove the detonator from the circuit. He could see where it was, and was just reaching for it when Kozlowski's voice came over the radio.

'Oh Mr Archer,' he said in a sing-song voice, 'I forgot to mention something. There is only one live device.'

Archer froze, cocking his head.

Kozlowski laughed. 'That's right. You're looking at two devices, but only one is live. Which one is it?' He chuckled again. 'You decide, Mr Archer. But make it snappy. Things are about to get hot in there.'

And in that moment, Archer knew without a doubt. Kozlowski would want to cause maximum pain. Killing intelligence bosses was not fatal to an organisation. Huge damage, no doubt, but not irreparable.

It was Archer that he wanted.

'Craig?' Izzy's voice wavered. 'I don't see any pressure pads, but I'm not sure. Can't tell without moving them.'

01:52. No time to fuck about now. This was do or die.

He leaned right over to the device between the VIPs, turned it gently in his hands, and ran through a mental checklist. It had everything it needed to go bang. Detonator, timer, explosive. It was a live bomb, ticking away towards detonation.

But if that was the case, he saw no need for the man in the suicide vest, standing just a few metres away, watching him intently. Thumb pressed down on the dead man's switch, jaw set, game face on. This guy was serious.

Either both bombs were live, or the one in his hands was a dud. The vest had to be live, and that was obviously Kozlowski's method of killing them all. There was no way Archer could get to the guy in time and prevent the switch being released. It was decision time.

01:43.

'Brace yourselves,' Archer muttered, even though no amount of bracing would do any of them any good at all.

He yanked the battery from the circuit with one hard jerk and the timer went dead. He froze.

There was no blinding, deafening explosion. He stayed where he was, battery pack in one hand, device in the other. His bladder was threatening to burst. The Director looked at him with wide eyes.

'What the...'

54

———

Rick felt his bladder contract when he saw the guy grip the device.

He knew what was about to happen and there was not a damn thing he could do to stop it. He half turned away but even as he did so, nothing happened. He saw the dismantled bomb in the guy's hands.

'What the fuck?' he muttered, pressing down harder on the trigger in his hand.

Somehow the guy had dismantled a live bomb without killing them all, in the crudest fashion possible. Unbelievable.

He saw Archer hold the device up to show Izzy.

'It's a dud,' he said hoarsely. 'A fake.'

Even as Rick was processing that thought, a realisation was pounding in his brain. If that one was fake, then...

He looked down at the device strapped to his chest.

01:28.

Archer and Izzy moved at the same time. The big man in the suicide vest was staring down at the timer on his chest, a confused look on his face. He was five metres away from Archer, four from Izzy.

He looked up as Izzy was almost on him, and threw a defensive fend into her face. She grabbed at him anyway, giving Archer a split second more to get on him. He clamped his left hand onto the guy's right, locking onto the thumb and holding on for dear life.

Rick got his free hand to Archer's face, scrabbling for his eyes, but that allowed Izzy to come in and throw an arm around his neck from behind. She was lifted off the floor as he bucked against her but she clung on, locking a forearm across his throat and securing the grip with her free hand.

Rick grabbed at her, Archer wrenched his arm and wrestled it behind him, gripping the thumb down hard. Rick was growling and they were staggering like drunks.

Archer could see only one solution if this guy wasn't going to surrender. Cranking the pressure on Rick's wrist, he lifted the man onto his tip-toes and manoeuvred him towards the floor to ceiling plate glass windows.

Izzy was still swinging on his neck, her legs flailing, and Rick seemed more interested in trying to tear her off than the guy trying to break his wrist. Archer used it to his advantage, stepping and staggering across the floor towards the windows. He wasn't sure if the suicide vest was actually rigged to the dead man's switch or if it was running on the timer, or maybe both as a failsafe.

But knowing the lethal effects of high explosives, he couldn't take the chance. They had to get this guy and his vest away from the hostages, and if that meant that Archer went out the window with him, then so be it.

Rick got a hand to Izzy's hair and was yanking at it but there was no way she was letting go. Archer got them closer to the windows, really piling the pressure on the big man's wrist now, just a few metres away from the glass, and the penny finally dropped.

Rick stopped grabbing at Izzy and went for Archer instead, trying to get a hand in his face. Archer ducked and dived, getting a couple of fingernail scrapes across his face, and Izzy dropped off the man's back.

Finally free of the weight, Rick reared up, swinging at Archer awkwardly. Izzy kicked him in the knee but he didn't even flinch, so she went higher, delivering a front snap kick straight in the balls.

He buckled forward, all thoughts of attack now gone, and Archer grabbed him by the back of the vest.

He charged for the window, powering hard with his legs and propelling Rick's weight, gaining momentum across the last few metres. Rick realised at the last second that he was going to lose this fight and let out a shriek or rage and fear, but it was too late.

He crashed head first into the plate glass window, powerless to stop himself, and hurtled out into space, both his arms wind milling wildly as if he could stop himself falling. The inevitable failure to stay airborne didn't matter, as the counter on his chest clicked from 00:01 to 00:00.

The explosion was enough to crack more windows on the hostages' floor as a cloud of red body parts and smoke filled the air outside.

Archer looked at Izzy lying sprawled on the floor near him.

'Okay?' he shouted.

She nodded and got to her feet. Archer rolled on his side and looked out the shattered window. Maybe his ears were tricks, but he thought he heard small arms fire out there.

55

―――

As they watched the death struggle taking place on the monitor, Kozlowski cursed to himself.

He grabbed the second radio from the table and pressed the talk button.

'All stations from Leader, stand by.'

The three gunners down on ground level would be readying themselves to attack, and not a moment too soon. Kozlowski could see what was going to happen, and he knew what would follow.

'The SAS will be coming straight through those doors any second and cut off our escape,' he said, 'we need to move.'

They saw Rick crash through the window and two seconds later there was an explosion outside.

'All stations from Leader, go go go! Big Bird, come and get us.' He shoved the radio in his pocket and stood, turning to the two gunners by the door. 'You two get down there and get me the girl. I want some collateral. Bring her to the roof.'

They left without a word, pistols drawn. Kozlowski closed the monitor down and stood up. Krystal looked at him with a raised eyebrow.

'Let's go,' he said.

THE DOOR CRASHED inwards at the same time as Archer was turning, and he saw the two grenades sailing inwards.

'Down!' His voice sounded detached to him. He threw himself sideways, arms over his head, eyes closed and mouth partially open.

The grenades went off almost simultaneously, but instead of shredding the occupants with shrapnel, they detonated with an ear-splitting series of bangs and blinding flashes of magnesium.

Archer kept his head down and moved his hands to his ears as the nine-bangers did their magic. Everybody within the room would be disoriented by the flashbangs, allowing whoever was coming through the door a momentary advantage.

He rolled onto his side as soon as he sensed the bangs had stopped, and saw two guys in jeans and jackets heading for the door, dragging someone else. One of the guys spotted him and raised a pistol, ripping off several shots as they got to the doorway.

Izzy was struggling in their grip and she slowed them down as they manoeuvred through the gap.

Archer got the Glock 26 out and fired a double tap, shooting instinctively rather than aiming. The pistol was an extension of him and he wanted to kill the two men.

The guy who'd fired took a round in the shoulder, pirouetted and took the second in the back.

The second guy returned fire and Archer felt an impact slam into his right forearm, throwing the Glock from his grasp. He rolled, pushing up and groping for the gun with his left hand.

Izzy and the guy were gone.

One quick look told him that the Director was out of the game, lolling drunkenly against his colleagues from the effects of the twin flashbangs. It struck Archer now that things were turning to shit, otherwise why would they grab Izzy? That seemed unplanned, just as the guy in the suicide vest had been surprised to realise he was about to blow up. Whatever the hell was going on, he had no time to figure it out right now. Izzy had been grabbed and he needed to get her back.

His right arm was numb and blood was flowing down inside his sleeve.

He stepped over the body of the man he'd dropped, putting a round through his head as he did so, and checked the hallway outside. Clear. Footsteps on the stairwell, going up.

He followed, ducking back when a shot pinged off the railing, then raced forward with his gun up. He was good enough with his left hand, but hopefully he wouldn't need a speedy mag change.

He continued up, the footsteps and sounds of a struggle still above him. One floor to go and he heard a door bang. Voices. He moved again, gun up, eyes everywhere, ears straining.

A creak, a sniff then a shadow moving. Archer pulled back slightly, two flights to go, the shadow on the top level, waiting for him. He scuffed his foot on the floor and the shadow moved.

A gunman showed himself over the top railing, a pistol pointing down towards Archer. Their eyes met.

Archer fired first, two shots. The gunman squeezed one off, took a hit to the torso and jerked sideways. Archer ripped off another double tap and another, the gunman jerking and twisting again before falling forward against the railing.

He hung like a rag doll, arms dangling, eyes staring at Archer. The gun was still in his hand, still pointing in Archer's direction.

The last shot blew a third nostril through his face and his head snapped back then lolled forward again. Fluid was drooling from the hole when Archer cleared the stairs. He left the guy hanging and paused, checking his surroundings, the Glock's slide locked open and gun smoke curling from the barrel and open chamber. The landing was small and had only one exit door, which opened outwards. Presumably a roof access point.

He could hear sounds beyond the door but couldn't make out what they were. A chopper, maybe? Probably cops or a news crew.

He took a knee and did a one-handed magazine change as quick as he could, shoving the empty mag back into his pocket. His right arm was throbbing like hell now and still bleeding. No time for repairs yet; he had to push on.

He cracked the door gently and paused. With no idea what was on the other side it was a death funnel, and he didn't want to wait around. Izzy had gone through here.

He took a breath, shouldered the door and charged through. Sunlight and open air all around him.

As soon as he cleared the door frame he threw himself to the right, hitting the ground and rolling once, coming up in a crouch. Punching the Glock out, he scanned.

He was on the rooftop, the cityscape all around. A chopper was hovering off the far side of the roof, a plain white Bell.

Facing him near the edge, maybe twenty metres away, was Izzy.

Her head was arched back painfully, the man behind her holding her savagely by the hair. An arm across her shoulder had a pistol aimed at Archer. Her eyes were on Archer, but it wasn't her he wanted to see. He shifted slightly so he could see better.

The man holding her also shifted, and Archer saw his face for the first time.

Viktor Kozlowski.

56

'Let her go, Kozlowski,' Archer bellowed. 'You've got nowhere to go.'

The Glock was up and his arm was steady.

Kozlowski shifted his stance, holding Izzy directly in front of him as a shield. Izzy grimaced as he pulled her into position by the hair.

'That's where you're wrong, Archer,' he shouted back. 'I have a helicopter and a hostage. What do you have?'

'Ten rounds and nothing better to do.' Archer ran his eyes over Izzy. He couldn't see any obvious injuries, and the clever bastard was perfectly shielded by her, even placing his legs directly behind hers.

Kozlowski laughed. 'So what're you gonna do, shoot down a helicopter with your little peashooter? Even if you did, you'd kill a lot of innocent people down there, and that wouldn't do, would it?'

He was right of course. A chopper plunging into the city streets was a disaster any way you looked at it. Beyond the terrorist and his hostage, Archer could see the side door of the chopper was open. A guy sat there with an assault rifle in his hands, good to go. No doubt he was in radio contact with Kozlowski and would happily drop Archer if given the command.

'No, Mr Archer,' Kozlowski continued. 'I think you need to just step away from this one. If you play nicely I'll let you live to fight another day. Maybe I won't even put a bullet in her brain, who knows.'

Izzy squirmed against him then cried out as he yanked savagely on her hair.

'No you won't,' Archer spat. 'Neither of us is walking away from here Kozlowski, and you know it.'

'You're partially right, Archer. I'll be flying out of here.'

At that the chopper moved closer, the *whupp-whupp* of its rotors loud and the down blast scattering leaves and debris across the roof.

Archer squinted against it, watching as Kozlowski shifted backwards, moving Izzy with him, closer to the edge. There was a low parapet around the lip of the roof.

Beyond them there was another chopper coming into view, heading in their direction.

'Back away and be a good boy, Archer,' Kozlowski shouted.

The white Bell came right in now, the door gunner ready with his weapon trained on Archer. The dust storm kicked up was almost blinding.

Archer edged forward, his left arm starting to ache deeply inside. Kozlowski moved back to the parapet, stepped up onto it awkwardly with Izzy still in front of him.

There would be a moment when he was exposed, there had to be, just a fleeting moment when he was out from cover. It was all that Archer would need to finish this.

But the risk was that Izzy would be killed anyway.

Archer edged forward, sliding his feet on the gritty surface of the roof, breathing slow and deep. The gunner moved to the side, maintaining a clear visual on Archer. The weapon in his hands was an M4 and at this range he couldn't miss.

'Back down, Mr Archer,' Kozlowski shouted, 'or I'll drop her right now.'

He yanked Izzy backwards over the parapet, her legs flying up in the air as she went off balance, her upper body out of sight for

Archer. Kozlowski was fully exposed now, but he was right – if Archer dropped him, he would drop Izzy.

The Bell nudged right up to the edge, the rotors whipping up a frenzy. It occurred to Archer that they might just blow Izzy and Kozlowski off the edge anyway and everything else would be moot.

The chopper in the background was closing in, and Archer saw Kozlowski's pilot glance that way.

'Okay, okay,' he bellowed, raising his hands in the air. 'I'm out.'

He saw Kozlowski grin and press the pistol in his hand against Izzy's body. The pilot was saying something and the door gunner cocked his head, momentarily distracted. Kozlowski twitched his head at the same time, his gaze shifting off Archer for the tiniest fraction of a second.

It was all it took for hell to break loose.

Archer's left hand dropped, the Glock arcing down on line to the door gunner. The first shot took the man straight in the forehead and knocked him backwards, spraying the interior of the cabin with blood and brain matter. The M4 fired as the gunner fell backwards, a burst of rounds chewing up the roof in a line to Archer's left.

The short barrel of the Glock swung right, his trigger finger closed smoothly, and a second round blasted through Kozlowski's right chest.

He flung his arm out for balance, released his grip on Izzy and wobbled backwards on the parapet. Kozlowski grabbed at his chest with his left hand, brought his gun back towards Izzy and pulled the trigger, and Archer fired a third shot. He heard a scream above the din of the rotors and saw Kozlowski take the second hit in the gut.

He was moving forward now, sprinting hard for the edge, seeing Kozlowski scrambling for the open door of the Bell. The chopper that was closing in had Police markings and was right there now, hovering off to the side. He could hear a voice over a loud hailer in the background.

He could do this, he knew he could. He was so close to getting his hands on Kozlowski and putting a stop to the madman, he could almost taste it. He was seconds away from success.

He was hit from behind with a crash, sending him sprawling to the ground, the Glock skidding loose. Krystal Raines had been hiding behind the rooftop hut that housed the access stairs and now made a break for it, shoulder charging him on the way past.

Archer rolled onto his back, saw her boot coming at his face and blocked it with both forearms, white hot pain bolting up to his right shoulder and causing a momentary burst of colours across his vision.

She went for another one and he grabbed her ankle with his left hand, yanking and twisting her off-balance, sweeping her leg with his.

She went down on her back and immediately vaulted back up, throwing herself forward onto him and going for his throat.

He tucked his chin down, grabbed her own throat and wrestled. She slid forward, straddling him until her knees were either side of his head, breaking his grip. She was breathing hard, a maniacal grin on her face as she clamped her knees on his head and shoved her thumbs into his eyes.

For some reason she was dressed like an engineer on a building site.

He squeezed his eyes shut tight and twisted his head away, but she was persistent and he could feel the intense pressure on his eyeballs.

He bucked hard, using his pelvis to throw her up, giving him enough room to get one hand onto her hair and jerk it back, the other one jabbing at her throat. She shrieked and went backwards off him.

He got up at the same time as her and she came at him again, claws out and her teeth bared, an animalistic growl coming from her throat.

Archer backed away, trying to judge the distance, and grabbed her by the front of her clothes as she got to him. He dropped, rammed his feet into her guts, and went down on his back. He jerked her upper body forward and shoved his legs out straight, still rolling back before he released her.

Krystal flew overhead, snatching at the air, and went straight over the edge of the building. A long scream sounded as she went down.

Archer was up immediately, seeing Izzy grappling with

Kozlowski. Despite his wounds Kozlowski was strong and determined, and he was getting the better of her. He hit her with a forearm across the throat, knocking her backwards.

Izzy's legs went up in the air and she went over backwards, one hand grabbing desperately at the edge of the parapet.

As Archer closed in, scooping up the fallen Glock, he could see a hand gripping the lip of the parapet, small white fingers clinging on for dear life. As he raced closer he saw a second hand join it, and he knew she was safe. The backdrop to the Bell was an office building with floor to ceiling glass, and even in the heat of the action he could clearly see people standing there, gaping.

It ruled out any shots at the helicopter from this angle.

Kozlowski was on board now, dragging himself up into the cabin and shouting at the pilot.

Fuck! In a few brief seconds they would be gone.

The Bell started to lift off, the down draft blasting Archer as he dug it in for the last few metres. No way was the bastard getting away now.

He dropped the Glock, leaped onto the parapet and threw himself off the edge of the building, arms outstretched.

57

His left arm caught the skid of the Bell and he locked on, heaving his aching right arm up over it as well.

The Bell lifted away with Archer's legs dangling in space, tossed about by the momentum, Kozlowski bellowing something unintelligible above him. As the craft banked around Archer caught a fleeting glimpse of Izzy dangling off the side of the building, trying to heave herself up.

For now she was on her own; he had enough to worry about.

The Bell banked hard left and built speed and Archer clung on for all he was worth. Buildings flashed by beneath him, terrifyingly fast and so close he could almost touch them. His right arm was almost numb from the strain and his left was locked tight over the skid. He had no idea how the hell he was going to finish this, but giving up was simply not an option.

Kozlowski had escaped him before, but today there would be no second chances.

The chopper lifted up sharply, throwing his weight off balance and dragging on his arms. He dug it in, fighting through the pain.

If he let go now he would fall to his death and one of the most wanted terrorists in the world would get away. In that moment the walls came up and blocked out the pain, and he had absolute clarity.

There was only one possible plan; kill Kozlowski. If he failed to do that, more people would die. If the chopper went down and killed innocents, well that would be a tragic consequence of saving even more innocents.

Either way, it had to be done.

The chopper was swooping low across rooftops, banking left and right, each movement bringing more drag on Archer's arms, his muscles straining to hold on. As the chopper dipped to the right he kicked up and used the motion of the aircraft to swing his right leg up onto the skid. He hooked his foot over, then his knee, and locked his foot around the skid to hold on.

'Shake the bastard off!' Kozlowski screamed above him, and Archer looked upwards. Kozlowski's face was only a metre away, spit flying from his lips as he shouted at the pilot. He was bloodied and enraged and Archer expected a bullet to come his way any moment.

He awkwardly manoeuvred his right hand under his jacket, got his fingertips to the butt of the holstered Kel-Tec, and tugged it free.

The chopper swung left and banked hard, forcing him to grab the skid with both arms again. Pain bolted up his arm into his shoulder and he felt a wave of nausea hit him. He clung on, the slipstream tearing at him as the aircraft dived towards the ground, bottomed out and rose sharply again. He caught a glimpse of the Police chopper over to the side, shadowing but unable to stop them.

Fuck it, if this didn't stop soon he was sure to be shaken off. If he could take out Kozlowski he could have a shot at climbing aboard and forcing the pilot to land at gunpoint.

Kozlowski's face appeared above him again and Archer saw a fire extinguisher swinging at his head. He ducked and slipped, swinging below the skid again, and the extinguisher clanged off the steel skid near his head.

He punched the Kel-Tec out and fired a shot, the round missing Kozlowski and pinging off the airframe.

The pilot banked hard right and Archer felt the muscles in his arms and shoulders screaming to hold on. They levelled out again and Kozlowski risked another glance, the fire extinguisher poised for another swing.

Archer fired a wild shot in the hopes of a lucky strike, but there was no such luck. The chopper banked and he saw the Thames hove into view below them, a dirty snake through the city dotted with boats of various sizes. They lifted again and he felt his weight shift, dragging his ankle free and throwing him into a pendulum swing.

His legs swung wildly beneath him and he gasped for breath. The chopper levelled then dipped again, heading low towards the water. They levelled off again so close that Archer could feel the spray on his face as they skimmed across the surface.

Kozlowski loomed above him, the fire extinguisher swung down and he felt an almighty impact on his left wrist. The thump was so powerful that he released his grip with that hand and dangled by his damaged right arm only, his feet brushing the river surface below.

He forced his left hand up again and secured a hold, glancing up as the chopper whipped beneath Tower Bridge.

The red steel cylinder of the fire extinguisher filled his vision as he looked up and Archer twisted his right hand, firing a single instinctive shot.

There was a loud bang and a burst of white powder filled the air, followed by an angry screech.

The chopper twisted, lifted and twisted again. Dry powder filled the cabin and billowed out the open door. Archer couldn't see it, but the pilot had been engulfed in it and not only couldn't see where he was going but had breathed it in and was fighting for air.

Archer hung on with all his remaining strength but he could feel himself slipping. He knew that if he didn't go now he'd end up going down with the chopper, and there was only one way that would end.

He braced himself, glanced down to see the river below him, and released his right arm, letting it hang free. He glanced back up one last time, and saw Kozlowski above him, climbing out of the cabin onto the skid. He raised his foot to stamp on Archer's hand, hanging onto the airframe with one hand.

The Kel-Tec came up and Archer fired a shot through Kozlowski's foot. The terrorist screamed, wind milling his free arm as he fought for balance.

Archer let go with his left hand, falling away as the nose of the chopper lifted again, white powder streaming from the cabin door. He fell backwards, eyes locked on Kozlowski who was grappling for the door, and he fired again. Kozlowski jerked with the impact and grabbed at the air.

The turbines were screaming as the chopper went almost vertical.

Archer squeezed the trigger again, then again, and the slide locked open. He caught a flash glimpse of Kozlowski falling from the stricken Bell, then clamped his arms across his chest as if in a coffin and made himself as straight as he could, ready for his landing.

The impact was harder than he'd anticipated and took his breath away as he knifed beneath the surface, plunging down into the murky depths of the River Thames.

Above him the chopper cut out and dropped like a stone, the rotor blades shearing off with the impact and spinning free, the chassis hitting the water with a crash and quickly submerging.

By the time Archer had kicked his way to the surface the Bell was almost completely under, drifting in the current away from him. He saw and heard the Police chopper coming in and the rotors whipped the water around him. Archer held onto the empty Kel-Tec as he tread water, kicking his legs to stay afloat. He would use the weapon to club Kozlowski to death as soon as he saw him.

He heard the roar of an engine approaching and turned to see a rigid inflatable approaching at speed, a pair of black-clad operators with MP5s at the ready. He prep'd himself to dive but as he took a deep breath he recognised a face behind the driver of the boat.

Ingoe.

The boat arced around and pulled up beside him, rocking on its own swell. Archer swum to the side and the two operators hauled him in. As soon as he was out of the water the driver gassed it and they were away again, skimming across the surface away from the wreckage.

'Kozlowski's there,' he bellowed above the din, 'we have to get him. Go back!'

An identical RIB raced past the other way with a full team of operators on board, blacked-up and carrying MP5s.

Ingoe jerked a thumb at them. 'They'll get him,' he shouted back.

Archer flopped against the side, exhausted. He gingerly cradled his wounded arm in his lap and looked at Ingoe, who crouched beside him.

'Did you hit Kozlowski?'

Archer took a moment to tip water from the barrel of the Kel-Tec. It would need a good clean after its swim. He met Ingoe's inquisitive gaze.

'I shot him four times,' he shouted above the din of the RIB's engine. 'And he went down with the chopper.' He paused for a breath. 'I don't know,' he said honestly. 'I don't know.'

'I saw it,' Ingoe said. 'Nobody could survive that.'

Archer cocked his head. 'You saw it?'

Ingoe looked grim. 'The whole thing was live streamed, there was a media crew in the air doing some aerials for the news. It's all over the internet.'

Archer shook his head and leaned back against the boat, rocking with the rhythm as they raced down the river. He closed his eyes for a minute and tried to get himself together.

But he couldn't fight the sick feeling in his gut.

58

T
he golden sand was hot beneath Archer's feet as he padded
down to the water.

The clear blue water glittered and foamed white as waves gently rolled in from the bay. A swimmer was making their way into shore. A large white cabin cruiser rolled its way easily across the mouth of the bay, trailing fishing lines behind it. Smaller fishing boats bobbed further out.

Behind Archer was the very private resort he had spent the last week at. Rest and recuperation, the doctors called it. They were worried about his mental state, not to mention the battering his body had taken.

The salt water had been good for his arm wound and the rehab he was doing to strengthen it was going well. The wound was still puckered pink and ugly and he would be having plastic surgery on it in the near future.

He was confident that in no time he'd be back to full fitness. He'd also strained ligaments in his left shoulder, which were taking some time to heal. Apparently hanging from the skid of a helicopter did that to you, although the doctors who treated him had never had a patient injured that way before.

The terror attack and successful hostage rescue in central London was fading from the news now, but there was still plenty of work going on behind the scenes. A staff member from GCSB had been quietly removed from their position and convicted on some fairly minor computer crime charges. No public mention was ever made of corruption.

The three Chechen gunmen had managed to shoot several bystanders and a couple of police officers before being dropped by snipers. All in all, two dead and nine wounded innocents was not bad, given the circumstances. The live footage was still a massive hit online, showing the explosive death of Rick, the fatal fall of Krystal Raines and the helicopter fight and crash.

There had been no trace of Kozlowski in the crashed copter or the river, and Archer knew within his bones that somehow, *somehow*, the man had managed to survive. The man was inde-fucking-structible.

The Director and his fellow hostages had escaped largely unscathed and slipped back into their agencies, working hard on rebuilding the Five Eyes network. Ethan Capstick was still in Canadian custody, whining endlessly. Lee Sweetman had turned dead in Dublin, but the supposed overdose was fooling no one. There was plenty more work to be done, and Archer felt the urge to get back to it.

He rubbed a hand over his face, the bristles of his beard rough on his palm. He wore only swimming togs, enjoying the heat of the sun on his skin.

He watched as the swimmer touched the bottom and stood.

Izzy was tanned and lean in a red bikini, rivulets of water running off her as she pushed her hair back from her face.

While dangling from the side of the hotel she'd taken a shot from Kozlowski, but it had only been a through and through flesh wound.

The entry wound above the front of her right hip and the larger exit wound behind it had also healed well and she wasn't bothered about trying to hide them.

Part of the fabric of life, she called them. Although she also noted that clearly she hadn't lived as much as Archer, with his ever growing collection of scars.

She wiped her face and made her way through the shallows, smiling when she saw him.

'Is it that time already?' she said.

'Time for what?'

She stood on tip toes to kiss him on the mouth. 'It's either drinks or sex,' she said. 'Take your pick.'

Archer grinned. 'Let's do both,' he said.

She slipped her arms around his waist and pulled him against her. 'I can think or worse ways to rehab, eh?'

Archer chuckled and kissed her again. 'It's a tough life,' he said.

They turned and headed up the sand towards the steps. The sun was warm on their backs.

59

———

Standing on the deck of the large white cabin cruiser, hidden in the shadow of the overhanging flight deck, the man in the black T-shirt lowered his binoculars.

The pilot of the craft increased power and the cruiser surged ahead easily.

He could still see the couple in the distance, taking the steps up towards the poolside bar. It was a nice resort, if expensive. He knew because he'd visited it under the cover of darkness.

He turned to the pilot, a man with burns to his expressionless face.

'There they are,' he said.

The other man nodded silently and turned his attention back to piloting the craft. It wouldn't do to accidentally run over a swimmer or hit a boat. Accidents brought attention and attention was bad.

'There they are,' the man in the black T-shirt said to himself. He pursed his lips thoughtfully before nodding to himself. He had seen enough.

He turned and limped into the cabin.

60

———

The ceiling fan whirring gently above the bed gave the first warning.

A gentle whiff of cigarette smoke in the air, not the stench of lighted tobacco, but the stale smell that clings to a dedicated smoker.

Archer twitched as the smell touched his nostrils and nudged his sixth sense. His internal clock told him it was the witching hour, maybe three or four a.m., when people were in their deepest sleep. The classic time for an assault.

He was aware of Izzy lying beside him, sleeping peacefully. The top sheet was light on his bare torso, the air cooled only by the fan. The instant that his sixth sense awoke and alerted him to danger, his body twitched and his senses sprang to life.

The softest footfall on the floor mat beside the bed, the slightest shift in the air pressure in the room. It was all he needed to know.

The sheet was flung back and his legs kicked out together as he snatched at the pillow he'd been resting on a moment ago. The attacker was just a dark shape in the semi-light of the room; Archer couldn't see how close he was, but he knew he was there. His feet connected weakly and he propelled the attacker back a step, dropped his feet to the floor and came up at an angle, swatting at the attacker with the pillow. It connected and there was a cry of surprise and Archer was moving, stepping fast to the right, away from the bed.

He heard a muffled sound somewhere behind him followed by a shriek – Izzy was being attacked too. At least two bad guys then, armed and there to kill.

The attacker came at him, a dark figure lunging forward, and Archer sensed the weapon coming at him. He blocked with the pillow and pushed away, stepping in and going for a knee strike. The attacker blocked him and wrenched at the pillow, throwing a jab at Archer's face in the meantime. Archer took it full on the cheek, a solid hit that sent him staggering back. He tripped on the rug and went over, knocking over a table with a crash.

The Kel-Tec was in the bedside table, if only he could get to it.

The guy followed through, coming in hard and fast, swiping at him. Archer heard the swish of a blade cutting through the air and felt the wind as it sliced past his face. He rolled to the side into a puddle, feeling shards of broken glass jabbing into his shoulder and bicep as he found the broken water jug. The sting was overridden by the adrenaline pumping through him, a massive drop of it as fight-or-flight syndrome kicked in. There was no option – this was always going to be a fight.

He scrambled to his knees, kicking out sideways at knee height, hoping for a lucky strike. The blade slashed across his left thigh with a whisper, and he knew the attacker would be off-balance. Bunching the floor rug in his fists, he yanked savagely at it, pushing up to his feet as it moved.

The attacker staggered, stumbled and went down to a knee. Archer was on him fast, blanketing him with the rug and getting it down over the guy's head and upper body. He crashed into him, slamming him to the floor and hearing a muted grunt from beneath the rug. He straddled the attacker, pushing the sides of the rug out to keep it tight and hopefully pin the guy's arms. The guy was bucking hard, going mental as he fought for his life, and Archer knew this was the pivotal moment.

If the guy got up, Archer was dead, and that meant Izzy would be too.

There was another crash behind him and he heard Izzy's voice. No time to help her.

The guy beneath him was like an oiled pig, threatening to slip out from beneath him, and Archer hammered the heel of his hand into what he figured was the head. A good hit, then another, but the guy got a hand free and was clawing for Archer's face.

Archer pulled his head back, getting a few fingernail scratches on his face but managing to protect his eyes. He hammered at the guy's head again then the hand was in his face, scratching and jabbing. A finger hooked into his mouth and Archer bit down hard, chomping on it, grinding it between his teeth until he tasted warm, salty blood.

The guy yelped and tried to free his hand but Archer bit harder, tearing at the finger.

There was a loud thump and crack as a gun went off close by and Archer felt the bullet rip past his shoulder. Another shot sounded and he felt a kick in his chest, rocking him backwards.

Fuck. Get into it.

Knowing the guy had somehow got his gun free and was shooting point blank, Archer went for it. He had no option now but to kill this guy as quickly as possible.

He rolled to his right, away from the gun, and saw the dark figure on the floor moving too, sitting up. Archer was up first, getting his footing then stepping into the guy again. A front kick to the head, his bare heel connecting hard and knocking the guy back. Following through, he stomped on the guy's torso, a third shot sounding, stomping down again and again at whatever he could get. He found the head and concentrated on that, three good stomps taking the fight out of the guy.

Archer dropped onto him, feeling the guy moving weakly, and yanked away the rug. The guy still held his pistol but didn't resist as Archer ripped it from him. He rammed the barrel against the guy's head and fired twice, feeling a wet splashback on his hand and forearm.

He pushed up to his feet and the lights came on, blindingly bright after the darkness.

A dead man all in black was at his feet, half covered with the floor rug, his head leaking blood and mush on the wooden floor.

Across the room by the window were two people. Kozlowski had Izzy by the hair, a pistol at her head. She was bleeding from a wound to her forehead and looked out of it, not resisting him as he manhandled her.

'Here we are again, Archer,' Kozlowski grinned. 'I see you met my friend, Constantine. Shame.'

'For him,' Archer said. His left side was feeling weak and his chest burned. He could feel blood running down his chest and back. The pistol grips in his right hand were slick with sweat and blood. 'There's no chopper coming to rescue you this time, Viktor. It's just you and me.'

'Just you and me,' Kozlowski repeated, still grinning. He gave Izzy a shake, producing a groan. 'I don't think she's going to help you, is she? Maybe I should just kill her.'

'It's me you want,' Archer said. 'Let's go to it, man to man. I'm already wounded.'

'So am I.' Kozlowski moved Izzy aside far enough to show a wet patch of blood on the chest of his dark top. 'The bitch stabbed me with a pen.'

'It is mightier than the sword,' Archer said.

'But not a forty cal.' Kozlowski jabbed the pistol against her head. 'Shall I do it, Archer? Just pop her now and we can get on with it?'

Archer half-shrugged, sucking down a breath. He felt surprisingly calm now. This was it. Game time.

'I think I...'

Archer's right hand came up fast and smooth and he fired, the report loud and final. The bullet took Kozlowski in the throat and he fired involuntarily as he fell backwards. Izzy dropped to the floor. Archer fired again, coming forward now, the second bullet impacting Kozlowski's chin and blasting a bloody hole.

The terrorist mastermind gaped, his jaw working uselessly, no sound coming forth. He stared at Archer in shock then lifted his own pistol. His mouth twisted into a grotesque smirk, blood spilling over his lips and dribbling down his chin. A chuckle sounded from somewhere deep in his chest.

Archer was barely a metre away when Kozlowski fired. The impact thudded into Archer's gut and he took an involuntary step backwards, too focussed on his goal to go down. He clapped his gun hand over the wound.

Kozlowski's eyes widened when he saw Archer still coming, staggering like a drunk with his left arm hanging uselessly at his side.

Kozlowski tried to raise his gun one last time but his body was shutting down, failing to obey his commands. He was helpless to defend himself and they both knew it.

Archer got to him, reaching out with his gun hand to push his enemy back against the wall. He leaned against him, barely able to stand, hot tingles running through his body. He tried to breathe but it was a battle. He struggled to stay upright.

Kozlowski rolled his head towards Archer, his jaw wobbling silently, blood running freely from the hideous wounds in his jaw and throat. Archer was amazed the man was still alive.

He knew time was running out fast. Either help would arrive and interrupt, or he would die. His vision was blurring and his head was starting to spin. He felt his legs wobble beneath him.

Leaning against the wall with his elbow, he rested the pistol on Kozlowski's shoulder, pressing the barrel against the man's ear. He noticed, with complete disinterest, that the pistol was a Glock 34. It was a damn good pistol, but he didn't care. He wouldn't need it for long.

His breathing was ragged and he could feel his boxer shorts soaked in blood. Thank God he had pants on. Wouldn't want to be found naked after this. He almost laughed.

Kozlowski made a chuckling sound again. He leaned his head forward, so close that Archer could smell his breath. Their foreheads were almost touching. Kozlowski worked his shattered jaw onto the barrel of the Glock, sliding the barrel into his mouth.

Archer was eyeball to eyeball with him, both men dead on their feet, neither man flinching.

'You...had,' Archer wheezed. 'Had your...chance.'

Kozlowski stared into his eyes as Archer squeezed the trigger and blew his brains out.

The Glock kicked in Archer's hand and he lost it. Kozlowski's body tumbled to the floor and Archer collapsed against the wall, slowly turning and sliding down into a sitting position. With his feet out and his left arm flopping at his side, Archer sat and waited.

It seemed like forever before the door crashed open and two resort staff rushed in, one carrying a baseball bat, the other a phone. They stopped still when they saw the four crumpled bodies, blood everywhere, the air reeking of burnt cordite.

'Oh my God, man,' the guy with the bat said. 'I t'ink we better call the po-lice.'

Archer closed his eyes.

61

———————

The hospital room was varying shades of off-white and cream, and smelled of disinfectant and flowers.

Ingoe stood at the foot of the bed, watching Archer sleep. His charge had been operated on again, the first surgery to close up his wounds being too rushed. They had missed a fragment of bullet in his gut and had to go back in to clean it up.

The Director stood beside him, trying to read the patient notes on the clipboard. Finally, he gave up and waved the clipboard at Ingoe. 'Good Lord, what does all this bloody gobbledegook mean, Jed?'

Ingoe spoke without turning his head. 'Ruptured spleen,' he said. 'Tissue damage. Lots of blood loss. Nerve damage.' He gave the Director a sideways glance. 'They're the highlights.'

'Then why don't they just bloody say that then?' The Director hooked the clipboard back over the end of Archer's bed, scowling. He hated hospitals and he hated when his men got hurt. He also hated having to explain to bloody politicians why they were getting bloody questions from foreign bloody governments.

It had been a hell of a couple of days. Kozlowski was dead, finally. Archer hadn't been spoken to yet, but they knew it was him. The other man, Constantine, was also dead. Wanted by various agencies, he would not be mourned. The Canadian, Isabella, had come through it with a few minor injuries to add to the ones she already had.

The Director had flown out with Ingoe as soon as they had heard. He was tired and hungry and had a thumping headache. Looking down at the sleeping man in the bed, though, he figured he was the lucky one.

'I'll go and check on the Canadian girl,' he grumbled. 'At least she's only got a concussion. Don't know why she's even still here.'

Ingoe almost smiled. 'Righto sir,' he said. 'I'll be here.'

'Let me know when he wakes up, would you?' The Director paused at the door, looking back at him. If Ingoe didn't know the man better, he'd have sworn there was a tenderness behind that gruff exterior. 'The sooner he gets back to work, the better. I've got things for him to do.'

Ingoe nodded and gave a wry smile. 'Of course, sir.'

The door closed and the room was silent again. Ingoe moved to the single chair beside the bed and sat. He moved the Sig from his hip holster to his lap, resting it there in the unlikely event he should need it. Kozlowski was dead, but the man had far-reaching tentacles.

While Archer slept, Ingoe sat and waited. He had barely closed his eyes the last two days, and he wouldn't until Archer came through this. It didn't matter; he was a seasoned warrior, fully alert and ready.

He sat, watching and waiting.

The protector.

END

The **Division** series continues...

BONUS CHAPTERS

Some would say I was paranoid, but they'd be wrong.

There's a difference between being paranoid and being smart.

To put it in real terms, if one President with a big red button and an ego problem butts heads with another with the same issues, it's probably a good time to start preparing for the worst. That's what I did, and every step of the way I prayed it would all be for nothing.

I wasn't the only one, but we were still the minority. Nobody wants their worst fears to be proved right, but I also didn't want to be one of the mindless sheeple that relied on someone else to pull their arse from the fire.

This was a country built by pioneers, tough resilient folk who travelled round the world to land on a handful of islands down near the bottom of the South Pacific. They battled adversity every step of the way, creating a national mindset of independence and humility. Shout your name from the rooftops? Expect to get cut down. Nobody round here likes a blowhard.

My name's Mark Dobson. I'm just the guy next door.

I don't care too much what people think of me, but of course there was another very good reason to keep my preparations quiet. If my predictions came true a lot of people would be caught short. Food and fuel would be the big issues. Lack of medicines. Unheated homes. Mental health issues would be exacerbated by the stress. Those that were desperate would steal to feed and clothe their families. The lowlifes would do that and more, whether they needed supplies or not. Violence would break out.

Those that were unprepared would fall victim to the predators. That wouldn't happen to my family, not on my watch.

No fucking way.

CHASE INVESTIGATIONS SERIES #1
OLD FRIENDS

The depot was quiet and still at 1am on a Monday, a light breeze flicking the odd leaf or piece of rubbish across the forecourt where the trucks came in and turned round to be loaded.

A row of semis lined one side of the compound, big and dark and empty, all emblazoned with Marcus Haulage markings. A security light flickered weakly and cast only a slight glow through the darkness. The chain link fence rattled and the gate squeaked as it was pushed open.

The man at the gate checked his watch nervously for the fourth time in as many minutes. He shivered even though it wasn't cold.

An engine could be heard and a second later bright headlights swept round the corner into the street and approached the end of the cul-de-sac where the man waited on the footpath by the open gate. It was an industrial area populated by trade centres and auto businesses and nobody was around at this time of night.

The lights blinded him as the truck swung easily through the gate and entered the depot, making a wide half circle before smoothly backing up to the loading bay. This wasn't a semi-truck like the ones parked up in a row at the side of the depot, but a smaller delivery truck with no markings. The man shut the gates and looped the chain through without locking it. He hurried over to the truck and met the driver and his passenger as they jumped down.

'Good work,' the driver told him with a smirk, 'let's get to it.'

He was a burly man with greasy hair showing under his cap. He had the strong forearms built from years of guiding 18-wheelers down the highways and the red nose of a hardened drinker. His companion was of a similar build but taller, with tattoos discolouring his own forearms. He also had a spider's web tattooed on the left side of his neck and several tear drops inked into the skin by his right eye. He was harder looking than the driver and didn't speak.

'Hurry,' the man who'd opened the gate said, checking his watch again, and the driver sneered at him with contempt.

'Just open up, fella,' he replied, hitching his jeans up, 'let us do our job.'

The first man unlocked the door beside the loading bay then lifted the roller door. He stood and watched as the other two men entered the warehouse, turned a couple of lights on and got to work. Within twenty minutes they had loaded the back of the truck with several pallets of boxes, replaced the forklift, turned out the lights and locked up again. It was a smooth, efficient operation, done with minimal fuss.

The driver and his companion climbed back into the truck and the nervous man went to the gate to let them out. The truck paused in the gateway and the driver wound down the window, leaning casually out.

'Cheers buddy,' he smirked, 'see ya next time. We'll be in touch, aye?'

The passenger stared at the nervous man with a blank expression, and the nervous man nodded glumly.

'Okay, okay,' he replied, 'just go. Just go.'

The driver laughed and the truck moved away up the road. The nervous man wiped his brow on the sleeve of his jacket, locked the gate again and hurried away into the darkness.

Silence returned to the depot.

The lady sitting on the red fabric sofa in the corner of the office was well dressed and smelt of expensive perfume. She appeared uncomfortable, as if she were waiting for the dentist or a mammogram. She was middle aged and had perfectly styled hair and flawless make up.

The man sitting on the matching chair at right angles to her was twenty years younger, with broad shoulders and a confident air about him. He had dark eyes and dark hair with a hint of grey at the temples, a full moustache, and was dressed in casual chinos and an open necked shirt.

He looked up from the notes he'd made on the pad on his knee and smiled at her. It was a calm reassuring smile, and it eased her discomfort a degree or two. He had a direct gaze and intelligent eyes, the sort of face that was more interesting than handsome. A faint scar showed at his chin, a patch where no stubble could grow.

'Okay Mrs MacNamara,' he said, 'is there anything else you can tell me that may help? Any particular routine that your husband follows that may help me narrow it down a bit?'

She thought for a moment.

'He plays squash every Monday and Thursday night right after work. He always starts work by seven and usually gets home about six.' She frowned. 'That's it I'm afraid. I can't think of anything else.'

'No problem.' He jotted it down, got the name of the squash club from her, and smiled again. 'That's it, Mrs MacNamara. We'll get onto it right away, and give you an update as soon as we know anything, okay?'

'How long will it take?' she asked, and for the first time her voice quavered. She paused to re-gather herself before continuing. 'I mean, will I hear from you this week?'

'It really depends on what your husband does and what we find, Mrs MacNamara.'

He stood and she followed suit, allowing herself to be ushered over to the desk by the door. 'We'll be in touch as soon as we can, hopefully in the next few days.'

She nodded and he gave her that reassuring smile again.

'If you can give your deposit to Molly I'll quickly print off a contract for you.'

He moved to the second desk in the office, which faced the first one across the floor space. Mrs MacNamara turned to the woman at the first desk-Molly-and passed her a gold Visa.

Molly took it and used it to take an electronic deposit of ten hours work. She was a striking woman of classical beauty, with wavy dark hair and sparkling, friendly green eyes. She had full red lips and wore little make up-mainly because she didn't need to. She had the sort of look that defied pigeonholing. She could pass for a European or a country girl, depending on what she wore. Today she wore a simple black skirt and silver blouse, elegant and understated.

Mrs MacNamara cast a furtive look at the man as he printed out a contract for her. He seemed like a nice person but she sensed he was not the sort to mess with. She glanced back at Molly, who was smiling at her and holding her card and receipt out for her. Her eyes smiled as well as her mouth, and Mrs MacNamara felt herself smile in return.

The man came over and gave her a copy of the contract and had her sign his copy. She folded it and put it in her bag with her card and receipt. Then he handed her a business card and smiled again. Molly smiled again too, and Mrs MacNamara felt a little better. She thanked them and allowed him to hold the door for her.

'We'll be in touch,' he told her, and closed the door behind her.

Mrs MacNamara walked towards the stairs down to the street. She could hear the motorway behind her on the other side of the building, and the main street of Ellerslie village was in front of her. She looked at the card in her hand.

Chase Investigations, it said. Dan Crowley, Director. It was a plain white card with blue lettering, the company's name in italicised lettering across the top as if it really was chasing something, his name and title below it in smaller letters. Address and contact details at the bottom.

She tucked it into her bag with the rest of the stuff, and checked her watch. It was 930am. Nearly time for her manicure.

Dan Crowley passed the notes and contract to his wife and went to the kitchenette off the office.

'What do you think?' he asked as he poured a coffee for himself and a green tea for her. 'If we could get a few more Mrs MacNamaras in here with their Remuera cheque books, I'd be happy.'

'If we get a few more Mrs MacNamaras in here, 'Molly replied, 'there won't be room to move. You've got a full week already, honey, and now this as well.'

'I'll give it to old Neil,' he told her, handing her a tea cup and perching on the corner of her desk.

'He's already got a full week as well.' She clicked open the weekly planner on her desktop and opened up the tab for Neil. 'He's in court for the Shelby theft case today, he's got the Parker and Philips fraud, four accident reports due in and he's got five processes.' She took a sip of tea and gave him a plaintive look. 'What, no biscuits this morning?'

Dan went to the kitchenette and brought back the cookie jar.

'How about you, could you squeeze it in?' He bit into a ginger crunch and showered crumbs down his front. He didn't seem to notice.

'I'll have to, won't I?' Molly sighed and frowned at him. He didn't seem to notice that either.

'We need to take someone else on though, honey. Neil's as slow as a wet week.'

'He is officially retired.'

'So he should retire properly then. I'm supposed to be part time but I'm practically full time and you did sixty hours last week.' She pouted at him. 'You need to get someone in.'

He sipped his coffee and nodded.

'You're right.' He smiled at her and patted her cheek affectionately. 'No worries gorgeous, I'll sort it out. I'll talk to Buck and see if he knows of anyone wanting to get out.'

The door opened and an elderly man with grey hair and a beer pot entered, a battered briefcase in one hand and a copy of the Racing Times in the other.

'Morning all,' he said cordially, kicking the door closed behind him, 'how are we?'

'We be fine,' Dan replied with an amused smile. 'How are ye?'

'Ye be good,' Neil replied, taking a seat at the third desk, the one in the corner with the empty file tray. He opened his briefcase and removed a thick manila folder. He carried it over to Molly's desk and put it down with a flourish.

'Here you go, my dear lady,' he said grandly, shooting the cuffs of his dark suit and smoothing his tie. 'All my files, up to date and complete.'

He looked across at Dan, who was coming from the kitchenette with a coffee for him.

'I'm retiring,' he announced, drinking in their surprised looks. 'Yep, I thought it was about time. I don't need to work; I've got my pension and not long left to spend it. June's found a place in Tauranga and put an offer in, it got accepted over the weekend and we move this week.'

'That soon?' Molly looked stunned.

'That soon,' he said. 'I'm sorry to drop it on you like this, but we got the word on Friday night. I cleaned up my files over the weekend, all the documents are served, the crash reports are done and photos on the disk, and I've done the preliminary work on the Parker and Philips job.' He glanced back to Dan. 'You'll just need to finish it off, Daniel.'

'Uh-huh.' Dan nodded and went to his desk. 'You're still in court today, I take it?'

'Indeed, indeed. The last time I'll be giving evidence, I should imagine.' He nodded solemnly. 'No more running round playing private eye for old Neil, it's time for fishing and golf.'

'And spending quality time with June,' Molly reminded him.

'Yeah, that too,' he conceded.

There was an awkward silence for a moment. Nobody seemed to

know what to say. Molly looked to her husband, but he remained silent. She felt her cheeks flush.

'Anyway, I better get to court,' Neil said eventually, 'justice waits for no man.'

'I think you mean time,' Dan told him.

'Don't I know it.'

Neil grabbed his briefcase, took a quick slurp of coffee and was gone, banging the door behind him again as he left.

Dan and Molly looked across the office at each other.

'Be careful what you wish for,' he said.

'D'you think he heard me?' she frowned.

'Probably.' He groaned and rubbed his face. 'Now we really need someone. Better book dinner for four at Luigi's, I guess.'

'Ooh, are you taking your wife out for dinner?' she cooed, making eyes at him across the room.

'Hmm, something like that.' He grinned. 'In company, of course, so you don't get any fancy ideas.'

'Typical. Where's the romance gone?'

'He could've given us more notice than a day,' Dan grumbled. He leaned back in his chair and put his feet up on the edge of the desk.

'That's what you get for taking on a contractor,' she told him, 'all care, no responsibility. I think we should take on a permanent employee this time.'

'Then I'd have to pay them holidays and sick and whatever else they can think of.' He shook his head in despair. 'Just can't get the staff.'

'You've gotta try first. What about Buck?'

'What, Buck himself? Na, he's got it too cushy where he is, why would he give that up?'

'Being the Ellerslie community cop can hardly be stimulating,' Molly opined.

'Not too taxing either, though. He hasn't got himself in trouble since...well...'

'Since he stopped working with you?'

'Exactly.'

His mobile bleeped on the desk with an incoming message. He smiled as he checked it.

'Mike,' he said, 'wants to meet for a coffee urgently.'

'Wonder who he's in love with now?' Molly speculated.

'You're such a cynic.'

'You know it's true. Ten to one it's a drama about some woman.' She gave him a challenging look. 'Go on, bet against me.'

Dan shook his head and got up.

'That's a sucker's bet.' He bent over her desk and kissed her softly on the cheek. 'And I'm no sucker.'

'No, you're a hot shot private eye.' Her eyes twinkled at him. 'But you know what it'll be.'

'Maybe.' He kissed her firmly on the mouth now. 'I'll shoot down and see Buck first, then go see him then head off and do the Parker and Philips case.'

'Hey.' Molly caught him by the sleeve. 'Maybe Mike wants a job?'

'You think?' He considered it for a second then shook his head. 'Na, can you really see him as a PI? Doubt it. We don't do debt collection.'

'You used to,' she reminded him, and he shrugged.

'Yeah, but now we're chasing better money than that. Any port in a storm I guess, but I'd rather Mrs MacNamara brought her friends to see us. At least you know you won't get your head stoved in investigating a cheating husband or corporate fraud.'

He leaned down and kissed her again.

'I'll call you later.'

He left the office, wondering what it was that Mike had got himself into now.

MESSAGE FROM THE AUTHOR

Thanks for taking the time to read *No Second Chance*. I hope you enjoyed this fifth book in the **Division** series. The sixth book in the series is coming soon. Watch this space.

I'd love it if you could please take the time to leave an online review of *No Second Chance* with your favourite book retailer.

If you'd like to know about new releases and receive a free book, sign up to my **Hitlist** on Facebook -

https://www.facebook.com/writer-angus-mclean

Cheers,
Angus McLean

ACKNOWLEDGMENTS

The author would like to thank the advisers who have assisted with the writing of this book. They must remain anonymous for security reasons, but they (and only they) know who they are.

They are the true heroes who put their lives on the line to protect our freedoms. My sincerest gratitude goes out to them.

And once again, huge thanks to "Tori" who does my covers and provides great advice. You rock.

This is a work of fiction, and all errors are the responsibility of the author.

ABOUT THE AUTHOR

Angus McLean is a South Auckland Police officer.

His experience as a cop and a private investigator give his writing a touch of realism. He believes reading should be escapist entertainment and is inspired by the TV shows he watched as a youngster.

His real identity remains a secret.

www.writerangusmclean.com